IRON HORSE

ROBERT VAUGHAN

WOLFPACK
PUBLISHING
— EST 2013 —

WOLFPACK PUBLISHING
— EST 2013 —

Text copyright © 2021 (As Revised) Robert Vaughan

Published by Wolfpack Publishing
5130 S. Fort Apache Road, 215-380
Las Vegas, NV 89148

Paperback IBSN 978-1-64734-651-5
eBook ISBN 978-1-64734-650-8

IRON HORSE

IRON HORSE

Dear Reader,

This is a story that I wrote several years ago that Wolfpack has graciously agreed to republish for me. While it is not the traditional western that I usually write, it is a story of the West. I hope you enjoy reading about Gabe and Makenna as the railroad moves across New Mexico.

Robert Vaughan

CHAPTER ONE

Makenna O'Shea was a young woman of twenty-two. Her black hair and green eyes combined to make a rather unusual but striking combination. Her face was dusted with a light spray of freckles, an effect which enhanced rather than detracted from her attractiveness.

Makenna's father, Kellen O'Shea, had returned from the battle of Shiloh minus one leg, a widower with an infant daughter to raise. He had been Makenna's sole parent since she was three months old and he still looked upon her as a young, innocent child. Young and innocent she was but Makenna was no child.

There was an excitement to meeting the midnight train that Makenna relished. There was always a carnival atmosphere about the crowd: laughter, good-natured joking, the constant cry of drummers who hawked their wares to midnight customers and, often, music from guitars or an occasional band.

What Makenna liked best, however, was the approach of the engine. The whistle could be heard first, far off and mournful, a lonesome wail that never failed to send chills through her body. "Here she comes," someone would shout and the laughter and talking would grow subdued as if everyone consciously gave the approaching train center stage.

Makenna stared down the track, waiting for the train. The first thing to come into view was the light, a huge, wavering, yellow disc, the gas flame and mirror reflector shining brightly in the distance. That sighting would be closely followed by the hollow sounds of puffing steam, like the gasps of some fire-breathing, serpentine monster. As if to add to the illusion, glowing sparks were whipped away in the black smoke clouds that billowed up into the night sky.

As the train pounded by, Makenna could feel her very body throb in rhythm with the engine's powerful beat. She watched the huge driver wheels, nearly as tall as she was, and the white wisps of steam that escaped from the thrusting piston rods. The engine rushed by with sparks flying from the pounding drive wheels and glowing hot embers dripping from its fire box. Then came the yellow squares of light that were the windows of the passenger cars. The cars would flash by, slowly, and finally grind to a halt with a shower of sparks and a hissing of air from the Westinghouse air brakes.

After the train was completely stopped and the doors to the cars started coming open, Makenna walked along the side of the train, headed for the engine.

Dudley Snider was the engineer and as Makenna approached his cab, she could see through the window the maze of pipes and valves that were Dudley's controls. She also saw Milo, the big Swedish fireman. He was grimy with soot, and sweaty, and he breathed hard as he sat on a bench to grab a breath of fresh air and rest his powerful, but aching muscles.

"Hello, Miss O'Shea," Dudley called down.

"Hello, Dudley," Makenna replied. "Did you have a nice trip?"

"We didn't get away from Trinidad until six forty-five," Dudley said.

"But you made it here on time. You must have really run fast."

"Sometimes better'n fifty-five miles per hour," Dudley said proudly.

"Ve haf the superintendent on board," Milo said. "Dudley vas showing off."

"Do you have our orders, girl?" Dudley asked.

"Yes, here in this envelope," Makenna said. She strained and stretched, reaching up to hand the envelope to Dudley but the envelope slipped from her fingers and bounced under the engine.

"Allow me, miss," a man's deep, resonant voice said.

The man who spoke was a stranger to Makenna. He was tall, with dark hair, and well-dressed in a russet brown jacket and brown riding breeches tucked into highly polished boots.

"I fear I'll cause you to soil your clothes, sir," Makenna said.

"Then I shall wear the grime as a medal of honor for having served you," the man replied. He handed the envelope to Makenna, then smiled as she stretched to hand it up to the engineer.

"Miss O'Shea, this here is Gabriel Hansen," Dudley said from the cab of his engine. "He's goin' to build him a railroad clear on to the Pacific Ocean."

"You're Gabe Hansen?" Makenna asked. For she had heard of him as had everyone in Albuquerque. The news that a new railroad, the Southern Continental, was going to connect Albuquerque with Phoenix and San Diego was on everyone's lips. But that a man so young could do all this? Gabe Hansen couldn't have been more than twenty-eight.

"I see you've heard of me," Gabe said. "I also know of you."

"You've heard of me?"

"Of course," Gabe said easily. "You are Makenna O'Shea, daughter of the man who is going to be my superintendent of station masters and telegraphers."

"What do you mean? Papa hasn't said anything about changing jobs. He has a good job with Western Pacific as station master of the Albuquerque Station."

"I'm sure your papa will want to work for me when I ask him," Gabe said. "I intend to raise his salary to three times what he now makes. That should interest him, don't you think?"

Makenna drew in her breath. That would raise her father's salary to sixty dollars a week. At that rate, he would be able to retire in one more year and go back to Missouri the way he'd always dreamed. Makenna had no personal desire to return to Missouri but she wanted it for her father since she knew that was what he lived for.

"Do you think your father would be interested?" Gabe asked again.

"Oh, I'm sorry," Makenna said when she realized he was talking to her and she was paying no attention. "Yes, yes, I think he would be."

"Fine. Perhaps you can intercede on my behalf if it becomes necessary."

A yard worker approached them and stood back quietly, waiting for recognition. Gabe saw him, smiled broadly, and stuck out his hand. "My name's Gabe Hansen," he said. "Who are you?"

"Al Blocker, sir," the man replied, surprised that he had been asked. "I've come to tell you that your private car has been detached from the end of the train and pushed onto a sidetrack."

"Good. Thank you, Al. I appreciate that."

Makenna was impressed with the way Gabe spoke to the man. Many, she knew, would have barely acknowledged him. They would have completely overlooked him as merely another piece of railroad equipment. Gabe had taken the time to introduce himself and learn the man's name then use it.

"That was nice," she said after Al had left.

"It was nice of them to take care of it for me," Gabe agreed.

"No, I meant that you took the time to speak with him."

"Friendliness is an investment, Miss O'Shea," Gabe said. "One which cost little and often gives great returns. Like now, for example. I'd like to make a friendly gesture and invite you to join me in my car for a small drink before I turn in. Would you be interested?" Gabe saw the shock in Makenna's eyes and he laughed. "No? Very well, then perhaps some other time. In the meantime, Miss O'Shea, I bid you good night."

Gabe gave a small bow almost mocking in its lack of movement, though made gracious by his style.

"Good night, Mr. Hansen," Makenna said.

CHAPTER TWO

Makenna worked her way back through the crowd to the station house, a small, wooden building. In front, was the station master's office and waiting room while in the rear there were small but comfortable living quarters. That was home for Makenna and her father and Makenna took a great deal of pride in making it an attractive place to live. She had bright splashes of color in the curtains and cushions, fresh flowers when she could get them, and Currier and Ives prints on the walls.

"I'm back, Papa," Makenna said cheerily as she stepped into the front office. Kellen O'Shea, her father, was sitting at the telegrapher's table. The instrument was clicking but Makenna, who had learned telegraphy from her father, knew that it wasn't important. It was only a time and line check and needed no answer. One pants leg of Kellen's trousers was flat, denoting an empty space. The leg that should have been there had been buried in the backyard of a small schoolhouse near Corinth, Mississippi, along with the thousands of other limbs lost during the battle of Shiloh.

"Papa, how many times do I have to tell you to keep that pants leg rolled up? When it flops loose like that, it could trip you and you could get hurt," Makenna said. She knelt in front of her father and began rolling up the pants leg.

"You're a fine broth of a daughter to be havin' around, Makenna O'Shea," Kellen said, rubbing his hand through her black hair affectionately. "Sure, 'n 'tis a shame your poor ma never lived to see you become such a beautiful child."

"I'm no longer a child, Papa," Makenna replied.

"Don't be in such a hurry to grow up, lassie," Kellen cautioned. "Age comes upon a person soon enough without a body rushing it."

"The girl is right, Kellen. She's full grown now," a voice said.

Makenna and her father looked up to see Superintendent Fletcher Whitney standing in the doorway. He was forty-five, overweight, and balding. He carried a solid gold pocket watch and wore the fob stretched across his vest as a badge of rank. Makenna remembered now that Milo had said the superintendent had been on the train. She didn't like him. His very presence could make her feel uneasy.

"Superintendent Whitney," Kellen said in greeting. "I didn't know you were in town."

"Came in on the midnight train," Whitney said. "I've some business discussions with Gabe Hansen tomorrow."

"Gabe Hansen?"

"He's here, Papa, in Albuquerque," Makenna said. "I just spoke to him."

Makenna wanted to tell her father about Gabe's offer but she had no desire to talk about it in front of Whitney.

"Is he really going to extend the track on to San Diego? I thought Western Pacific was going to do that," she asked.

"Western Pacific has the exclusive right-of-way across the desert," Whitney said. "It was granted to us by the

United States government. But it would be foolish at this point for us to build out in the wasteland. So, we are going to allow young Gabe Hansen to try."

"I can't see Western Pacific just giving up like that," Kellen said. "What's in it for them?"

"Gabe Hansen gets a grant of sixteen thousand dollars per mile for every mile of track he builds. We are giving up our right-of-way for one half of his government grant. In addition, we have exclusive shipping rights for all materials across our tracks and extensive track rental agreements for equipment that stands on Western Pacific property." Whitney laughed. "There's not a chance in the world he can do the job."

"Then why is Western Pacific willing to sell him the right-of-way?" Makenna asked.

"Quite simple, my dear," Whitney said. For every mile he does build, we will get eight thousand dollars."

"That doesn't sound fair," Makenna said.

"It's the way of business," Whitney replied. "It's a hard world you're growing into, girl."

"Who brought the train in, lass?" Kellen asked.

"Dudley Snider."

Kellen reached for his crutches. "I think I'll walk down and say a word or two to him. Dudley 'n I have been friends since we worked on the Cairo and Fulton Railroad in Missouri back before the war."

Makenna was afraid that Whitney would hang on to talk to her if Kellen left, so she yawned and pretended sleepiness though, in fact, she would have preferred staying awake until after the train left.

"I'm going to go on to bed, Papa," she said, yawning and stretching. "I'm really bushed."

"Well, I guess I'll see who's out and around," Whitney

said. "I hope it isn't too late to get a hotel room."

Makenna knew that Whitney was hinting for Kellen to invite him to stay with them and she held her breath.

"It's never too late," Kellen said. "I'll find a place for you. They've always got room for one more in the hotel."

"Good night, Papa," Makenna said with a thankful smile.

"Good night, my darlin'," Kellen answered. The twinkle in his eyes told Makenna that he had understood her plight and had taken care of it.

After the two men left, Makenna turned down the lantern, then went into her bedroom just off the office. She undressed in the dark so she could look through the window at the train without being seen.

The train was surrounded by people and the windows of the cars shone bright yellow. Inside, there were people moving about and she wondered about them—who they were, and where they had been.

At breakfast the next morning, Makenna asked her father about Gabe Hansen.

"I'm afraid the lad's goin' to be in for a bit o' disappointment," Kellen said.

"Why?"

"Whitney is right. Without money to develop the land, he'll lose it. It's a shame to see such dreams go for naught."

"Maybe he can do it," Makenna suggested.

"No, lass. There's just no way. And besides, what has your interest so aroused?" Kellen asked.

"It's just that he's going to offer you a job," she said.

"Gabe Hansen is going to offer me a job?" Kellen asked in amazement. "As what?"

"As superintendent of the line. And he'll pay you three times what you are making now," Makenna said.

"Three times you say? Faith, 'n 'tis a shame the lad can't afford to do it. For that would be a fine job, I'm thinkin'."

"Perhaps he can, Papa," Makenna said. "If what I've heard of Gabe Hansen is true, he isn't likely to be the kind of man who would throw money away."

"He's a dreamer, lass," Kellen said. "And sometimes a dreamer becomes so blinded with the glory of his vision that he loses sight of the reality. 'Tis dangerous to get caught up in another man's dreams."

The telegraph instrument started clicking and Makenna recognized the call.

"Do you want me to take the message, Papa?"

Kellen laughed. "Sure 'n if someone saw you handlin' my instrument now, I'd be out a job for teachin' a woman the science. You pour me another cup of coffee, lass, 'n I'll take the message."

Kellen walked over to the table where the instrument sat and flashed back a message that he was ready to receive. Makenna poured another cup of coffee and took it to her father, then stood by him as the message came clacking over the wire:

Message to Gabe Hansen from Emory Van Zandt/ stop/ Agree to the terms you propose/ stop/ Will provide such financial backing as is required to make the railroad a reality/ stop/ As per our agreement am sending my son Peter as liaison between us/ stop/ Good luck on our new venture/ stop/ Emory Van Zandt.

"Papa, Emory Van Zandt?" Makenna asked.

"That's what the message says," Kellen replied.

"Isn't he that rich banker from San Francisco?"

"Honey, he's much more than just a rich banker. He is one of the richest men in the country. Maybe in the world."

"If he's going to back Gabe Hansen, then Whitney is wrong and Gabe Hansen does have a chance, doesn't he?"

"I'd say a very good chance," Kellen said. He rubbed his chin and looked at the message again, reading it over for the second time. "I'm afraid I'd better tell Whitney of this. Western Pacific should know about it."

"Why?"

"Don't you see, darlin'? Western Pacific figured that Gabe Hansen would go broke. I don't think they would have let their right-of-way go if they thought he had a chance."

"In other words, they were trying to cheat Gabe Hansen but they are winding up by cheating themselves. Is that it?" Makenna asked.

"I wouldn't put it that way," Kellen said mildly.

"Why not?"

Kellen scratched his head. "It was just a smart business move."

"Well, Mr. Hansen is evidently smarter than Mr. Whitney and the Western Pacific," Makenna said.

"I still think I should tell. After all, I'm an employee of Western Pacific."

"You are now. But you are about to become an employee of Southern Continental," Makenna said. "Besides, this message was a commercial message. You are under no obligation to Western Pacific."

Kellen tapped his fingers on the table, then looked up at Makenna and smiled. "You are right." He folded the message over and put it in an envelope, then handed it to Makenna. "Would you like to deliver it, darlin'?"

"Yes, I think I would," Makenna said. "And when he asks me if you'll go to work for him, what shall I say?"

"Tell him to come see me," Kellen said. "I'll listen to any man's offer."

The wires that were connected to Kellen O'Shea's telegraph instrument ran up the wall of the station house, then out through a small hole where they attached to a tall telegraph pole. The pole was one of many. Some ran north, along the spur line to Santa Fe. Others ran east along the main track, leading back to Trinidad, where connections were made with Kansas City and points east, or Denver and points west. The poles stretched for as far as the eye could see until they were only black dots in the distance.

The twin steel ribbons of track and the graceful curving of the copper wires between the poles, cut across the desert and mountains, visible evidence of man's invasion. They crossed miles of uninhabited country and it was very easy for someone to make minor alterations without being seen. Thus it was that a totally unauthorized wire branched off the telegraph poles at an unobserved spot. That wire ran over a system of poles not quite as uniform as the official line but every bit as effective. The unauthorized line stretched over cactus and rock, through mountain pass and along canyons, until it reached a fertile valley wherein stood a well-ordered ranch known as Rancho Sombra de las Montanas.

Rancho Sombra de las Montanas was the ranch of Don Esteban de Tafoya, the sixth generation Tafoya to occupy the land, on an original land grant made in the year 1610 by Don Pedro de Peralta, third governor of New Mexico. When New Mexico was ceded to the United States, the validity of the original Spanish land grant was questioned and some of the land was set aside to be given or sold to the railroads. Don Esteban looked on the deal with misgivings. He wrote a strong letter to the United States government and to the president of Western Pacific Railroad when they began surveying route rights-of-way through his land. The letter was ignored.

Don Esteban was sixty-three years old and the letter was the strongest form of protest he could manage. But his son, Bernardo, was only twenty-seven and capable of a much stronger protest. Bernardo had fought for one year in the New Mexico border guards against marauding Indians and bandits who would strike across the border, then retreat back into Mexico. He was a skilled and brave warrior and it was not in his hot, Latin blood to stand by impotently while his land was invaded by the railroad magnates of the east.

Rancho Sombra de las Montanas consisted of a main building and several smaller ones. The main building was large and brown with a red tile roof. A cloister with an arched colonnade stretched from the main house to one of the smaller buildings, and the telegraph line ran into that building where it attached to an instrument. The message that had been received by Kellen O'Shea was also received by this instrument.

"Bernardo, the message says that the new man, Gabe Hansen, will have money for his railroad," the telegraph operator said.

"*Damn!*" Bernardo swore. "Now we have a new enemy."

"Perhaps the new man can be reasoned with."

"There is no reasoning with the Yanquis who build the roads," Bernardo said. He crumbled the message in his fist and tossed it to one side.

"Let us destroy the track before the train can bring the new money," someone suggested.

"No," Bernardo said. "The track that they now have does not violate our land. We are sworn only to keep our land from being violated, not destroy that which doesn't offend us."

"But in so doing, we can prevent the money from reaching them and prevent the new track from being laid," the man reasoned.

"No," Bernardo said. "I don't like that idea."

"Why don't you just take the money?" a woman's voice said.

The men turned to see a beautiful young woman who stood in the doorway. She had the same flashing black eyes and dark rings of hair as Bernardo, though her hair was much longer and fell in soft folds across her shoulders. Her name was Teresina and she was Bernardo's sister.

"*Sí*, just take the money," one of the men laughed. "It is not that easy."

"Why not? If it comes on a special train, we will know of it," Teresina said. She pointed to the telegraph set.

"My sister has a point," Bernardo said. "Perhaps, we could take the money."

"Caramba, you mean rob the train?" one of the men asked.

"Yes," Bernardo said. "I think this could be done."

"Ah, chihuahua, what a victory this would be over the Yanquis!" one of the men said excitedly. "Let's do it."

"We will," Bernardo said. "But first, I must ride into Albuquerque. I want to have a look around."

CHAPTER THREE

Makenna stood on the platform at the rear of the special car Gabe Hansen was using and knocked on the door. She waited for a few minutes, knocked a second time, and called his name. There was still no response. As she started to leave, she heard a noise from within as if someone were scurrying about.

"Just a minute." The voice was muffled but it was clearly Gabe.

Makenna felt embarrassed. Gabe Hansen was obviously still in bed, probably tired from the long trip. She should have shown more discretion than to come over at this early hour. Besides, it made it appear as if she were anxious and that was unbecoming a lady.

Makenna wished she could just leave quietly. But the fact that he had answered her made that impossible. She was stuck with the situation and waited self-consciously.

The door opened and Gabe's face peered through the crack. When he saw Makenna, he smiled.

"Why, Miss O'Shea, how nice of you to call," he said. He opened the door wide and stepped back into the room. "Won't you come in?"

Makenna knew that it would have been more proper for her to just hand him the telegram and leave but she was consumed with curiosity, so she accepted the invitation. In spite of herself, she gasped when she saw the inside of Gabe's private car. She had seen living quarters on wheels before, mostly crew quarters, but never had she seen anything like this. The end of the car where she stood was the living room-dining room. It was paneled in mahogany, hung with rich, red velour draperies, lighted with a crystal chandelier and carpeted with a plush, maroon carpet.

"What do you think?" Gabe asked, amused by her look of wonder.

"I've never seen anything like it," Makenna said finally.

Gabe smiled. "I don't want you to get the wrong impression of me. I'm not this much of a dandy. But I ramrodded construction on the Central Mountain and brought the road in three months ahead of schedule. This private car was my bonus. It's a bit gaudy for my tastes, and not all that practical, but a man has to live somewhere. Perhaps you've reconsidered my offer?"

"Your offer?" Makenna asked, puzzled by the remark.

"For a drink."

"At this hour? Besides, this isn't a social call, Mr. Hansen," Makenna said.

"If it isn't a social call, Miss O'Shea, then what can I do for you?"

"I have a telegram for you."

"Thank you," Gabe said. He took it from her and pitched it carelessly onto a nearby table.

"Aren't you going to read it?"

"What for?"

"Because. It may be important. It is important," she sputtered, then she flushed with embarrassment for having disclosed that she knew the telegram's contents.

"I don't need to read it," Gabe said. "I already know it's from Emory Van Zandt. He has wired me his decision, so I assume he has agreed to back me. Had he decided otherwise, a letter would have been quick enough to suit him."

Gabe was opening a bottle of wine as he spoke and he poured two glasses, then handed one to Makenna.

"Wine, at this time of the morning?" she said again.

"There are men of medicine who recommend a glass of wine for breakfast," Gabe replied. "And don't you celebrate communion with wine? Besides, this is a celebration of sorts. Surely you wouldn't make me celebrate alone?"

"No, Mr. Hansen," she said, returning his smile. "I won't make you celebrate alone."

The wine was light and dry and had a very pleasant bouquet.

"Did you tell your father of my offer?"

"Yes."

"What did he say?"

"He will listen to you, Mr. Hansen."

"It's Gabe," he said, holding the bottle of wine over Makenna's glass.

Makenna covered the glass with her hand and smiled. "No, Mr. Hansen, I don't care for anymore, thank you. I'll celebrate with you but I'll not get tipsy."

Gabe pulled the bottle back and poured another for himself. "Then will you strike a bargain?"

"What sort of bargain?"

"I'll not try and get you tipsy if you'll call me Gabe."

"In due time, Mr. Hansen. In due time."

Makenna finished her glass of wine, then set it on the table. "I really must be going," she said. "I must admit that

I felt excited for you when I read that you were going to get the backing you need."

"Then he did agree," Gabe said, letting out a sigh of relief.

"Why, yes, of course. I thought you knew. I mean the celebration and all," Makenna said, confusion showing on her face.

Gabe gave a slow, almost embarrassed smile. "The truth is, I was too nervous to look. I just ran a bluff, figuring that if I was wrong, you'd tell me." He laughed. "This is great! I mean really great!" He poured himself a third glass, then offered to pour another for her. "Have one more. This time for real."

"No, one is enough," Makenna said. "Besides, we have a bargain now, remember, Gabe?"

"Right you are," Gabe agreed. He drained the glass, then set it down and rubbed his hands together briskly. "Well, I've much to do today. And I intend to start with your father. Please tell him that I shall call on him this morning."

"I will do so."

"Thank you, Miss O'Shea."

Four regular trains daily made the run into Albuquerque: at midnight, nine A.M., noon, and four P.M. It was nearly time for the nine A.M. train and, already, a large crowd had gathered at the platform.

The coming of a train, any train, was a public event in Albuquerque. Trains brought visitors, friends and relatives. They brought mail, mail order goods, newspapers and treasures. They were visible proof that Albuquerque, so far from everything, was not totally isolated from the world.

Makenna had observed that the composition of the crowd around each train was unique and identifiable. She believed that she could tell which train was coming, without seeing a clock, just by observing the behavior of the crowds.

The midnight train was the most exciting...the crowd was gayer and noisier as if the coming of the train was the feature attraction at a gala party. The day train-watchers were more business-minded—merchants waiting for their wares, businessmen waiting for appointments—and though there were always vendors selling to the midnight crowd, there were even more during the day.

There was a crowd gathered around one of the vendors: a patent medicine man. Makenna drifted over to watch him and listen to his pitch. He was tall and thin and wearing a black suit that was badly in need of a cleaning. His long, bony finger jabbed at the air as he spoke.

"Yes, ladies and gentlemen, I have come bearing a new miracle drug that will work wonders for all illnesses. If you suffer from ulceration of the kidneys, loss of memory, weak nerves, hot hands, flushing in the body, consumption, torpidity of the liver, costiveness, hot spells, bearing down feelings, or cancer, this marvelous Extract of Buchu will be your salvation."

Makenna smiled as she left the crowd. If all these marvelous elixirs did what the vendors claimed they would do, there would be no need for doctors.

The whistle of the arriving train interrupted her thoughts.

Bull Blackwell was a huge man. He stood six feet, nine inches tall and weighed two hundred and eighty-five pounds. He had flaming red hair and a bushy beard of the same color. His legs were like tree trunks and his arms larger around than most men's legs. He was section foreman the time the Central Pacific laid ten miles of track in a single day to set the record and his name was spoken in work camps from the Mississippi to the Pacific. He stepped off the train right in front of Makenna and looked around with a bemused expression on his face.

"You, girl," he said when he saw her. "Would you know where to find Gabe Hansen?"

Makenna had never seen anyone as large and she stared in silence for a moment before she replied. Bull realized that he was awe inspiring to most people, so he just laughed and held his hand out, spreading the palm open for her.

"This big mitt would make three of yours, I reckon," he said good-naturedly. "When the good Lord started makin' me, he just didn't know when to stop."

"Oh, I'm sorry," Makenna said, suddenly realizing that she had been staring. "You wanted to know where Mr. Hansen is?"

"Yes, ma'am."

"He's in his private car." She pointed to Gabe's car which stood on a side switch.

"Thank you kindly, ma'am," Bull said. He started through the crowd toward the switch and Makenna watched him for several seconds. He wasn't swallowed up by the crowd; his head and shoulders stuck up above everyone else's and he moved through as if he were wading in a pond.

"What is Bull Blackwell doing here?" a voice asked.

Makenna turned to see Superintendent Whitney.

"I don't know," she said

"I understand Gabe Hansen has offered your papa a job."

"He has."

"Did he turn it down?"

"It's a much better job than he has now and he's considering it."

Whitney smiled, a slow, evil smile. "That's fine," he said. "See to it that you are all moved out by noon. The rooms where you live belong to Western Pacific, you know."

"By noon? That's impossible, where will we go?"

"That's not my problem."

Makenna turned away, tears burning her eyes. Why had she spoken out? Now her father had no job and they had no place to live. It was all her fault.

"Remember, girl, if your papa isn't out of there by noon, I'll have the sheriff run him out," Superintendent Whitney's voice called after her.

Makenna worked her way through the crowd of people, fighting the urge to cry, blinking rapidly to try and keep the tears in. Here and there she recognized someone and tried to return a greeting but, for the most part, she thought only of getting back to the safety of her house. Her house? *It's the Western Pacific's house*, she thought bitterly.

"Hello, darlin'," Kellen greeted when Makenna returned. "Say, look on the table in the kitchen. We got a case of those canned peaches in the mail order. Why don't we have some at noon?" When she heard her father say the word noon, Makenna could no longer keep it inside. She began crying in earnest.

"Makenna, darlin', what is it?"

Makenna went to her father's chair, then dropped to her knees beside him. She leaned her head against him and wept as if there were no end to her tears.

"Lass, here now, what could be botherin' you so?"

"Papa, we won't be here at noon. I did a terrible thing."

"What?" he asked, stroking her hair.

"I...I told Whitney you were considering Gabe Hansen's offer and he got mad. He said we had to be out of our house by noon today."

"That bastard!" Kellen said. He stood up and grabbed his crutches. "I'm going to have a word with him."

"Papa, no, please," Makenna said. "Leave it alone. Nothing happened."

"What do you mean, nothing happened?" Kellen asked, his voice raised now in anger. "Something happened. Something bad enough to bring you home in tears. And I intend to have words with the man."

"Please, Papa, you'll be hurt. You know you can't..."

"Can't what?" Kellen replied. He looked at Makenna. "Honey, I left my leg at Shiloh, not my manhood."

"Please, no; don't go see him," Makenna said. She grabbed him but Kellen pulled away, gently though firmly.

"Darlin', I will do this," he said. "If you've no wish to watch, you stay here." He moved quickly through the door and Makenna watched him through tear-dimmed eyes as he swung angrily on his crutches, hurrying along the station platform, bound toward the crowd to seek out Superintendent Whitney.

A moment after Kellen O'Shea left, Makenna heard the door to the front office open, and a voice called for her father. She went to see who it was.

"Well, Miss O'Shea," Gabe Hansen said. "It's nice to see you again. Is your father in?"

"Oh, Gabe," she cried impulsively. "Gabe, you've got to help...please!"

"Help? Of course, what is it?"

"It's Papa. He's gone to call out Superintendent Whitney. Whitney said we had to be out of here by noon and I think he's going to challenge him to a fight."

"A fight? Then I take it he's ready to leave his job and work for me?" Gabe asked.

"Yes. Gabe, you may not know this but my father only has one leg. And Whitney is younger. Papa can't fight Whitney!"

"Evidently, he feels that he can," Gabe said.

"Oh, Gabe, please...go stop him. Talk to Whitney."

"Makenna, I couldn't do that to your father. This is his fight. He'd never forgive me if I interfered."

"Oh, my god, what's happening? Has everyone gone mad?" Makenna said.

"I'll tell you what I'll do. I'll go keep an eye on him. I won't let your father be seriously hurt. But I won't fight his fight."

"Wait, I'm going with you," Makenna said.

It wasn't difficult to find them. The crowd at the station had gathered in a large circle and there was little doubt as to what was going on inside.

"Hurry," Makenna urged.

"Didn't your daughter get the message right?" they heard Whitney say as they approached. "I want you out of here by noon."

Makenna and Gabe forced their way through the crowd until they stood near the large circle that had been formed by the onlookers. Whitney and Kellen O'Shea were facing each other inside the circle. Kellen O'Shea was tall and lean, his leanness intensified by the fact that he had only one leg. Kellen's eyes flashed in anger as he stared at Whitney.

Whitney was about five years younger than Kellen and forty pounds heavier. And Whitney had two good legs. He was smiling confidently, almost eagerly, tauntingly.

Kellen brought his left hand up quickly, then slashed it across Whitney's face in a wicked backhand smash. The blow surprised and stunned Whitney and a trickle of blood began coming from his nose. "You...you one legged son-of-a-bitch," Whitney sputtered. "You think I'm going to let half a man get away with that?"

Whitney swung at Kellen but Kellen caught Whitney's wrist in his hand. He began squeezing and Whitney let out a surprised yelp of pain then, gradually, was forced to his knees by the strength of Kellen's grip.

"As you can see, Mr. Whitney, I may have only one leg but there is nothing wrong with my grip," Kellen said.

It was only then that those in the crowd realized that years of supporting himself with crutches had given Kellen O'Shea's upper torso great strength. They had thought, like Whitney, that the lack of a leg would render Kellen completely helpless. But they, like Whitney, were wrong.

Whitney was on his knees now, gasping in pain.

Kellen let go of the whimpering superintendent, then stepped back. "I'll be off Western Pacific property by noon, sir," he said.

As Kellen turned to walk away, a cheer rose from the crowd.

"Thank God, he wasn't hurt," Makenna said.

"You do not do justice to your father," Gabe replied.

Makenna and Gabe turned to follow Kellen and didn't see the signal that passed between Whitney and two rough-looking characters who were standing in the crowd. They also didn't see the two men drift away and start toward the station house.

But one huge, red-headed man did see them and he started walking, slowly, just behind them.

The two men waited until they were free of the crowd, then they darted across a switch track whereon stood a line of empty boxcars. They ran on silent feet behind the line of cars, then emerged at the far end, perfectly positioned to waylay Kellen O'Shea as he returned to his house.

The big red-headed man came up behind the line of cars, moving as silently as had the men before him. He reached the end, then stood there quietly, watching the two as they waited for Kellen to approach.

Kellen was swinging along the track on his crutches, moving quickly toward the house. Makenna and Gabe were several feet behind him, following. As Kellen reached the end of the cars, the two ruffians stepped out in front of him, smiling wickedly.

"Well, now, for half a man, you did pretty good," one of the men said.

Kellen stopped, then took a half step back. Though the words were complimentary, the tone of voice was not and Kellen sensed danger. "What do you want?" he asked.

"Fifty dollars," the other man said.

"Fifty dollars?"

"Yeah. That's what we're bein' given to beat you up. Now it don't make no never mind to us, one way or the other. You give us the fifty, 'n we'll leave you alone."

"I certainly will not give you fifty dollars," Kellen said. He braced himself, then saw something that made him lose all hope of defending himself. A huge man, larger than anyone he had ever seen, stepped out from behind the cars and stood behind and between the two men. Kellen assumed that he was with the two scoundrels.

"The odds don't seem right to me," the big man said. "Two to one is unfair. I'll make it two to two, if you gents don't mind."

The two waylayers turned around and saw that they were looking into the chest of the man who spoke. "What the hell?" one of them said. "Who are you?"

"Bull Blackwell," the man said easily. "I guess you got a right to know the name of the man who's going to break your neck."

"Let's go!" one of the two shouted and he broke into a dead run, his partner right behind him.

Kellen began laughing and Bull joined him in laughter. They were still laughing when Gabe and Makenna approached a moment later.

"Papa, what is it? Why are those men running?"

"I guess they just didn't like our company," Kellen said. He stuck his hand out toward Bull. "Mr. Blackwell, I'm obliged. My name is Kellen O'Shea."

"Pleased to meet you, Mr. O'Shea."

"Bull Blackwell is my track foreman," Gabe said, smiling. "You two will be seeing a lot of each other if you decide to work for me, Mr. O'Shea."

Kellen nodded. "I don't reckon I've got much choice," he said. "I'd be proud to work for you."

"Well, that calls for a celebration. What say we get you folks moved out of your place, then go over to Delmonico's for lunch?"

"Oh, Papa, where are we going to live?" Makenna asked, suddenly thinking of it.

"How about my railroad car?" Gabe offered.

"Thank you kindly, Mr. Hansen…" Kellen started.

"It's Gabe."

"Thank you, Gabe, but we couldn't do that."

"Why not? You were living rent free on Western Pacific property. Just look at this the same way."

"But where will you live?"

"I've got ten crew cars arriving tomorrow," Gabe replied. "One of them is the car I lived in on my last site. It's quite comfortable and I'm used to it. I'll live there."

"Well, then, if you're certain," Kellen said. "I'd be honored to live in your railroad car."

"Good. We'll get you moved into it right away and I'll stay at the hotel tonight."

"I hate putting you out this way," Kellen protested.

"Please don't worry about it," Gabe assured him. "I'm going to be celebrating tonight. Chances are, I won't be in bed before one or two o'clock anyway. Uh, beg your pardon, Miss O'Shea."

"You owe me no apology," Makenna answered. "And it's Makenna."

The largest crowd ever to greet a train in Albuquerque turned out early the next morning for the arrival of the Honest Abe. Honest Abe pulled a train composed of bunkhouse cars, a rolling kitchen, and a field office, all part of Gabe Hansen's new railroad. The engine was the first of the new line. It was a beautiful Baldwin 4-4-0 fast passenger engine with huge driver wheels and a diamond stack. The body was green and it and the green wheels were trimmed in bright red. All the fittings and the bell were of shining brass. The tender, also green and trimmed in red, had the logo SCRR in huge, gilt letters, denoting Southern Continental Railroad.

As the engine rolled to a stop, the engineer blew the whistle, then leaned out the cab window. He smiled down at Makenna, who was standing on the platform.

"What do you think of her, Miss O'Shea? Ain't she a beaut?"

"Dudley, you? What are you doing up there?"

"Me 'n Milo pulled the pin on Western Pacific," Dudley said, using the railroad slang for quitting.

The big Swede suddenly appeared beside Dudley in the cab window, white teeth showing through a soot-blackened face.

"Yah," he said. "Dudley 'n me, will not be stayin' with railroad when they not do right by such fine man as your papa. And Dudley is the best hoghead in the business, so Mr. Hansen hire him 'n me right away."

"Oh, I'm glad," Makenna said.

There was a sudden strange cacophony of voices and Makenna looked back along the train to see several Chinese detraining. She had heard that Chinese labor was being used in building the Western railroads but this was the first time she had ever seen a large number of them.

"Long Li, you old yellow-skinned heathen, how are you?" Makenna heard someone shout. It was Bull Blackwell, walking over to greet one of them, shaking the man's hand warmly. Bull would have made two of the small Long Li but, in terms of affection, they were equal.

"You know that Chinaman?" Dudley called back to Bull.

"Hell yes, I know him," Bull answered. "He was the boss of my Chinese on the old Central Pacific. Best damn slave driver you ever saw. Long Li, what are you doing here? I thought you were through with railroads."

"I no like San Francisco," Long Li replied. "All Chinamen in San Francisco run laundry or place to eat. I no like either, so I come back to work on railroad. Maybe we do good, set another record same-same like in old days."

"You better believe it," Bull said. He looked at the group of Chinese workers who were climbing off the train. "Have we got any of our boys back?"

"I no can tell," Long Li said. "All Chinamen look same to me," he added with a straight face.

Bull laughed uproariously, then threw his great arm around the small man's shoulders. "Come on, li'l buddy. Let's you 'n me go get drunker'n hell."

"Bull, will they let Chinamen drink at this bar?" Dudley asked from the cab of his engine.

"Now, by God, Dudley, who the hell's goin' to tell me I can't buy my li'l buddy a drink?" Bull asked.

Dudley laughed. "I can't think of a soul."

"I can't either," Bull replied. "Come on, Long Li, let's go."

Makenna saw Gabe moving through the crowd, smiling as he approached her.

"Here's your new engine, Mr. Hansen," Dudley said. He had a cloth in his hand and he rubbed along the bottom frame of the cab window, polishing an imaginary spot.

"Pretty, ain't she? I'll tell you somethin' else. Me 'n Milo had her up to fifty miles an hour on the way down here, 'n she had a lot left. I wouldn't be surprised if she wouldn't make seventy."

"You're going to get a chance to find out," Gabe said. "I want you to kick these cars over onto the spur line, then deadhead back up to Trinidad and pick up a string of cars loaded with new rails. I just got the message that they arrived."

"We'll be back in ten hours," Dudley guaranteed.

"Ten hours?" Makenna said in wonder. "To Trinidad and back is four hundred and fifty miles. You can't make that speed."

"Miss, with the big Swede here keepin' my fire hot, we'll sing on the iron, you mark my words."

The brakeman came up to the engine to join the group. His name was Davis and he, too, had worked for the Western Pacific before coming to work with Gabe Hansen. Makenna thought it spoke well for Gabe, that he could hire so many good men away from WP on the promise of a dream.

"Davis, we've got to kick these cars free," Dudley said. "We're headed back for Trinidad."

"We've got a problem," Davis said.

"What?" Gabe asked.

"We can't park our cars on the spur line."

"What? Why the hell not?"

"There's a couple of armed galoots at the switch. The

switch is locked closed and they won't open it. They say they have orders to leave it closed until they get word from the station agent."

"I wonder what the hell this is all about?" Gabe mused.

"The two guys on the switch say it's something about paying the track rent," Davis said.

"Track rent? That's all been taken care of. We don't have to pay the track rent until we get our first loan payment from Van Zandt."

"All I know is what they said," Davis replied.

"Damnit," Gabe swore. He rubbed his hand through his hair and looked at Makenna. "Makenna, do you know this agent? This new guy? What's his name?"

"Yes," Makenna said. "His name is Wayne Gerhard. He was Whitney's assistant before he came here."

"Gerhard, Gerhard," Gabe mused. "I've heard of him somewhere, haven't I?"

"He's the one who was found negligent in the cornfield meet outside Dodge City," Dudley reminded him.

"Yes, yes; I remember now," Gabe said. Cornfield meet was another way of saying a head-on collision. A train wreck between a west-bound passenger train and an eastbound freight had killed forty-three people near Dodge City, Kansas. Investigation revealed that Wayne Gerhard, the station agent at Dodge City, had received a message ordering him to hold the freight train on a side track until the unscheduled passenger train had passed. But, Gerhard, who was a petty man, was arguing with a rancher over the bill of lading for a shipment of cattle and the freight train went right on through. It wasn't until fifteen minutes after the train passed that Gerhard remembered. He hired a fast horse and tried to chase after it, but arrived to find broken rails and twisted cars scattered on both sides of the track. The field was strewn with the dead and dying and the sound of hissing steam and anguished screams filled the air.

"What's he doing running a station again?" Gabe asked. "I thought they found him negligent."

"They did," Davis said. "He was fined one hundred dollars and returned to full duty."

"And now he's here to plague us," Gabe said. "I won't have the money until tomorrow. It's arriving on a special train. I wonder if he'll wait until then?"

"Not likely," Davis guessed. "He's still a stickler for petty things."

"It's always the case with men like that," Gabe said. "They can't handle the major things, so they tie themselves down with the small." He sighed. "Well, I guess I'll go see what I can do." Gabe left to talk with Wayne Gerhard and Makenna began walking around, enjoying the crowd that the special train had drawn. As she stepped down from the platform, a man on horseback galloped by. He was going so fast and came so close to Makenna that she let out a short scream and jumped back, only to trip and fall.

"*Señorita*, are you all right?" The man who spoke was Mexican, dressed in solid black, with silver conchos and a silver buckle fastening a gun belt, which held a pearl-handled pistol. His face was shaded by a large sombrero.

"Yes, I'm all right," she answered, struggling to regain her balance and her dignity.

"Please, permit me to help you stand," the man offered, extending his hand to her. He smiled and Makenna noticed that he was in his late twenties, extremely handsome in a darkly Latin way.

"Thank you." Makenna took his hand, allowing him to help her up. She brushed herself off with what dignity she could muster.

"I saw the man's face, *Señorita*. If you like, I will bring him here and he will get on his knees to apologize to you."

"No, no, don't do that," Makenna protested. "But thank you for your help, *Señor*... I'm afraid I don't know your name."

"Tafoya," the man said. He smiled broadly, then removed his hat and gave a graceful, unaffected bow.

"Tafoya? You are the don?"

"No, *Señorita*, that is my father, Don Esteban Tafoya. I am Bernardo."

"The bandit?" Makenna asked impulsively.

Bernardo laughed. "Some may call me a *bandido*," he said. "There are others who call me patriot. I prefer to think of myself as a simple rancher."

"There is nothing simple about Rancho Sombra de las Montanas, Señor Tafoya," Makenna said. "I've heard that it stretches from here to the Arizona territory."

"*Sí*, this is true," Bernardo agreed. "You can see why we fight so to defend it."

"I remember now," Makenna said. "You destroyed some railroad equipment and you shot many men in a surveying party."

"I did destroy railroad equipment, *Señorita*, but only because they slaughtered some of my cattle. But I did not shoot any of the surveying party though I did embarrass them."

Bernardo laughed and Makenna remembered the incident. Four men had come riding into town, their legs tied beneath the bellies of their horses, their hands tied to the saddle horn. Their entrance into town had been met with great laughter because all four men were stark naked.

"You are a wanted man, Señor Tafoya," Makenna said. "I've seen the posters on you. What are you doing here?

Aren't you afraid you'll get caught?"

"No, *Señorita*. I have come only to scout the enemy. I will go quietly before anyone knows I have been here."

"But I know you are here."

"*Sí*, but you won't say anything."

"How do you know I won't?"

"Because, Señorita O'Shea, I can see it in your face."

"Do you know me?"

"I make it a point to know everyone who has anything to do with the railroad. I know all about you and your father and I know about Gabe Hansen and the money he is getting from Emory Van Zandt."

"How do you know that?"

Bernardo laughed. "An interesting thing about the telegraph wires, *Señorita*. If you have a wire and a machine, you can read the taps even though the message isn't addressed to you."

"That's against the law," Makenna said sharply.

"Oh? Haven't you heard? I am already a wanted man," Bernardo said mildly. He took Makenna's hand and raised it to his lips, then brushed it lightly with a kiss.

Bernardo laughed, then dropped her hand and took a step back. He touched his hand to his hat. "*Adiós*, my pretty one."

Makenna watched him walk through the crowd with as little concern as if he were strolling through his own house. She knew she should tell someone. He was a wanted man, an avowed enemy of the railroad. To let him remain free was to invite trouble. But for some inexplicable reason, she didn't want to turn him in.

CHAPTER FIVE

After Gabe left the train, he started toward the station house with angry, purposeful strides. As he passed the switch, he saw two men standing there, both carrying sawed-off shotguns. He recognized them as the two men who had accosted Kellen O'Shea the day before.

"Hey, Hansen," one of the men called. "Why don't you send that big red-headed son-of-a-bitch over here to open the switch?"

"Yeah," the other said, laughing: "I'd like to see how the big bastard would act with a load of buckshot in his belly."

Both men laughed and Gabe walked by without answering them.

When Gabe pushed his way into the station house, he saw Kellen O'Shea's replacement. Wayne Gerhard was a small man who wore wire-rim eyeglasses and suffered with a nervous tic in his jaw.

"Gerhard, my name is Gabe Hansen."

"I know who you are, sir," Gerhard said easily.

"Why won't you let my cars onto the spur track?"

"I'll let them on as soon as you pay the first month's rent," Gerhard said.

"Whitney never said anything to me about paying in advance," Gabe said.

"I'm afraid he said something to me," Gerhard said. He put his glasses on, looping them over one ear at a time, and pulled a message from his pocket. He cleared his throat.

"I just got this over the wire this morning," he said. "WP order number eleven, dated June 15,1881. 'All rolling stock of any railroad other than Western Pacific must pay track rental fees in advance, at the rate of ten dollars per standing car, per day, one month minimum.'" Gerhard folded the message up and put it in his pocket, then removed his glasses and looked at Gabe. "You have ten cars, Mr. Hansen. Your rent for the first month is three thousand dollars."

"Very well, I'll pay it tomorrow."

"No, sir, Mr. Hansen. It must be paid today."

"Do you think I carry that kind of money with me?" Gabe asked angrily, fighting to maintain his control. "I'll have the funds tomorrow."

"I'm afraid Superintendent Whitney's instructions were very explicit, sir," Gerhard said. "I was ordered to collect the rent in advance. That means today."

"Why don't you wire Whitney and tell him that I paid it? I'll have it for you by tomorrow and he'll never know the difference."

"I'm sorry. I can't do that."

Gabe slapped his hand on the desk angrily.

"All right, you dried-up little bastard. I'll get the money today."

"When you give me the money, I'll open the switch," Gerhard replied.

Gabe stepped out onto the station platform and thrust his hands in his pocket. He knew there would be many more aggravations before he brought this railroad in. This was only the first. It wouldn't do to let it get to him. A handsome phaeton passed by and Gabe saw Rosie Cleveland sitting in the rear seat, shielding herself from the sun with a parasol. Rosie was the madam of the local brothel. Though Gabe had never done business with her enough of his men had that he had, of necessity, made her acquaintance. He got an idea.

"Hello, Rosie," he called.

"Driver, stop," Rosie said. The liveried driver pulled the team to a stop and Rosie looked out at Gabe and smiled. "Well, Gabe, I see your first crew of workers have arrived."

"That they have."

"I hope they aren't all Chinese," she said. "That would be awful."

"Why, Rosie, you mean your girls don't like the Chinese?" Gabe teased.

"Don't be ridiculous. In this business you don't have any choice as to likes or dislikes. It's just that the Chinese don't spend their money as freely as the others do."

Gabe stepped down off the platform and stood by the carriage. "Out to look over the clientele?" he asked.

"If they're Chinese, I've seen them," she said. She patted the seat beside her. "Would you join me?"

"Maybe I would at that," Gabe said. He climbed in beside her. "Perhaps a ride to the hotel?"

Rosie smiled broadly. "Of course. Driver, to the hotel, please."

"Yes'm," the driver said.

The carriage rolled through the streets of Albuquerque and Gabe was strangely quiet. Finally, Rosie spoke.

"What is it, Gabe? You aren't your usual, jovial self."

Gabe laughed. "No, I guess you've got me there,

Rosie. The truth is, I need something and I'm going to ask you for it."

"What do you need?"

"I need three thousand dollars," Gabe said.

"Are you serious?"

"Very."

Rosie turned in her seat to Gabe, a look of disbelief on her face. "Gabe, how do you plan to get this railroad off the ground if you don't even have three thousand dollars?"

Gabe explained the problem to Rosie, assuring her that he would have the money the next day when Emory Van Zandt and the special train arrived. "So you see," he concluded. "It's to your advantage to let me have it, just long enough to get started. Because if this thing falls through before it ever gets going, you stand to lose a good deal too."

Rosie looked through her purse and pulled out a small cigar. She stuck it in her mouth and lit it before she answered. "You've got a point there. All right, come on up to my room. I'll get the money for you."

"Thanks, Rosie. I'm going to owe you for this."

Makenna thought about her meeting with Bernardo. There was something he had said that vaguely disturbed her but she couldn't quite put her finger on it. Then, as clearly as a lightning flash in a summer sky, she realized what it had been. Bernardo said that he had a wire connected to the telegraph lines! That meant that he knew everything that was going on and he knew it as soon as anyone else did.

If Bernardo knew that Emory Van Zandt was supplying money to Gabe's operation, then he also knew how and when it was coming. And that could be dangerous. Gabe had to be warned.

Makenna saw the unmistakable bulk of Bull Blackwell and she called out to him, asking him if he knew where she could find Gabe.

"Yes'm, I just saw him over at the hotel," Bull answered.

Makenna hurried to the hotel. Somehow, she felt guilty about telling Gabe as if she were betraying Bernardo's trust. But Bernardo had no right to expect her to honor a trust between them. She didn't owe him anything. On the other hand, she owed Gabe Hansen a great deal or, at least, she owed the fledgling railroad her loyalty. She had burned her father's bridges behind him. There was no place left for him to go, except Gabe's railroad, and if Bernardo meant to destroy it, then she would have to stop him in whatever way she could.

"Hello, Miss O'Shea," the desk clerk said, looking up as Makenna went inside.

"Hello, Harry. Is Gabe Hansen in the dining room?"

"No, ma'am, I just saw him go upstairs."

Makenna started upstairs. Of course, Gabe would be here. He spent the night here last night and he would be moving his things back to the crew car. She would help him and tell him about Bernardo as they worked.

When Makenna reached the second-floor landing, she saw a maid about to knock on a door. The maid was holding a tray with a bottle of wine.

"Excuse me, do you know where I might find Gabe Hansen?" Makenna inquired.

"Why, yes, ma'am. He's right in here," the maid answered. "I'm about to deliver this bottle of wine to him."

"I will deliver the wine," Makenna said, "as a surprise."

"But, ma'am..."

"You shall have your gratuity," Makenna assured the girl.

"Yes, ma'am," the maid said, surrendering the tray to Makenna.

Makenna drew in her breath and knocked on the door. "It's the wine, sir," she called, disguising her voice and swallowing the lump of excitement that had risen in her throat.

"Bring it on in," Gabe called.

Makenna opened the door and stepped inside. She was surprised to see a woman in the room with him. The wine was for the two of them.

Makenna let out a gasp and dropped the wine bottle along with the tray.

Gabe looked around at the crash of sound. "Makenna! What the hell are you doing here?"

Makenna turned and ran from the room

"Makenna, wait! It isn't what it looks like," Gabe called.

"I shouldn't have come here like this. It's none of my business who you bring to your room!" Makenna shouted back at him. Embarrassed, she ran down the stairs, through the small lobby, and out the front door—right into Bernardo Tafoya's arms.

"You," she said angrily. "Let me pass." Bernardo pulled his pistol from the holster and held it to her head.

"Now," he shouted past her. "I think I have the advantage, no?"

"What? What is this?" Makenna asked.

It wasn't until that moment that she realized what she had done. The street was full of armed and angry men and it seemed that she had saved Bernardo Tafoya from a certain hanging. But, apparently, she had saved him at the expense of her own liberty.

"Let her go, Tafoya," one of the men shouted.

"This I cannot do, *Señor*," Bernardo said. "Now, the

señorita and I will stay right here until someone is so kind as to bring my horse."

"Don't be a fool, Tafoya, you'll never get away with this."

"My horse, please," Bernardo said calmly.

"Do as he says," Kellen O'Shea spoke out from the crowd. "Makenna, you just stay calm, honey, and we'll get you out of this."

"What is this? What's happening?" Makenna asked, her mind swirling in confusion.

"Unfortunately, one of the gentleman I ran into recognized me," Bernardo said. "He told the others and, before I knew it, I was about to attend a lynching party. As the guest of honor. You came along just in time, *Señorita*."

"Let me go," Makenna asked. "I didn't have anything to do with this. I didn't tell anyone you were here."

"It doesn't matter now, *Señorita*," Bernardo said. "I can't let you go. You are my only means of escape."

A man started toward them leading a big, black horse.

"Ah, Diablo, my beauty. I must apologize to you. You will have to carry double. But the *señorita*, she is so beautiful, this is not a chore you will dislike, no? Come, *Señorita*, get on the horse." Bernardo prodded her gently with the gun.

The two of them swung into the saddle and Bernardo looked back at the crowd. "If anyone comes after me, I shall be forced to put a bullet into this lovely head. I'm sure you agree with me that it would be a terrible waste, yes?"

"If you hurt that girl, all the demons of hell won't keep me from you," Kellen O'Shea shouted.

"The girl will not be hurt if no one acts foolishly," Bernardo said. "*Adiós, amigos.*" He slapped his feet against the horse's side and they left in the thunder of hoofbeats.

CHAPTER SIX

Makenna did not fight as they rode out of town because to fight would only make matters worse. Bernardo rode at full speed and only after he was sure that he wasn't being pursued, did he allow the horse to slow to a walk.

"Get down, *Señorita*," he said.

"You're going to make me walk?"

Bernardo lifted Makenna out of the saddle and put her on the ground, then swung off his horse behind her. "We are both going to walk for a while," he said. "Diablo needs the rest."

"You shouldn't have taken me," Makenna said, after a moment. "They will come after you and they'll kill you."

"Will you cry for me when that happens?" Bernardo asked, his eyes sparkling as he teased her.

"No, not one tear," Makenna replied hotly. Bernardo clucked his tongue at her.

"Ah, you are a cruel woman."

"And why shouldn't I be? You were willing to shoot me if you had to."

Bernardo laughed. "I wouldn't have shot you, *Señorita*. But it was good that the others thought that I would."

"Are you going to let me go now?" she asked, looking around her.

"I think not," Bernardo said. "I think it is better if you stay with me for a while."

"Well, I certainly will not stay with you!"

Bernardo smiled easily. "You have no choice, *Señorita*. You are my prisoner."

Makenna saw riders approaching from the west and a quick surge of hope flashed through her. They were her rescuers! She looked at Bernardo and saw that he, too, saw the riders. But he was smiling as if welcoming them; then Makenna realized that, coming from the west, they would have to be his own men.

Four men and a woman reined up just in front of them. The woman was a feminine copy of Bernardo. And she was beautiful.

"Who have you here, my brother?" she asked, looking at Makenna.

"Allow me to introduce you," Bernardo said.

"Señorita Makenna O'Shea, this is my sister, Teresina Tafoya."

"Why did you bring her?" Teresina asked, her eyes never leaving Makenna's face.

"I had no choice. I was recognized. The girl was my ticket out of town."

Teresina sighed, nodded at Makenna, and turned to her brother. "What will we do with her?"

"Take her back to the rancho," one of the men said. He looked at Makenna and smiled lecherously. "I know what I can do with her."

Bernardo said something in Spanish. Makenna couldn't understand what it was but it was sharp and angry and the Mexican replied in Spanish in a tone of voice just as angry. A few more words were exchanged, then the air hung heavy with tension. Without understanding a word, Makenna realized that the two men were having some sort of confrontation.

"Draw your gun, Garcia," Bernardo said in quiet English. "Draw your gun or ride out of here."

Garcia glared at Bernardo angrily and, for a moment, Makenna was certain that he was going to draw his pistol. No one made a sound, looking from one man to the other. Bernardo remained calm, not a tremor in his hands, nor a flicker in his eye. Garcia, on the other hand, began shaking. Sweat popped out on his face. Finally, with an oath muttered in Spanish, he slapped his legs against the side of his horse, turned, and rode away.

"You shouldn't have done that, my brother," Teresina scolded.

"He was a pig," Bernardo said easily.

"And so, to defend this gringo girl, you have made an enemy? You know he will go straight to the railroad."

Bernardo shrugged. "What harm can he do?" he asked.

"He can alert them that we intend to rob the special train tomorrow," Teresina said. "Without the element of surprise, we have no chance."

"Then we will not rob the train," Bernardo said easily. "Besides, as long as we have the girl, we have no need to rob the train. We will hold her until the railroad sends its tracks elsewhere."

"We can't take her to the Casa Grande," Teresina cautioned. "Padre would not approve."

"You are right. The don, unlike his children, is an honorable man," Bernardo said. "We will take her to the old place."

Bernardo regained his saddle, then reached for Makenna.

"It will be a lighter load if she rides with me," Teresina said. She called Makenna over to her horse, then helped her mount. They started out at a brief trot, Bernardo in the lead, the other two men behind him.

They rode hard for four hours, switching Makenna from horse to horse to keep the mounts from tiring. Finally, when Makenna felt as if she couldn't ride another minute, they approached the Rio Puerco and she saw a cluster of houses along the west bank. The horses rode through the shallow river, throwing water and sand up from the hooves, then onto the other side where they were welcomed by a group of men, women and children.

"What is this place?" Makenna asked as they dismounted.

"It was our family home for many years," Bernardo said. "Now the don lives in the new casa, ten miles from here. He has given these houses over to the families of our vaqueros." There was a great deal of talking and wild gesturing and, several times, someone would look toward Makenna and laugh. It made her extremely uncomfortable.

"What is it?" she asked. "What is everyone laughing about?"

Bernardo smiled. "They want to hold a party in your honor."

"In my honor? Why? I'm a prisoner here, I'm not a guest," Makenna said.

"My people are happy people," Bernardo said. "It takes little excuse for them to have a party. And if they prefer to think of you as a guest rather than a prisoner, why should you object? They are a generous people."

Makenna started to protest again but suddenly realized that a party might occupy everyone's attention enough to allow her to escape. She forced herself to smile.

"All right," she said. "It might be fun."

"There now, that's the way to look at it," Bernardo said. "After all, *Señorita*, you and I are not enemies, no? It is only the railroad which causes the trouble. Come, we will have our party."

The word spread to the others and, in an amazingly short time, the atmosphere changed to one of gaiety. Tables were placed on a shaded patio and, as if materializing from thin air, they were covered with food. There was much wine in evidence and soon there was singing and dancing to the music of two excellent guitarists.

"*Señorita, Señorita*, you will strike at the *piñata*, yes?" the children urged.

"What do they want me to do?"

"Break the *piñata*," Bernardo answered. "Sweets are placed in a clay jar, then tied to a rope. The rope is thrown over a tree limb. You are blindfolded and given a stick and you try to break the *piñata* while it's moved around by the rope. If you break it, the children win."

"Will you do this, *Señorita?*"

Makenna looked at the children and laughed. "Yes," she said.

The children cheered and two of the older ones took her by the hand and led her to a tree. She was blindfolded and given a stick. She swung several times, missing every time and bringing forth peals of laughter.

"I will help," Bernardo said.

Makenna felt Bernardo's arms go around her, then take her hands in his. She tensed.

"Easy, *muchacha*," Bernardo said. "I'm just going to help you break the *piñata*. The children grow restless."

Bernardo swung her arms and she felt the stick hit the clay jar. There was a satisfying crash, then squeals of delight from the children as the contents rained down.

"You may remove your blindfold," Bernardo said.

Makenna took the blindfold off, then laughed. The music swelled and the party went on.

"Now, isn't this the way to be a prisoner?" Bernardo asked.

A prisoner! For a moment Makenna had nearly forgotten.

"Bernardo, you must let me go," she said quietly. "They will come after me and there will be bloodshed."

"Makenna, there is going to be bloodshed anyway and there is little we can do about it," Bernardo answered.

"Then you must let me go."

"I cannot," Bernardo said. "I intend to use you to bargain with Gabe Hansen."

"You're a fool," Makenna said. "You will accomplish nothing this way."

"Perhaps not," Bernardo agreed. "But let us talk of this no longer. Are you hungry? Come, we will eat now."

Makenna walked with him to one of the tables and Bernardo began preparing a plate. "You must eat something," he said. "It is very good." Makenna began filling a plate with the highly spiced foods. She looked at the far end of the table and saw someone riding up. The rider dismounted, then walked over to talk to Bernardo.

They were speaking in Spanish and Makenna couldn't understand them but she wasn't trying. Her attention was held by the horse.

The horse was standing where the rider left him, less than ten feet away from Makenna. There were no other horses anywhere close and, by now, many of the men were pretty drunk. If she could just get on that horse, Makenna thought, she could ride out of here!

Makenna eased on down the table, still putting things

on her plate, but now using it only as an excuse to reach the horse. Finally, she was right there! She set the plate down and quietly swung up into the saddle.

"Makenna!" Bernardo called, seeing then what she was doing.

Makenna slapped the reins against the horse and the horse broke into a gallop.

Makenna was a good rider and the horse cleared the courtyard before anyone was able to react. She heard Bernardo call her name, then shout to the others, but she thought only of getting away.

Makenna bent low over the horse's neck, riding as fast as she could. She looked around to see Bernardo on Diablo, gaining fast.

"Oh, come on, horse, go faster, go faster," she pleaded.

Bernardo overtook her easily, then reached out and grabbed the reins of Makenna's horse. He got them both stopped. "I'm sorry," he said soberly. "We must go back now."

"Damn it," Makenna cried out in frustration.

Bernardo smiled. "Do not be angry with yourself. It was a good try. But I am the owner of this ranch. Do you not think I would keep the fastest horse for myself?"

They rode back to the party, then dismounted. "Teresina," Bernardo called.

"Yes?" She joined them quickly.

"Our guest of honor tried to leave the party early. Perhaps you can think of a way to discourage her."

Teresina smiled. "I can think of a way. Come with me, Señorita O'Shea," she said.

Makenna followed Teresina inside the house. They walked down a long hallway, then Teresina stopped just outside a door. "In here," she said, opening the door to a room. "You could have been our guest. Now, you are our prisoner."

Teresina pushed Makenna into the room, then closed the door behind her. Makenna heard the door lock.

About an hour later, Makenna heard shooting outside. Not the occasional shots of the party that she'd been hearing but rapid and angry firing. The sounds of music and laughter changed to cries of fear and rage and then she heard Gabe's voice.

"Save Bernardo for me! If he's done anything to that girl, I'll carve the bastard's heart out!" There were more shooting and more shouts, then the sound of several horses galloping off. "Mr. Hansen, they're gettin' away!"

"After them, men," Gabe shouted. "I'm going to look for Makenna."

Makenna heard noises in the house. Doors were being kicked open and boots stomped down the hallway. She quailed in her bed and, seconds later, her door exploded into the room, flying off its hinges in splinters.

Gabe stood just on the other side of the smashed door, looking in curiously.

"Gabe, oh Gabe, thank God it's you," Makenna said.

"Makenna, are you all right?"

"Yes, I'm all right, thank you, thank you," Makenna replied.

CHAPTER SEVEN

The morning light spilled in through the window and the plush draperies of the railroad car which was serving as home to Makenna and her father. The noises of a train being worked on drifted in and Makenna found herself slowly abandoning sleep.

"Makenna, girl, will you be sleepin' the entire mornin' away now?" her father's voice called from outside the door.

"I'm up, Papa," Makenna said. "I'll be out shortly."

When Makenna was dressed, she left her bedroom and saw two men with her father. One of them was Gabe Hansen.

"Good morning, Gabe."

"Sure now, 'n that's all you've to say to the man who risked his neck to rescue yours?" her father chastised her. "I'm thinkin' a more proper thank you would be in order."

"It isn't necessary, Mr. O'Shea," Gabe put in quickly. "Makenna has undergone quite an ordeal."

"You haven't introduced our guest," Makenna said.

"I haven't at that," Kellen said. "Makenna, darlin', this is Peter Van Zandt, the son of Mr. Emory Van Zandt. Peter here will be lookin' out for his father's investment."

Peter Van Zandt looked to be a year or so younger than Gabe. He had wavy brown hair, insolent blue eyes, and a somewhat world-weary look. He had neither the ruggedness nor the look of strength about him that one saw in Gabe. In fact, Peter's classic good looks were almost feminine. But Makenna sensed something about him—a current of danger seemed to flow through him. She instinctively knew that no man who valued his life would lock horns with the young man before her.

"I do hope you will do me the honor of dining with me tonight. Of course, this invitation includes your father as well," he added quickly.

"Sure 'n we'd be glad to," Kellen answered for the two of them. "Wouldn't we darlin'?"

"Yes, of course," Makenna said. She had no choice in the matter now; her father had preempted that by his acceptance.

"Wonderful. I shall call for you here at seven this evening," Peter said. He gave the two of them another wide smile, then turned to Gabe. "Mr. Hansen, if you would care to show me how you are spending my father's money, I shall be glad to accompany you now."

"Of course," Gabe said. "Come along, I'll show you the crew cars, then we'll walk out to End-of-Track. It's only a short walk today but, within a week, we'll have to take a locomotive or go on horseback."

"I find the whole idea of laying track across a desert inconceivable," Peter said. "I feel I must warn you now that I don't share my father's enthusiasm for this project. I intend to keep a very close watch on every penny and hold you absolutely to the contract."

"Not one cent will be squandered," Gabe promised as they left the car.

Kellen watched them through the door for a moment, then he turned to face Makenna.

"Makenna, girl. Did that Mexican bandit hurt you in any way?"

"I wasn't physically harmed, other than being held as a prisoner," Makenna said.

"We'll be thankin' the good Lord for that," Kellen said.

Gabe and Peter walked out to End-of-Track, now just a few hundred yards beyond the western limits of Albuquerque, and watched the activity of the men laying the new track. Ties without rails were stretched several hundred feet beyond, already in place. Then forty men, twenty to each rail, would snake the long piece of steel ribbon into place, laying it just so on the ties. They would leave and their places would be taken immediately by others who would swing sledge hammers driving the huge spikes home, ringing out, steel on steel. The railroad was growing right before the men's eyes, stretching out nearly as fast as a man could walk.

The Chinese workers were scurrying about like ants working a hill, each indistinguishable from the other. But one of them, who was carrying a bucket of dirt used for setting the ties, tripped and the dirt spilled over Peter Van Zandt's polished shoes. The laborer was on his feet immediately, bowing apologetically to Peter, unable to express himself in English.

Peter's eyes grew very cold and his hand slipped in under his coat. Bull Blackwell, who was standing nearby, saw the move and let out a bellow.

"Long Li, take that clumsy son-of-a-bitch out of here and teach him some manners."

Long Li, who had seen Peter's move just as Bull had,

reacted quickly. He shouted something in Chinese and, within a second, the man was surrounded by dozens of his countrymen. They were shouting and cursing him but, more effectively, they were shielding him, for by now, Peter, who had removed his pistol, was unable to get a clear shot at him. In fact, within an instant, Peter could no longer tell which of the Chinese it was who had offended him.

"Don't you worry none, Mr. Van Zandt," Bull said, walking over to the two men and towering over both of them. "We'll strip the hide off the little bugger."

Peter's face showed that he had been denied his satisfaction but since it was so adroitly handled, he replaced his pistol without a word.

"Would you really have shot him just for spilling dirt on your shoes?" Gabe asked.

"Yes," Peter said easily.

"That doesn't seem like enough to kill a man over."

"He was a coolie," Peter said as if that justified his action.

"The Chinese were printing with movable type when our ancestors were still writing on the walls of caves," Gabe said.

"Mr. Hansen, I hope you don't let your tender feelings for these creatures extend into the work you get from them. I expect to see a full measure of work extracted for the money my father invests," Peter said.

"You need have no fear on that score," Gabe replied. "There's not a crew in the world who can outwork this one. Bull Blackwell and Long Li are the best in the business."

"Long Li? A Chinese? You have a Chinese in authority? Over white men?" Peter asked incredulously.

"No," Gabe said. "He supervises only the Chinese labor."

A train whistle was heard in the distance and the two men looked back toward town, at the track stretching beyond the town to the other side. There, still a couple of miles away, they saw an approaching train, its stack drawing a pencil line of smoke in the clear, blue sky.

"That'll be another crew coming in," Gabe said. "I'd best be getting back to meet them."

"More Chinese?"

"Irish," Gabe said. "I don't think you'll care much for them either."

As Gabe started back, Peter called to him. "I hope you aren't upset over my inviting Miss O'Shea to dinner tonight."

Gabe stopped and looked back. "Upset? No, why should I be?"

"It's just that I thought I perceived something between the two of you. No? Well, then there is no problem. Makenna O'Shea may prove to be a delightful diversion in this otherwise Godforsaken place."

"Miss O'Shea is a big girl and can do as she pleases," Gabe said.

Peter smiled an easy, but disquieting, smile. "I thank you for your permission," he said. "It will make it easier."

"It is not my permission to give," Gabe said. He turned away then and hurried to meet the train.

Makenna was very excited as she readied herself for the dinner that evening. She had eaten in the hotel restaurant before but almost always it had been as a matter of necessity or convenience. This would be the very first dinner she had ever eaten out, just for the purpose of eating out. She wished for a moment that it was Gabe who would be eating with them but almost as quickly as that ungrateful thought arose, she put it aside. Peter Van Zandt, after all, was a very handsome man and a gracious one. She was flattered by his attentions and she knew that her evening with him would be an event to remember.

Peter was exactly on time and Makenna made a last-minute adjustment to her hair as she heard her father letting him into the living room. She pinched her cheeks to bring out the rose glow, then walked out to greet him.

"Good evening, Mr. Van Zandt," Makenna said.

Kellen O'Shea was in the midst of a story and he was smiling as he was talking. He looked around at his daughter and the smile left his face to be replaced by an expression of surprise and awe. It was as if he were seeing his daughter for the first time. And, in fact, this was the first time he had ever been aware of her as others saw her.

Makenna was standing in the doorway wearing a golden colored silk gown. Kellen remembered when she had sent away for it from the mail order catalog. It was high-necked but close-fitting at the bosom and pinched-in at the waist, then flaring out into many tiers. Her skin glowed and her eyes sparkled. A flash of light sparkled from the dancing ear bobs she was wearing.

"My God, daughter," Kellen breathed reverently. "I have never seen you look so beautiful." He continued to stare as if it were a stranger who stood before him.

"I must say that I agree completely," Peter said easily. He crossed the room and offered his arm to her. "I have a phaeton waiting outside. Shall we go?"

"You went to all that trouble?" Makenna asked in surprise. "It's only a few blocks walk."

"My dear, one does not walk to an occasion such as this. One arrives," Peter informed her.

The phaeton was elegantly upholstered and Makenna

sat back in the luxuriously cushioned seat and drank in the sights, sounds, and feel of the evening. Never had she done anything like this and she wanted to savor every bit of it.

When the phaeton drew up to the front of the hotel, the hotel doorman and the concierge met them and helped Makenna out of the carriage.

"I have opened the special dining room, sir," the concierge said.

"Thank you," Peter replied.

"Did you prepare the wine I selected?" Peter asked the sommelier.

"I did, sir, and I have allowed it to breathe for one hour. It is ready now."

"I will decide that," Peter answered.

"Yes, sir, of course," the sommelier agreed.

Makenna almost gasped when she saw the private dining room. She had glimpsed it before but never had she seen it when it was laid out for serving. It was the most beautiful room she had ever seen. The chandelier was lighted by gas and it glowed in a soft, gold light, with the hundreds of glass facets exploding in spectrums of rainbow color. The table was covered with a beautifully worked damask cloth and laid with bone china which seemed to glow, from some soft, inner light. The eating utensils were of gold and the wine cups silver.

"I will test the wine now," Peter said.

The sommelier who was standing by poured a little wine in a glass goblet and handed it to Peter. Peter held it up to the light, swirled it about in the goblet as he sniffed its bouquet, then tasted it. Finally, he nodded at the sommelier, signaling that it could be served. The sommelier, with a visible look of relief on his face, poured the deep red liquid into the silver goblet at Makenna's setting.

From the serving of the wine through the beef tournedos to the peach flambé, Peter supervised everything. It was the most elegant and exciting evening Makenna had ever spent.

"And now, Mr. O'Shea, I have a Havana cigar for you, which you may smoke as we take a ride through the countryside to enjoy the starlit scenery of your great Southwest," Peter offered.

Kellen laughed. "I've seen enough of the mountains to last me a lifetime. For my money, I'll take the swamps and forests of Southeast Missouri. Why don't you two young people take a ride? But, leave the cigar with me."

"That sounds fair enough," Peter said. "Makenna?"

"Yes," Makenna said. "I'll ride with you, Peter." After all, Makenna thought, the driver of the phaeton will be with them. It won't be as if she were going out alone.

Makenna waved to her father as the driver called to the horses and the phaeton rolled away from the hotel. The pair of horses trotted easily down the main street, then took the desert road. Within moments, the town of Albuquerque lay behind them, little more than a few yellow lights on the desert floor.

"I don't care what Papa says," Makenna said, leaning back and looking out. "I think it is beautiful out here. Look at those stars. There are so many, and they are so bright; it's almost as if they are going to fall on you. Oh, look!" she said, laughing and pointing to a flash of light streaking through the sky. "One of them is falling!"

"I arranged that for you," Peter said easily.

"Where do the stars go when they fall?"

"They aren't really stars, you know. They are meteorites. Little pieces of heavenly bodies falling into the earth's atmosphere from space," Peter said.

"Oh, I wonder what they look like? They must be as beautiful as diamonds," Makenna said.

Peter laughed. "No, not really. They just look like any rock you might find on the ground anywhere. They have one in the museum in San Francisco."

"I would love to see it sometime."

"As I said, my dear, it is just a rock, nothing worth seeing."

CHAPTER EIGHT

The train whistle echoed through the canyons and Bernardo's horse took a few nervous steps.

"Easy, Diablo," Bernardo said, patting the horse on the neck, calming him. "Soon we will have action!"

Four men came running up the hill from the track and retrieved their horses from four others who were holding the reins for them.

"Did you grease the tracks well?" Bernardo asked.

"*Sí*. The engineer is in for one big surprise when he finds that his locomotive cannot climb such a little hill."

"Are you certain this will work, my brother?" Teresina asked.

"It will work. I saw it used in the border wars," Bernardo replied. "The driver wheels will slip on the grease and the train will stop."

"I think it would have been better to put dynamite on the track and explode it under the train."

"And perhaps kill the engineer and other innocent people?" Bernardo said. "They are not our enemies, Teresina. It is the railroad that is our enemy, not the people who ride the trains."

"You have a soft heart," she said derisively.

"And you, my sister, for the beautiful woman that you are, have a heart of ice. Ah, but such is the way of women. It is a well-known fact that the fighting bulls get their strength from their fathers and their blood lust from their mothers."

"There, the train comes around the bend and is starting up the hill," one of the men said.

"Get ready," Bernardo ordered. He pulled his pistol from his holster and checked each of his men. Teresina had her pistol drawn as well.

"You stay here," Bernardo ordered.

"You try and make me stay here," she replied.

The train was traveling at fifty miles an hour when it hit the greased tracks. The pounding drive wheels suddenly began spinning and the train slowed, then came to a complete halt and started sliding backwards down the hill.

"Aiieee, it worked," one of the men shouted happily.

"Now," Bernardo called. "We attack!"

Bernardo led his group of men out of the rocks and down the hill. They fired their pistols in the air as they galloped toward the train. They reached it just as the train slid to the bottom of the hill. The engineer, perceiving what was happening, threw the engine into reverse and tried to back away from them but Bernardo had anticipated that and the grease was the heaviest there. The engine stood still even though the wheels spun rapidly.

Bernardo rode up to the cabin window of the engine and, as a warning, fired a bullet into the large steam pressure gauge inside. The cab began to fill with steam. He smiled at the engineer and the engineer closed the throttle.

"That is good, *Señor*," Bernardo called to him. "Now if you and the fireman would be so good as to step down?"

A few cars back, a man leaned out from the vestibule. He was holding a gun and Bernardo shot him, hitting him in the arm. The gun fell to the ground.

"I am sorry, *Señor*," Bernardo called out, "but guns make me nervous. If you'll please return to the car, one of my men will attend to your needs shortly."

"You are Bernardo Tafoya," the engineer said.

"At your service," Bernardo said, giving the engineer a salute. He pointed to the baggage car. "Tell whoever is inside to open the door."

"Open up," the engineer shouted.

The door slid open and a small man started pitching bags out onto the ground, even before he was asked.

"*Gracias*," Bernardo said. "You are being most cooperative." Bernardo swung down from his horse and picked up the bags. He handed them up to his sister and she affixed them to her saddle horn.

"If you will forgive me, I have been most rude in keeping the passengers waiting," Bernardo said. "Come, my *amigos*, we must see to them now."

Bernardo climbed to the first car and kicked the door open and stepped inside. A woman screamed and a man shouted a curse toward him. He smiled back pleasantly and tipped his hat.

"*Buenos dias, Señores and Señoras*," he said. "My name is Bernardo Tafoya. I have robbed this train but I am here to tell you that you need have no fear. I have no intention of robbing any of you and none of you will be hurt."

"What about the man you shot?" someone challenged.

"Oh, yes. For that I am truly sorry but he was about to shoot me and I feared that perhaps he could not shoot as well as I. I shot him in the arm only. He may have shot me in the heart and I would not like that."

A little girl of about five, too young to be frightened, had been looking at Bernardo's scarf, which was held around his neck by a large silver and turquoise slide ring. "Mama," she said, pointing at the scarf. "Isn't that pretty?"

"Hush," the girl's mother said.

Bernardo smiled. "No," he said. "You should never stifle a child's appreciation for beautiful things." He removed the scarf and ring and handed them to the little girl. "To remember me by, *poca Señorita*," he said.

"Bernardo, we are ready to ride," someone called from outside.

Bernardo gave a parting wave to the passengers inside. "I must go now. I wish you a pleasant and safe journey."

Bernardo's horse was brought alongside and he leaped onto the horse's back, then slapped his legs against the animal's side. They rode along the track for several hundred feet so as not to present a target to anyone on the train, then turned and headed out across the desert, back to the Tafoya ranch.

They rode for nearly an hour before they stopped to rest the horses and themselves.

"Look at how the bags bulge," one of the men said. "I wonder how much money they contain."

"It doesn't matter," Bernardo said.

"Of course, it matters."

"It matters only that this is the payroll," Bernardo said. "That means that the workers don't get paid and if they don't get paid, they don't work. If they don't work, the railroad doesn't get built. That's all that matters."

"But think of the fun we could have with this money."

"No," Bernardo said loudly. He stood up and walked over to stand near the money, then turned to look at the others. "You know why we do this," he said. "It is not because we are thieves but because we are patriots. Each of you has been given land by my family and now each of you has your own interest in seeing that the railroad does not take our lands from us. Think of this and of your families and of the generations to come who will enjoy your land. It is for this that we took the money, not so that you may get drunk and visit with a whore."

"You are right, Bernardo," said the man who had spoken. "I meant nothing. I was only talking."

"The horses have rested. We must be going," Bernardo said.

The train was late in reaching Albuquerque and the crowd was growing very restless. There was some speculation as to whether or not the train had been involved in a wreck and some were talking of organizing a posse to ride out and look for it. The crowd was much larger than usual because the work crews knew that they were going to be paid when it arrived. Therefore, in addition to the usual people who met the train, there were a couple hundred workers. The Irish, many of whom had already begun to celebrate, were singing, drinking, and laughing amongst themselves, and the Chinese, who were standing or squatting in groups, were just waiting quietly.

Makenna, her father, Gabe, and Peter were sitting in a buckboard, waiting with the others. Bull Blackwell and Long Li, who were to help Gabe with the payroll, were standing beside the buckboard.

"What time is it now?" Gabe asked.

"Five minutes later than it was the last time you asked," Peter said, looking at his watch. "It is nine-forty-five."

"Forty-five minutes late," Gabe said.

"Maybe Gerhard has telegraphed back to check on it,"

Makenna suggested.

"No," Kellen said easily. The regulations say wait one hour before telegraphing and you can bet that Gerhard will be waitin' the full hour."

"My father's bank in Denver put the money on the train," Peter said. "We've got a telegram to that effect. That means the money is now your responsibility. If anything has happened to it, you'll bear the loss."

"I know, I know," Gabe said.

"Mr. Hansen, you think maybe something has happened?" Bull asked.

"I don't know, Bull. But I'm afraid it has. I can't think of any other reason the train would be this late."

"She's on her way in," a man on horseback yelled, galloping down the track toward the station. "I just seen her light from Lookout Point."

There were cheers from the men who were waiting to get paid and an excited babble of voices from the others in the crowd. The Chinese remained silent.

"Listen," Gabe suddenly said, holding his hand up. "Damnit, there's been trouble, I knew it."

"Why do you say that?" Makenna asked.

"Listen," Gabe said again.

Makenna heard it then. The engineer was blowing his whistle but not in the long, mournful wail which normally marked the entrance to Albuquerque. Instead, it was a series of short blasts...the sign of trouble.

The men who were waiting to be paid heard the whistle then and their cheering and boisterousness suddenly died. They had all worked the railroads long enough to recognize the signal for trouble and it didn't take a genius to figure out what the trouble probably was.

"Mr. Hansen, what are you going to do about getting

us paid?" one of the men shouted.

"Yeah," another put in. "We've broke our backs on this damned railroad and we're entitled to a fair wage."

"Wait a minute," Gabe said. "You don't know that the payroll was taken."

"The hell we don't," another said.

"At least wait until the train gets here and find out," Gabe pleaded.

"We'll wait, but if there ain't no pay, there ain't no work."

"That ain't enough by me, gents," one of the others called. "If I don't get paid, I intend to tear up the work I already done."

"Bull, what do we owe that man?" Gabe asked, pointing to the one who had just spoken.

"Twenty dollars, Mr. Hansen, same as the rest of them," Bull answered.

Gabe pulled his billfold from his pocket and took out twenty dollars. "Pay him," he said. "Then fire him."

"Yes, sir," Bull replied, smiling. "I never cared much for that troublemaking son-of-a-bitch anyway."

"Oh, Gabe, what if the train has been robbed?" Makenna asked. "How will you handle this mob?"

"I'm interested in seeing that myself," Peter said with a smug smile.

The train pounded into the station with the hissing of steam and the grinding of metal, then came to a stop. Almost as soon as the train stopped, people were jumping off the cars.

"We were robbed!" the first man off the train cried. "Bernardo Tafoya and his men held us up."

The crowd of track workers began shouting angrily.

"Now what are you going to do?" Peter asked.

Gabe stood up and held his hands out, asking for quiet. "Men," he said. "Listen to me. There's no cause for alarm yet."

"What do you mean there's no cause for alarm? Didn't you just hear that the train was robbed?"

"Trust me," Gabe said. "Bull, keep the men quiet for a while longer. I've got to check on something."

"All right, boss," Bull said.

"What on earth do you plan to do?" Kellen asked. "We don't have nearly enough money in the safe to pay these men."

"I'll be right back," Gabe answered cryptically. He hopped out of the buckboard and walked over to the baggage car. He rapped on the door, and after the door slid open, climbed inside. The door closed behind him and remained closed for several minutes.

"Do you think you can hide in there, Hansen?" one of the men shouted.

"Yeah," another called. "You've gotta come out of there sometime and that train ain't leavin' until you do."

"Peter, can't you do something?" Makenna asked.

"It's Hansen's problem," Peter said. "Besides, I don't have sufficient funds to pay this unruly mob. I'm afraid there's nothing I can do."

The door suddenly slid open again and Gabe stood on the edge of the car. He held both hands out for quiet. "Men, I'm happy to report that they didn't get the payroll. We'll begin paying immediately."

A loud cheer went up from the crowd and Makenna gasped in surprise. "Is he serious?"

"Yes, ma'am," Bull said, grinning. "I guess our little plan worked."

"What plan?" Kellen asked.

"When the money was put on board in Trinidad, it was put into bags marked 'seed.' The money bags were filled with paper. Bernardo and his men didn't get nothin' but four bags of junk."

"Paper!" Teresina shrieked angrily. "The son-of-a-bitch tricked us!"

"Paper?" Bernardo asked in disbelief.

"Look!"

Teresina dumped one of the bags on the ground in front of her brother. He stooped down and picked one of the bundles up. It was as his sister said, nothing but old newspaper, cut into the size of money and secured in bundles. He began to laugh.

"You are laughing," she snapped. "You think it's funny?"

"Yes," Bernardo said. "You've got to give him credit for a sense of humor. He played a joke on us. A brilliant joke."

"He made fools of us," Teresina spat.

"Of course, my sister," Bernardo said easily. "That is what a joke is supposed to do."

"Well, what are you going to do about it?"

"About this? Nothing," Bernardo said. "But now that I know our friend has a sense of humor, perhaps he will appreciate a joke of our own sometime soon."

CHAPTER NINE

"Makenna, darlin', I've got to take the train into Santa Fe 'n I won't be back 'til tomorrow mornin'," Kellen said. "But I've a whole pile of paperwork I've been meanin' to get around to 'n now I just don't have time."

Makenna smiled. "Papa, why didn't you just ask me to do it instead of putting it off? You know I would have been glad to."

"Still 'n all, it's not right that I should have you doin' my work for me. I'm the one hired on, not you."

Makenna got on her knees in front of her father and began rolling up her father's empty pants leg. "It just so happens that I anticipated this," she said. "And I've already started, so you go on into Santa Fe and don't worry about a thing."

Kellen ran his hand affectionately through Makenna's hair. "'Tis a good 'n lovin' daughter you are, lass.

Kellen stood up and reached for his crutches. A train whistle hooted in the distance and Kellen took his hat from a peg on the wall. "That'll be the mornin' Santa Fe train. I'd best be goin'. You'll be all right 'til mornin'?"

"I'll be fine, Papa."

Not long after Kellen left, the door to the engineering car opened and Gabe stepped in at that moment.

"Where is Kellen?" Gabe asked. "I must send a message to Denver."

"He's gone to Santa Fe," Makenna said. "He won't be back until tomorrow."

"That'll be too late," Gabe said. He sighed. "I suppose I can have Gerhard send it commercially and pay the rate,"

"That isn't necessary," Makenna said easily. She took the lock from the sending key. "I'll send it."

"You'll send it?" Gabe asked, laughing. "Are you crazy?"

"What do you mean, crazy?" Makenna replied.

"I've never heard of a woman telegrapher."

"Well, you've heard of one now," Makenna said. She reached for the message in Gabe's hand but he pulled it back.

"Look," she said angrily. "You said it was important."

"I don't know," Gabe hesitated.

Makenna started operating the key. The small room of the engineering car began echoing with the metallic clacks as her fingers opened and closed the switch in a rapid series of dots and dashes.

"What are you doing?"

"I'm clearing the lines for your message," Makenna answered. She reached up and took the paper from Gabe's hand. "Is this it?"

"Yes," Gabe said, letting her have the paper. "I didn't get the timbers for the trestle across Prealta's Gulch."

Makenna sent the message and after a moment, another message came flashing back.

"What does it say?" Gabe asked anxiously.

"It says the timber order was killed by Peter Van Zandt."

"What? Are you sure?"

"You heard the message, same as I did." Makenna replied sarcastically.

"I don't know telegraphy."

"Why not? You're a man, aren't you? Surely a mere woman can't do something you couldn't do."

Gabe chuckled. "I guess you got me on that one." He picked up the message and stared at it. "Why would he cancel the timber order?" he asked angrily.

"I don't know. You would think that, because of his father, he would want the railroad to succeed," Makenna said.

Gabe was silent for a moment as he studied the message in his hand. "I don't like what the message said but I appreciate you sending the telegram for me."

As Gabe rode into the wind he could feel and smell in the breeze the dampness of an upcoming rain. He reined in his horse and pulled his poncho from the saddle roll, then slipped it over his head. He examined the track as he spread the poncho to provide as much protection for the horse as he could. Twin steel ribbons, straight as an arrow, shining brightly as they stretched back into Albuquerque, now some five miles behind him, and on to End-of-Track, a good twenty miles in front. Tomorrow, the engineering car which was the headquarters of the operation, and Kellen O'Shea's quarters car, would be moved out to End-of-Track to set up operation there. The twenty-five-mile run with the locomotive wasn't too bad when it was available but it was generally too busy hauling materials from Albuquerque to the site to be used for transportation. That meant a long horseback ride every time something came up.

Dark, ominous clouds moved across the gray sky, preceded by a rolling column of dust. Gabe squinted his eyes and pressed on.

The rain was coming in full force by the time Gabe reached End-of-Track and he hurried his horse into the canvas shelter erected for the remuda, then ran over to the mess tent to get out of the rain. He removed his hat and poured water out of the brim and crown, then stripped off the poncho and hung it across one of the tent support ropes. The rain was drumming loudly on the canvas and, here and there, it was dripping through, making little pools on the tables.

"Want a cup of coffee, Mr. Hansen?" the cook asked.

"Yes," Gabe answered. "Thanks."

He turned to look back through the tent opening at the activity on the roadbed. The rain hadn't stopped the work and the crews were still laying track with a well-established rhythm.

"Here you go, fresh made," the cook said, handing a blue tin cup to Gabe.

Gabe blew on the coffee to cool it, then slurped a drink through lips extended to prevent burning. He had seen Peter Van Zandt sitting quietly at the other end of the tent when he arrived but had said nothing to him as yet. Finally, he spoke.

"I reordered the timber," he said.

"You won't need it," Peter replied, without turning around.

"How else do you propose we cross Prealta's Gulch?" Gabe asked. "Lay the track on thin air?"

Peter turned now to face him. "You won't be going through Prealta's Gulch. I told the surveyors to lay a course around the gulch."

"What are you talking about? There is no way to go around it. The mountains north of it are virtually impassable."

"We're going south."

"South! That's right through the middle of Tafoya land. If you think we've got troubles now, you just try that. He'll have the government on his side if we do that."

"The government won't do anything after the tracks are already laid and you know it. They are so anxious to have a railroad through here that they'll back our play. Besides, my father has enough congressmen on the payroll to insure that there will be no trouble."

"I don't care if he has the President," Gabe said. "We are not going south of Prealta's Gulch."

"Hansen, I had the engineers prepare the cost estimates for me. We can lay track south of Prealta's Gulch for less than half what it's going to take to go across it."

"No."

"You seem to forget whose money is backing this operation of yours," Peter said.

"I'm using your father's money, Van Zandt, not your ideas. This is my railroad, and we'll build it the way I say, or you can take your money and go. I'll find backing somewhere else."

"Oh, yeah? Where?"

"Your father wasn't the only one interested," Gabe said. "Now you make up your mind, Van Zandt. You let me build this railroad the way I see fit or just get the hell out of here altogether."

Peter stood up and began putting on his raincoat. "Very well," he said. "Build your trestle. But you go one penny over budget and you'll default everything you've got to us. That is in the contract." He smiled. "I've got time to wait you out, Hansen. And a pleasant way to pass the time while I'm waiting. I see that the train is about to run into Albuquerque. I think I'll just hop a ride into town and visit Rosie Cleveland."

"Fine," Gabe said. "It'll keep you out of the way."

"One penny over budget and it'll be my railroad," Peter said.

He laughed cruelly, then darted through the rain toward the single passenger car the engine was pulling. Gabe watched him with cold fury seething inside. He wrapped both hands around the hot tin cup, so angry that it was several seconds before he felt the heat building up in the palms of his hands.

"Don't let Mr. Van Zandt rile you up none, Mr. Hansen," the cook said quietly. "His kind is like a cat. They like to torment people when they see they can get to them and he's gettin' your goat good."

Gabe looked at the cook, embarrassed that his emotions were showing so strongly. Finally, he set the cup on the table and reached for his poncho. "I'd better see how the work is going," he said. "Thanks for the coffee."

CHAPTER TEN

The next morning, Makenna went down to the depot to await her father's train.

Near the tracks, there was a crowd gathered around a buckboard where an itinerant preacher was standing on the buckboard giving a sermon. Makenna drifted over to listen, to kill the time while she waited for the train.

The man was of average size and build with a full head of thick, black hair. He jabbed his finger toward the crowd as he spoke to them.

"And here's another reason why there shouldn't be no trains," the man was saying. "It's done been proven in Arkansas that them heavy trains shakes the ground so that the hogs is kept too nervous to eat. They don't fatten up and folks is goin' without pig meat. The live steam wilts the grass and spoils the pasture and the horses and cows won't eat 'n there goes your beef. 'N as if it warn't bad enough for the train to kill pigs, cows and horses, it'll even kill little children what gets on the tracks, 'n yes, old folks who are goin' to church in their buggy. 'N hear this. Them steel rails lyin' out there on the ground," he pointed to the track, "draws lightnin' better'n a dog's tail, 'n ever'one knows to stay away from dogs durin' a lightnin' storm. Now what'll you think all that electricity runnin' loose in the ground'll do to you? I'll tell you what it'll do to you. It'll make you sturl. You know what sturl means? It means the men folks will all be turned into geldin's and no more children will be born. And that means the end of the human race. I tell you, folks, what you're seein' here is the Antichrist come in the form of a fire-breathin' steel monster."

"I'll give you this, preacher man," one of the men in the crowd called, "you got guts. Don't you know most ever'one in this town makes their livin' off the railroad?"

"You should all turn your efforts to more Godly pursuits," the preacher replied.

Makenna turned away from the preacher and saw the engine arriving from End-of-Track. Gabe was standing on the platform between the engine and the tender, holding onto the assist bar, leaning out and looking down the track.

The engine stopped and Makenna walked over to speak to him.

"Hello, Gabe," she said brightly.

"Good morning, Makenna," Gabe replied with a welcoming smile. "Oh,

I see my trestle timber has arrived."

Gabe jumped off the platform and walked down the track toward the flatcars, which were loaded with the large twelve by twelve timbers he would use for constructing the trestle across the Prealta Gulch. The engine, which had brought Gabe to town, backed down the track and hooked onto the engineering car that served as the office and then to the plush, private car that Gabe had given over to Makenna and her father for living quarters. After the connection with those two cars was made, it moved back to hook up with the flatcars loaded with timber.

"Miss O'Shea," one of the brakemen said, approaching Makenna then. "Dudley told me to tell you he would hold the train 'til you got on board."

"Tell Dudley to go without me," Makenna said. "I'm going to wait here for Papa."

"Very well, miss," the brakeman said. He turned and gave a signal to Dudley and Dudley blew his whistle a couple of times, then the engine jerked forward. Dudley gave Makenna a wave as the engine chugged by and the brakeman swung onto one of the rapidly rolling cars with ease.

The train had gathered speed by the time the last car passed her by and Makenna saw Gabe on that car walking along the top of the load carrying a bill of lading, inspecting his timber.

"Miss O'Shea?"

Makenna turned to see one of the men who worked for Wayne Gerhard.

"Yes?"

"We just got word that the train is going to be late. Your father won't be in until this afternoon."

"Thank you," Makenna replied.

Prealta's Gulch is a deep, wide canyon that lays its scar across the land for some fifteen miles, stretching north and south. At its narrowest and most shallow point, it is three hundred feet deep and one thousand feet across. But at that point the approach from the opposite side wouldn't allow track to be laid, so the engineers had very carefully determined a location for the crossing, which was designed to give the best approaches from the east and west, with the smallest distance and over shallowest canyon possible under the circumstances.

Survey stakes were placed to mark the path and, as the track was laid, the construction crews followed the line of stakes that were tipped by little blue flags as they stretched out before them like a perfect row of desert flowers.

It was three days from the time the timber arrived until the construction crew had laid track to Prealta. Now the timber cars were backed to the canyon's edge, and the precut timbers were snaked off and placed into position. It was nearly four hours before Bull noticed something was wrong and he got on a handcar and pumped his way back to the main camp to talk to Gabe.

Gabe had a map spread-before him and he was examining routes when Bull knocked on the door.

"What are you doing here?" Gabe asked easily. "I thought you had a bridge to build."

"Boss, didn't the engineers send the numbers in for the timbers to be precut?" Bull asked.

"Yes, of course they did," Gabe replied, looking up. "Why?"

"Well, somebody made a mistake," Bull said.

"What kind of a mistake? What do you mean?"

"I mean the timbers don't fit. They aren't the right size."

"Are you sure?"

"Boss, you wanna come look for yourself? I tell you the damn timbers aren't right. It's impossible to bridge the gulch where we are, with the timbers we have."

"Damn," Gabe swore. "I think I know the problem."

Gabe had been looking at the map in his crew car, and he stepped out the back door and walked along the track to the engineering car.

Bull was right beside him. When he reached the engineering car, he saw Makenna drinking coffee.

"Where's Kellen?" Gabe asked.

"He just stepped out," Makenna said. "Why, what's wrong?"

"The timber order that you telegraphed for me. Did you get it right?"

"Of course I did," Makenna answered. "There was nothing to it. I just asked that they reactivate the order you had already submitted. Why?"

"Because it's wrong," Gabe said. "The sizes are all wrong. They made the wrong cuts."

"Don't be blamin' her for that, Gabe," Kellen O'Shea said, returning to the car at that moment.

"Have you heard?" Gabe asked.

"Aye, I've heard. And I'm about to check on the order to make sure they got it good and proper when I sent it the first time."

Kellen laid his crutches on the platform of the train, then swung himself aboard. He came inside and started riffling through the pigeon holes until he found the original message. He showed it to Gabe.

"These are the numbers, are they not, lad?"

"Yes," Gabe said after looking them over. "Well then, we'll just wire back to Denver and see what numbers they used, if not these." Kellen removed the key lock and began sending his message.

"Boss, you wanna go take a look at the timbers?" Bull asked.

"Yes," Gabe agreed.

As he hopped off the platform Bull said, "I've got the handcar; we can take a run out there."

The two men pumped their way out to the edge of the gulch and saw the confusion the mistake had caused. The workers were all sitting or standing around, taking advantage of their unexpected break. The section leaders had the timbers laid out and were looking at them with puzzled expressions on their faces when Gabe arrived.

"Boss, somethin' is mighty wrong," one of the men said.

"I know. Bull told me about getting the wrong timbers."

"No, that ain't what I mean," the man said. "These here are the right timbers but they still won't work."

"What do you mean they are the right timbers?"

"This here bridge plan has all the sizes marked on it," the man said. "And we done checked 'em out. The sizes is right."

"Then what the bloody hell is wrong?" Gabe sputtered.

"I think I see," Bull said suddenly. "I don't know why I didn't notice this before."

"What is it?"

"Look, do you see that rock ledge there? When I come out here with the surveyors, that ledge was some half mile or so to the north. Now, it's about a half mile south. We're at the wrong spot."

"We can't be! We followed the stakes just like they were laid," the man with the bridge plan said.

"The stakes!" Gabe said. "They must've been moved!"

"That don't make sense. Who would move them?" Bull asked.

"Bernardo Tafoya," Gabe said. He cursed angrily. "It'll take us two days to get the surveyors back and another two days to lay in the corrections. There's no telling how far back the error was made. We may have lost as much as two weeks."

"What'll we do with the men in the meantime?" Bull asked.

"Start pulling up the track," Gabe said. "I can't afford to waste any of it. Take it up all the way back to the main camp."

The section leaders began yelling instructions and the men, amidst much grumbling and cursing and wondering what they would be asked to do next, began taking up the rails they had just worked so hard to lay.

Gabe walked out to stand on the edge of the gulch. He looked out across the wide expanse and down into the deep valley below. Bull came to stand beside him and handed him a bottle. "Thought you might be able to use a little snort."

"Thanks," Gabe replied. He turned the bottle up and took several swallows, then handed it back.

"What do you think Bernardo's purpose was in doing this?" Bull asked. "Surely he didn't think this would stop us."

"I don't think he intended it to," Gabe said. "I think he just wanted to pay us back for giving him a payroll of cut newspaper."

"I'll bet you're right," Bull said. "The son-of-a-bitch is probably out there somewhere laughing his ass off."

CHAPTER ELEVEN

Don Esteban de la Tafoya, Bernardo's father, was a citizen of the United States by virtue of the fact that his ranch and all of New Mexico had been ceded to the United States. But though he was an American citizen, he was no less Mexican and was an adherent of the Spanish customs and the old ways. Thus, it was that when Vicente, his younger brother who lived in Mexico, wished to remarry after having been a widower for years, he felt it necessary to visit Don Esteban and secure his brother's blessings.

Vicente traveled all the way up from Buenaventura to see his brother and he brought several of his servants, his bride-to-be and her daughter, and their servants with him. The woman he was to marry was Camila Botin, a handsome and elegant widow of fine background. Camila's daughter, who also made the journey, was a lovely eighteen-year-old, with flashing black eyes and beautiful white teeth, and a smile that lit up her whole face. Her name was Alexia and she had become the object of attention of every eligible man on Sombra de las Montanas.

Don Esteban, his brother Vicente, and Vicente's fiancée, Camila, were taking the grand tour of the ranch, a journey which would take several days to complete. Alexia remained at the main house where Teresina and Bernardo held a fiesta in her honor. Amidst the food and drink, music and dance, there were also games and, as a result of the games, a great tension had developed at Sombra de las Montanas. It wasn't an uneasy tension but rather a sense of excitement as everyone gathered around to see how Bernardo would answer the challenge.

The excitement had started thusly: Bernardo and Santiago, who were raised almost as brothers, were, as was their custom on such occasions, playing a game they called "one better." It was a game of such skill that only those two of all who lived on the ranch could play, though when they were younger, Teresina had sometimes joined in and, to the chagrin of Bernardo and Santiago, had often outclassed them.

Today's game had gone far beyond Teresina's skills, however, and had in fact taxed the limits of both men. Santiago had just performed a feat of horsemanship that seemingly assured him of victory on the afternoon. He had placed his horse side by side with Bernardo's horse, then standing with one foot on the back of each animal and holding the reins from each, he rode at breakneck speed through a complicated obstacle course.

Now the pressure was on Bernardo to match him if he could.

"Give up now, my brother," Santiago teased. "It will be no disgrace. You have lost to me before."

"But I've no desire to lose to you now," Bernardo said. "And I shan't."

"Very well, match my ride if you can."

"I will more than match your ride," Bernardo boasted. "I will better it."

"How?"

Bernardo went to the table where the food and wine were laid out. He picked up six empty wine bottles, then handed them to a couple of the vaqueros. "Place these on the course," he instructed. He smiled at Santiago. "I will ride the course just as you did," he said. "In addition I will shoot all these bottles, breaking every one of them."

"But there are six bottles, Bernardo. That's all the bullets you have in your gun. That means you cannot miss, even one shot. And you'll be standing on the backs of two horses."

"I will not miss," Bernardo smiled.

"I do not believe you can do this," Santiago said.

"If I do this, will you concede I am the better man?" Bernardo challenged.

"*Sí*, if you concede that I am the better if you miss," Santiago replied.

"Done," Bernardo agreed. "But we should have some form of wager."

"What could we wager?" Santiago asked. "I have nothing you want."

"I will be the prize," Alexia suddenly said. "I will go with the winner."

The others whistled and shouted and Bernardo broke into a big smile. "I accept that wager," he said. "The question is, will my sister allow Santiago to accept?"

The others laughed again, then Teresina called out hotly, "Santiago may do as he pleases. I certainly do."

"Ah, but not to worry, my sister," Bernardo said, looking at the beautiful young girl who had offered herself as prize. "One short ride and this girl is mine anyway."

"We shall see," Santiago countered.

Bernardo pulled his pistol from his holster and spun the

cylinder, checking to see that every chamber had a bullet. Then he signaled for Alexia to approach him. When she did, he kissed her. "That is for luck," he said.

Bernardo swung into Diablo's saddle and rode to the far end of the course, leading Santiago's horse with him. When he reached the end of the course, he stood on Diablo's back, then guided Santiago's horse into place. He put one leg over onto Santiago's horse and stayed that way for a long moment. Finally, he gave a shout to the horses and they broke into a run. He leaned over and bent his legs so that his knees acted as springs, taking up the shocks of the horses as they ran. After he negotiated the first two obstacles in the course, he pulled his pistol and prepared for the six wine bottles.

Bernardo did not hesitate as he approached the bottles. He shot quickly, first to one side of the horse and then to the other, the gun popping six times, then he holstered his pistol in time for the final two obstacles. The horses came pounding up to the finish line and he jumped down.

"Well?" he asked, breathless, "how did I do?"

"You rode well," Santiago admitted. "It remains to be seen how your marksmanship was."

"He broke them all!" the two men who had gone to check on the bottles shouted. "A dead hit on each of the bottles."

"Ai, yi, yi, what shooting!" Santiago said in genuine admiration. He took Bernardo's hand and shook it in congratulations. "You have won, my friend, and I do not hesitate to call you the better man."

"And to the victor go the spoils," Bernardo said. "I claim my prize." He put his arm around Alexia.

"You have won as well," Teresina said to Santiago.

"How have I won?"

"Now, you will not feel my anger," Teresina said

laughing.

The others joined in the laughter and they were still teasing Santiago when a messenger approached them.

"Bernardo, I have good news," the messenger said. "The railroad was fooled as you said they would be. They have built their tracks right up to the Prealta Gulch but they cannot build the bridge. Now they must tear the tracks out and build again."

Bernardo laughed at the news, then walked over and grabbed another wine bottle, this one nearly full. He held it over his head and called out to the others: "*Amigos*, let us drink a toast to Gabe Hansen and to the men who must undo what they have done."

"You mean undo what we did, don't you, Bernardo?" someone shouted.

"Yes," Bernardo said. "They must undo what we did. And now my friend, Señor Hansen, we are even with the jokes. What passes between us from now on will be no joke."

Bernardo held the bottle out in the general direction of the railroad, then turned it up and took several swallows.

"Are you going to claim your prize?" Alexia asked softly.

Bernardo brought the bottle of wine down from his lips and wiped his mouth with the back of his hand. He looked at Alexia. She was as slender as the ocotillo bloom and quite as lovely. He held his arm out for her and she came to him, then they walked together into the hacienda.

It took an entire week to pull up the track and lay it again in the right place. That had the end result of costing three times as much to cover the same territory since once the track was laid, then pulled up, then re-laid, the workers had covered ground three times. It required the same amount of work whether they were laying track or pulling it up and the fact that they were covering the same ground again meant nothing to them as far as their pay was concerned. They were paid just the same.

But Gabe was acutely aware of the increased cost of the operation. And he dispersed practically his entire reserve for equipment and supplies. He was in Albuquerque to take care of such business and most important to pick up more loan money from Peter Van Zandt. He waited at the bank for Van Zandt and, when Van Zandt didn't show at the usual time, he left the bank to look for him. He found him playing poker in the hotel bar.

Peter glanced up as Gabe came into the bar. He held up his cards and smiled. "Some of your bad luck must be rubbing off on me," he said. "I haven't had a decent hand all morning."

Gabe looked around the room. It was full of gamblers, drummers, and camp followers of the railroad. He considered them all scavengers, unable to make their own way, subsisting on the efforts of others. He placed Peter, whom he considered a scavenger of his father's money, in the same boat as the rest.

"It's after ten o'clock," Gabe said.

Peter reached into his vest pocket and pulled out a gold watch. He opened the case and looked at it, then looked back at Gabe and smiled. "I do believe you are correct. Say, if you can tell time that well, you should get a job with the railroad."

Everyone in the room laughed at the joke and Gabe felt a flush of anger burning his cheeks. "You know what I mean," Gabe said angrily. "You were supposed to meet me at the bank."

"Really, my good man? I was supposed to meet you at

ten o'clock? For what reason?" Peter asked. He put three cards down on the table. "I'll take three," he said to the dealer as if the game were much more important than his conversation with Gabe.

Gabe felt the rage building inside him and he grabbed the edge of the table and flipped it over. Cards and chips slid from the table to the floor, and the players yelled in protest and jumped out of the way causing their chairs to tumble as well, adding to the noise and confusion. Peter stood up slowly and turned to face Gabe. He adjusted his jacket so that it hung open slightly, allowing him access to the gun he wore on the shoulder holster.

The motion didn't go unnoticed by anyone in the bar and they moved quickly out of the way, giving the two men room.

"Are you bracing me, Van Zandt," Gabe asked, calmly. "You do see that I'm unarmed, don't you?"

"You wear a gun sometimes, Hansen. The next time I'll make certain you are armed. Now what is all this about?"

"You know damned well what it's about," Gabe said. "I have an agreement with your father. A business agreement. He is advancing money for the construction of the railroad. Your only function is as messenger boy, to carry the money from him to me. I was due a payment at ten o'clock this morning and you weren't there."

"You are due no such payment," Van Zandt replied.

"What do you mean, I'm due no such payment," Gabe demanded. "The agreement is that at ten o'clock every Monday morning, I will draw funds based on the miles of track I laid the week before."

"And what secures that loan?" Peter asked.

"The government grant," Gabe said.

"Precisely," Peter replied. "The government grant, payable when you cross the territorial line, will recompense you for the total track mileage. They will not pay you for the miles of track you laid twice. Therefore, I have made the decision not to advance you any more money until enough progress has been made to once again earn credit toward the government grant. My father has put me in charge of this and I know he will abide by my decision."

"I see," Gabe said quietly. He felt a sinking sensation in his stomach as he realized what was happening.

Peter chuckled, then pulled a long thin cigar out of his pocket. He stuck it in his mouth at a jaunty angle and held fire to it. Finally, when his head was wreathed in blue smoke, he spoke. "However, we may be able to work out something. Would you like to come to my room with me? Or do you want the whole world to listen to your business?"

Gabe looked around the room to see that the dialogue he and Van Zandt were having was being very closely followed.

"I'll go with you," Gabe said.

"I thought you would."

Peter Van Zandt's room was actually a two-room suite on the second floor of the hotel. It was the finest suite in the hotel and, in fact, the finest suite in the entire city. When Gabe saw the creature comforts of the room, he understood why Van Zandt spent most of the time in Albuquerque and came out to End-of-Track only every other day or so.

"Would you like a drink?" Peter invited, holding up a bottle.

"No," Gabe said. "It's a little early."

"Very well, I was just trying to be hospitable," Peter said. He put the bottle down and looked at Gabe through the cloud of smoke from his cigar. "I've got the money you need," he said. "But it's going to cost you."

"Cost me how?"

"First, you are to transfer final control of construction policy to me. That means how we build and where we build. Secondly, I'll have my accountants establish a rate of stock exchange. For every dollar I provide above the original agreement, you'll transfer stock into my name."

"Those are pretty harsh terms," Gabe said.

"Nevertheless, they are my terms," Peter replied.

"I'll have to think about it."

Peter smiled. "Take your time, Hansen. But if you don't go along, you are going to lose everything. This way, at least, you'll manage to salvage some interest in the railroad if not maintain control."

Gabe looked at Peter and at the smug expression of confidence on Peter's face. He saw the cigar at its jaunty angle and wanted to knock it right out of his mouth. Instead, he tried to put what he hoped was a very calm expression on his face. "I'll let you know," he said.

CHAPTER TWELVE

Gabe kept the problem to himself for the rest of the day. He worked down at the depot, checking incoming shipments of rails and ties as if nothing had happened. Finally, he took the last train back to End-of-Track, spending the entire three-hour trip atop one of the boxcars, watching as the sun set over the magnificent landscape, underlighting the purple clouds with gold and bringing fire to the mountains. It was a soul-inspiring sight and brought some degree of perspective, if not a solution, to his problem.

It was dark by the time the train reached End-of-Track. Gabe could see campfires going on both sides of the track. He could hear singing around the fires of the Irish workers. There was a high-pitched chatter coming from the fires of the Chinese workers and he knew they were probably engaged in their incessant gambling, their one vice.

Lights were coming from Kellen O'Shea's car and, as he looked at it, he thought of Makenna. She was one of the prettiest women he had ever known and he couldn't help but wonder how things might have been between them if they had met under different circumstances.

Gabe looked over the rest of the camp. The work train—sometimes called the perpetual train because it was always on the move—sat just behind the freshly laid track. The train was pushed by the engine, which sat at the furthermost point back on the track. In front of the train, at the point closest to the construction, several flat cars bore the tools and a blacksmith shop. Next came the crew cars, each one eighty-five feet long, with interiors lined with triple tiers of bunks. The tops of the crew cars sported tents and there were hammocks slung beneath them. In all, some 400 men were billeted this way. After the crew cars came the dining car with a single table running its full length. The dining car, which augmented the mess tents, fed in shifts of fifty men each, with three minutes between shifts to allow the tin eating plates to be cleaned. They could be cleaned in three minutes because they were nailed to the table and swabbed out with a hand mop. The dining car was followed by the kitchen car and storeroom. The outside of the kitchen car was festooned with quarters of beef, provided by the company herd that grazed nearby. Occasionally, the beef would be augmented by freshly hunted buffalo and quarters of that meat would hang red and glistening alongside the quarters of beef.

After the kitchen car came the engineers' car, the office or brain-center of the entire operation. It was here that Gabe made his own office and here that Kellen O'Shea kept them all in contact with the outside world through the telegraph key. Behind the engineers' office, there was a caboose, which Gabe was using as his living quarters, then the car in which Kellen O'Shea and Makenna lived, then several flat cars that were used for the daily trips back for new rails and ties. On each side of the track, there were tents erected by the camp followers: a preacher, a doctor, a saloon keeper, a general store, a hotel of sorts, and a mess tent to supplement the dining car.

It was a heady feeling to be in charge of an operation this large and Gabe felt a pang of remorse over the prospect of losing it.

"Gabe, lad, come in and have coffee with us."

Gabe had been standing just outside Kellen's car and Kellen's voice snapped him out of his reverie. He looked up at the old man. "Thanks, Kellen, I just may do that," he agreed.

Makenna poured the coffee for them, then took a cup herself and sat with them, smiling prettily at Gabe.

"Why so pensive, lad?" Kellen finally asked after they had sipped coffee in silence for several minutes.

"I may be losing everything," Gabe said without fanfare.

"Oh, Gabe, why?" Makenna asked showing her concern over his comment.

Gabe explained the costs incurred by having to tear up the track, then lay it a second time. Then he told them of Peter's offer.

"So either way, I figure to be out of it soon," he finally concluded.

"Makenna, darlin', you'll be handin' me a bit o' the Irish sweetenin' for the coffee, if you please," Kellen said, to cover his shock.

Makenna handed a flask of whiskey to her father and he poured a generous amount into his coffee, then added an equal portion to Gabe's cup. He put the cap back on and sighed.

"Have you got any ideas, lad?" he asked.

"Not a one, I'm afraid."

"Oh, Gabe, what are you going to do?" Makenna asked. "This is your dream. You can't lose it after having come this far."

Gabe looked at Makenna and smiled. "Thanks," he said. "I appreciate your concern but I don't know yet what I can do."

There was a knock on the door then, and Makenna got up to answer it. The giant figure of Bull Blackwell stood on the other side.

"Ma'am, did Mr. Hansen come back on the train?"

"Yes, he's in here," Makenna said. "Won't you come in?"

"Well, I've got Long Li with me, ma'am," Bull said and, only then, did Makenna see the diminutive Oriental standing behind him. The juxtaposition of the two of them was startling.

"Mr. Cho is welcome as well," Makenna said. "In fact, if you'd like, I'll boil some tea," she added.

"Thank you, missy, I don't wish to bother," Long Li said.

"It's no bother, believe me."

The two men came in and Gabe stood to greet them.

"We got troubles, boss," Bull said.

"What more?" Gabe asked.

"The survey engineers say we are going to have to blast our way through Fence Lake Pass."

"I thought they said we wouldn't have to," Gabe replied. "That's why we decided to cross there instead of Pie Town."

"I thought so, too," Bull said. "But they've changed their mind."

"That's all I need," Gabe replied glumly. "Do you have any idea what blasting engineers are going to cost us?"

"Chinese do blasting," Long Li said quietly.

"Long Li, I don't want to sound negative but it's a pretty sophisticated operation to handle dynamite. It takes a tremendous amount of skill."

"Chinese have skill," Long Li insisted. "Chinese invented blasting."

Gabe laughed. "I guess you're right about that. Bull, what do you think?"

"Boss, if Long Li says them little fellas can handle dynamite, then I say let's give it a try."

Gabe ran his hand through his hair. "All right; I guess we got nothing to lose. Your Chinese can try it," he agreed.

"We do good job for you," Long Li said gratefully, "You see."

"Come on, little buddy, we better go now," Bull said. "We got some plannin' to do."

"You know, I would hate to let them down almost as bad as I would hate losing the railroad," Gabe commented after they left.

"Maybe things'll work out all right," Makenna said hopefully.

Gabe smiled. "Hang on to your optimism, Makenna, right now it's about all we've got."

"Gabe, when do you get the government grant?" Makenna asked.

"As soon as I lay continuous tracks to the Territorial Line," Gabe answered.

"Could you borrow from anyone else against that money?"

"I'm afraid not," Gabe said. "The money that isn't committed to Emory Van Zandt is committed to Western Pacific. I have nothing left to borrow money against. It's a shame, too, because I believe Pacific Trust Bank in San Francisco would lend me money if I had some collateral."

"What about the equipment? The engines, the cars, the tools?" Makenna asked.

"Most of the cars are leased from Western Pacific," Gabe said. "The rest is already committed to Van Zandt."

"But there must be something we could do," Makenna suggested.

"There's nothing," Gabe said. "There is only so much money to work with, and we've used it up." He stood and stretched. "I've had a rough day. I think I'll go to bed and sleep on it. Maybe I'll get an idea in the morning."

"You'll be havin' our prayers, lad," Kellen promised as Gabe started to leave.

"Thanks," Gabe said. He looked at Makenna. "And thank you," he added.

"For what? I haven't been of any help."

"Yes, you have," Gabe said. "More than you realize. I needed someone to talk to tonight and you were kind enough to listen. Good night."

"Good night," Makenna replied.

She stood at the door for a moment after Gabe left.

Makenna sat up long after her father had gone to bed. She had no idea what time it was but realized it must be quite late because she heard no sound from the workers outside and knew they must all be asleep.

At first, Makenna stayed awake because she was too upset to go to sleep. Then, more to pass the time than to actively look for a solution, she began reading the government regulations pertaining to the requirements to qualify for a Congressional Railroaders' Building Grant. For the construction of the Central Pacific, there had been a government loan of $16,000 per mile of flat land and $48,000 per mile of mountain land crossed, along with a land grant of ten miles to either side of the track. But that had been during the great rush to link the Pacific and Atlantic oceans. Now the government was less generous. The maximum grant was $16,000 per mile, regardless of the type of terrain the railroad crossed, and land grants were for one mile to either side of the right-of-way only. Makenna knew $8,000 per mile was committed to Western Pacific and that left Gabe with little enough to work with. To make matters worse, the track had to cross a state or territorial line in order for the grant to be paid. In this case, the line had to be crossed by the end of the ninetieth day and that was only twenty-three days away.

Makenna was about to close the book when her eyes caught a supplemental paragraph. At first, she read it with curiosity, then with interest, and finally with a growing sense of excitement.

"This is it!" she said aloud. "This may be the answer!"

Makenna held the pages of the book open with an ashtray, then looked at the map on the wall. She searched for Fence Lake Pass, the point at which Bull said they would have to cross, then ran her finger down the line of mountains until she found Pie Town. "Yes!" she said excitedly. "It will work, I know it will!"

Excitement had built to such a pitch that Makenna was unable to prevent the words from spilling out and she looked around sheepishly, aware that she was talking to herself. At first, she thought to awaken her father and tell him of what she had discovered but then decided to take it directly to Gabe. After all, he was the one who would have to make the ultimate decision.

Makenna was wearing her nightgown and robe, and she started to go to get dressed, but was too excited to take the time. Besides, her robe was modest enough, she decided.

Makenna closed the book and stepped outside. The desert ground was spotted with piles of glowing coals, all that was left of the campfires. The men were asleep now, resting for the five-thirty wake-up call the next morning. The night air was cool and Makenna shivered slightly as she clutched at the neck of her robe and hurried back to the caboose, which served as Gabe's living quarters. She wasn't sure whether the shivering was from the cold or from the excitement of her discovery.

Makenna knocked on the door. She heard nothing, so she knocked again. Finally, she heard Gabe call from inside.

"What is it? Who's there?"

"Gabe, it's me, Makenna."

"Makenna? What is it? What's wrong?"

"Nothing. Gabe, let me in, please. I must talk to you."

"All right, just a minute."

Makenna waited for a moment longer, then the door was opened. Gabe was standing on the other side, wrapped up in a blanket. He looked like an Indian and she chuckled at the sight.

"Excuse the wardrobe," Gabe said. "I was in bed and I don't own a robe. What is it? What are you doing here this late at night?"

"Gabe, I've come up with a way to raise the money," Makenna said.

"What are you talking about? There is no way."

"Yes, there is," Makenna said. She went past him into the darkened caboose. "Light a lamp." Gabe did as she instructed and turned the lamp up. The mantle glowed white and the room was bathed in light. She put the book on his desk.

"Do you know what this is?" she asked, pointing to it.

"Yes. It's the government regulations pertaining to railroad grants."

"I have found an additional four hundred ninety-seven thousand dollars in this book," Makenna said.

"What?" Gabe asked, his mouth dropping open in surprise. "What are you talking about?"

"Here," Makenna said, opening the book. "Read this paragraph."

"Exceptions to the above conditions," Gabe read aloud. "Additional funds may be made available in those areas where easement must be purchased from private property owners." He looked at Makenna. "That won't do us any good," he said.

"Read on," she instructed.

"Railroads which serve military installations may receive additional funding from the Department of War, depending upon the recommendations of the Secretary of War. No, nothing here," he murmured. "Wait a minute, is this what you mean? One thousand dollars per mile above the basic grant will be allocated for each previously settled community the railroad serves."

"That's it," Makenna said excitedly. "Look," she added, pointing to the map, which hung on his wall. "You are going to have to blast your way through here anyway. Why not swing south and go through at Pie Town? That way you can pick up Hickman and Tres Laguanas, then Pie Town, Omega, Quemado, Red Hill, and Springerville over on the Arizona side. That's seventy-one miles and seven towns, or four hundred ninety-seven thousand dollars."

"I don't know," Gabe said slowly. "Some of those places are nothing more than mining camps, just spots on the map. There may not even be anyone living there."

"But they are on the maps," Makenna said. "Gabe, if

you have to, you could put people there."

"How do you mean?"

"You've made Papa your line supervisor. He could put railroad agents and their families in each of those places. They are already listed on the map, so we wouldn't be just creating them to get the money. And if someone lived there, they would certainly qualify as settled towns, even if by one family only."

Gabe smiled broadly. "You know, Makenna, that head on your shoulders is as smart as it is pretty."

"Thank you for noticing," Makenna said.

"That you're smart?"

"No, that I'm pretty," Makenna replied with a broad smile.

"I've always known that."

"I must get back before Papa wakes up and misses me."

"I'll go with you."

"Go with me? Whatever for?"

"I want to tell him what a brilliant daughter he has," Gabe said affectionately. "Also, I'm going to ask you to do something for me and I want him in on it."

"What do you want me to do?"

"I want you to go to San Francisco," Gabe said easily.

"Why?"

"I'm going to write a letter, which I want you to deliver personally to Ernest Carr of the Pacific Trust Bank. I am authorizing you to ask for a loan on our behalf of one hundred fifty thousand dollars, securing it with the new grant money, we expect to receive."

"Gabe, you want me to ask for a one hundred fifty thousand-dollar loan?"

"Yes."

"But I couldn't do that."

"Why not?"

"Why, I wouldn't know what to say, what to do, or how to act! I mean, how will it look for a woman to go in there and talk business with a man like Ernest Carr?"

"Ah, but you aren't just any woman," Gabe countered. "You're Makenna O'Shea."

"Well, if you think I can do it…but don't you think you should send a wire first?"

"Absolutely not," Gabe said. "Makenna, this has to be kept secret. You mustn't tell anyone where you are going or why. And especially not Peter."

"Can Papa know?"

"He's the only one we can tell," Gabe said. "Is it agreed?"

"Very well," Makenna said.

The two slipped through the darkness, and just before they went into Makenna's car, Gabe hugged her.

"I'll get Papa," she said, after they went inside.

Makenna left Gabe looking at the map and went into the compartment that served as her father's bedroom. He was sleeping soundly, snoring contentedly. Makenna shook him awake.

"What is it? What do you want?" Kellen said groggily.

"Papa, wake up. Gabe Hansen is here. He has something he wants to tell you."

"Can't it wait until morning?" Kellen burrowed into his pillow.

"No, Papa. He needs to tell you now."

"All right," Kellen said. "Give me a moment."

Makenna returned to the front room to find Gabe still studying the map.

"I think we can do it," he said, looking over at her. "The whole secret is going to be in making it to the Arizona line within twenty-three days."

"How long would it take you to make the border if you blast through at Fence Creek?" Makenna asked.

"I figured ten days at the outside," Gabe said. "It's only half as far. This way we'll have to push it to make it in time. But I still think we can do it."

"Do what?" Kellen asked, swinging into the room on his crutches.

"Save the railroad," Gabe said. "I'd like to tell you about an idea that a very smart person gave me."

Gabe proceeded to explain Makenna's plan to Kellen. He ended by telling of the necessity for Makenna to make her secret trip to San Francisco.

"I see," Kellen said. "And you want my permission for her to go?"

"Yes," Gabe said.

"Then I say, how soon can she leave?"

CHAPTER THIRTEEN

The train ride to Denver was uneventful and as Makenna had been there once before, there was nothing new in the way of adventure. She picked up a week's worth of copies of the Albuquerque Daily Journal and read every article as the train sped on to Denver. It was such a pleasant way to pass the time that she took scarce notice of the cinders and dust or the discomfort of spending the night in a cramped coach car since there were no sleeping cars available for the Albuquerque to Denver run.

Once Makenna reached Denver though, the situation changed drastically. There she entrained aboard the Pacific Parlor Express, a luxurious eight-car train that ran from Kansas City to San Francisco. The Pacific Parlor Express boasted two libraries, a hair-dressing salon, two organs, and its own private newspaper. The parlor car was resplendent in plush upholstery, rich hangings and hand-carved inlaid paneling. Makenna, who had been raised as a railroader's daughter, had never seen anything to match the luxury and elegance of the train and its pure grandeur was enough to bring her out of her reading in order to observe the wonder of it all.

"Mademoiselle O'Shea?" a uniformed steward inquired as soon as Makenna's luggage was stowed and she had settled into a large, overstuffed chair.

"Yes?"

"Welcome aboard the Pacific Parlor Express, *Mademoiselle*," the steward said. He handed her a menu. "There are seats available in the dining car at eleven-thirty, noon and one o'clock. Which would you prefer?" The steward had an accent but Makenna didn't know whether it was genuinely French or put on just for the overall effect of elegance.

"I think I will take the one o'clock sitting," Makenna said.

"Would *Mademoiselle* care to select from the menu?"

Makenna's previous experience with meals on board trains had been limited to sack lunches or the very unappetizing fare served at stations along the way. Now she saw a veritable feast offered. The menu featured blue-winged teal, antelope steaks, roast beef, boiled ham and tongue, broiled chicken, corn on the cob, fresh fruit, hot rolls and cornbread.

"I'll have broiled chicken, please," she said, returning the menu to the steward.

"An excellent choice," the steward assured her. "Your table companion will be a Señorita Alexia Botin. She is a young Mexican lady and exceptionally well-cultured. Do you mind?"

"Mind? No, of course not," Makenna replied. "Why should I?"

"There are those who do," the steward said. "I've had two refuse."

"Then you may schedule me as her dining companion for the duration of the journey," Makenna said.

"Thank you, *Mademoiselle*, that is most kind," the

steward said. "Your chicken will be ready at one o'clock. I hope you enjoy your trip."

After the steward left, Makenna looked through the large windows at the beautiful scenery. Huge purple mountains hung in the distance, while in the meadows and plains alongside the track, wild flowers grew in colorful profusion. As the train passed, it gathered the curious at trackside and Makenna saw hundreds of children waving gaily as they sped along. At first, she returned their waves but soon grew tired from the sheer effort of it and settled back to read her newspapers.

The dining car began serving at eleven and by one o'clock, when the third call for lunch was issued, Makenna was ravenously hungry.

The elegance of the dining car was in keeping with the rest of the train and Makenna saw richly paneled walls, plush drapes and upholstery, and flower-bedecked tables. She was met by a waiter as soon as she stepped through the door.

"Your name, miss?"

"Makenna O'Shea."

"Ah, yes, your dining companion is already seated. This way, please."

As Makenna approached the table, she saw a beautiful young Mexican girl sitting quietly. The girl was wearing an elegant gown of pale gold and it made her dark, flawless skin even more beautiful. She greeted Makenna with sparkling eyes and a dazzling smile.

"Hello," Makenna said. "My name is Makenna O'Shea."

Makenna thought she saw something pass over the girl's eyes—recognition, maybe? But that couldn't be. Makenna had never met this girl. She wouldn't be likely to forget her if she had. Besides, the look passed away as quickly as it arrived.

"I am Alexia Botin," the girl said. "I am very pleased to meet you."

"Alexia...what a beautiful name!" Makenna answered warmly.

The waiters brought their lunch then and the two women got to know more of each other as they enjoyed their meal. Makenna learned that Alexia had just become the stepdaughter of a very wealthy Mexican and was being sent to San Francisco by her new stepfather to enjoy a vacation.

"I think he is embarrassed to have me around during the—what do you call it, the early part of the marriage?"

"The honeymoon?" Makenna suggested.

"*Sí*," the girl said with a smile. "The honeymoon."

"But it will be such a wonderful thing to visit San Francisco, don't you think?" Makenna asked.

"I have never been before," Alexia said. "Although I have an uncle who lives there. Have you ever visited San Francisco?"

"No," Makenna said. "This is my first."

"Why have you come?"

"I," Makenna started, then hesitated. "I have come on business."

"Forgive me, it was rude to ask," Alexia apologized.

"No, not at all," Makenna replied. "It is just business to do with a railroad my friend is building. It isn't very interesting, I'm afraid."

"Perhaps we can do something together while we are in the city," Alexia suggested. "I would very much like to see the opera. Wouldn't you?"

"Yes, very much," Makenna replied.

After the meal, Makenna excused herself and returned

to the parlor car where she read for a while, then listened to the steady clicking of the wheels on the tracks. She knew from her long association with railroads that the number of clicks she heard in twenty seconds was roughly equal to the speed of travel in miles per hour. She counted fifty-five clicks.

Makenna looked around the parlor car at the other passengers. They were probably unaware of the speed they were traveling and totally unconcerned over their safety. The comfort of the chairs and the luxury of the car seemed to mock the possibility of an accident. And yet Makenna had seen "cornfield meets," and knew, from ghastly observation, what a four hundred ton train traveling at nearly a mile a minute could do.

Makenna was probably the only passenger in the car to have ridden in an engine cab. She knew what it was like to see the narrow bright line of rails and the slender points of switches as the train rushed forward. She had heard the thunder of the bridges and seen the track shut in by rocky bluffs as the train swept around sharp curves. She had also seen it during a dark and rainy night, when the headlight revealed only a few yards of glistening rail and the ghostly telegraph poles lit up, then whipped by so fast as to be a blur. Makenna knew full well that by the time the headlight picked up anything, it would be far too late to stop.

And yet, knowing all this, she, too, was as content as any of the passengers on board and in a short while the steady clicking of the rails and the comfort of the reclining seat lulled her into sleep, where she slept peacefully.

There was a bustle of activity at the station when the train arrived in San Francisco two days later. It was a huge crowd but, unlike the crowds of people who came to meet the trains at Albuquerque, these people all seemed to have a purpose. There were no fewer than fifteen tracks running under the awning at the station and a train sat on each track. Out of the awning in the yard, there were more tracks and switches than Makenna could effectively count and everywhere she saw engines puffing about, making up new trains. Her father had been a train man for his entire life but Makenna knew he had never seen anything this magnificent. She wished that he had been able to come with her to share the pure excitement of such a sight.

"Makenna!" Makenna heard someone call and she looked around to see Alexia Botin standing with an attractive Mexican gentleman. "Makenna, have you made plans where to stay? Is anyone meeting you?"

"I am staying at the St. Mark's Hotel," Makenna said. "No one is meeting me. I thought I would hail a carriage."

"My Uncle Armando is here," Alexia said. "Perhaps you will allow us to give you a ride?"

"I don't wish to put you to any trouble," Makenna said.

"It is no trouble, *Señorita*," Armando said, smiling broadly at her. "We will be going right by the hotel."

"Well, I thank you very much," Makenna said.

"Where is your baggage?"

"There," Makenna said, pointing to two pieces of luggage.

Armando spoke in Spanish and an older man, obviously his servant, stooped to pick up her bags.

"But what about Alexia's baggage?" Makenna asked.

Armando laughed. "I'm afraid my sister's daughter brought all of Mexico with her. We have another wagon taking her things."

"I did not know what to bring," Alexia shrugged, "so I brought everything."

Makenna joined the others in laughter, then followed them through the huge station to the street out front. There, dozens upon dozens of carriages sat and hundreds of people walked by quickly as if hurrying to make an important engagement. Everyone seemed to be yelling at everyone else and the noise was deafening. She caught a strong, fishy smell and commented on it.

"We are but a short way from the docks," Armando explained. "What you smell is the sea!"

"The sea!" Makenna said excitedly. "Oh, I've never seen an ocean. I am going to enjoy this trip ever so much."

"Don't forget we have a date for the opera," Alexia said. "Uncle Armando tells me there is one tomorrow night. Would you like to go then?"

"Yes, that would be nice," Makenna answered. "My business with the bank should be concluded by then."

"Fine," Alexia said. "We will call for you at your hotel tomorrow evening at seven-thirty."

"That would be delightful," Makenna replied.

CHAPTER FOURTEEN

During the heyday of building rails across the country, there were those smart, if somewhat unscrupulous, men who realized that more money could be made in building a railroad than in actually running one. The government advances and land grants were so generous as to invite speculative building when indeed no railroad was actually planned. The land was divided up into profitable parcels and sold, tracks were shoddily laid across land that dishonest surveyors certified to qualify for the government money and the get-rich-quick schemes left the Comstock Lodes and flocked to the railroads.

Perhaps, the most grandiose scheme of all was the Credit Mobilier scheme. Credit Mobilier was a construction company organized by the directors of Union Pacific Railroad. The railroad paid for all work through Credit Mobilier which set its own charges for goods and services. Of the seventy-three million dollars that poured into the Union Pacific construction funds, no more than fifty million dollars went for actual cost. The remaining twenty-three million dollars were divided among the principal stockholders of Credit Mobilier: a brilliant and zany man named George Francis Train; Thomas Durant, one of the principals of the Union Pacific; Oakes Ames, a United States Congressman, and Schuyler Colfax, Vice-President of the United States.

The Credit Mobilier bubble burst in the summer of 1872, however, and the days of highhanded railroad financing had ended. From that day forward, there was very little of the get-rich-quick appeal to railroad building and backing was much more difficult to obtain. Thus it was that the letter, which Makenna carried with her to present to Ernest Carr of the Pacific Trust Bank, had a complete accounting of all funds acquired and expended by the Southern Continental Railroad as well as the anticipated route of travel that would increase the government grant.

Makenna had the letter in her purse as she stood in the lobby of the Pacific Trust Bank. She had asked a clerk for permission to speak with Ernest Carr and now cooled her heels as the clerk held a whispered conversation in the back of the room. Makenna was aware that the men in the bank were staring at the upstart woman who would invade their domain and she tried not to return their stares or to show embarrassment over being the center of their attention. Finally, the clerk returned.

"You may see Mr. Carr," he said.

"Thank you."

Ernest Carr was a portly man with a thick curving mustache over drooping jowls. He stood as Makenna approached his desk, walked around it, and held a chair for her to be seated. "Now, Miss O'Shea, what can I do for you?" he asked after he returned to his own chair.

Makenna opened her purse and removed the envelope she had been given by Gabe.

"Mr. Carr, I believe you recall a Mr. Gabe Hansen who

came to see you a few months ago concerning a loan?"

"Gabe Hansen. Yes, he's building a railroad somewhere I think. Texas or Arizona."

"New Mexico," Makenna said. She handed the envelope to Carr. "Here is a complete accounting of the operation to date. We've made excellent progress but now we find that we need an additional one hundred and fifty thousand."

"One hundred and fifty thousand?" Carr repeated. He read the letter carefully, then read it again. "That isn't an excessive amount. That is, if it offers our depositors a fair chance of return. Tell Mr. Hansen I will be happy to speak with him."

Makenna felt a sinking sensation in the pit of her stomach. He hadn't even understood that she was asking for the money. She took a deep breath and tried again.

"He won't be able to come see you, Mr. Carr," she said. "If we are to get the government grant that we are using to secure this loan, we have to lay track across the Arizona line by a set deadline. Mr. Hansen can't leave the construction. That's why he authorized me to apply for the loan."

Carr looked up in some surprise. "You? You're a woman."

"Yes, Mr. Carr, I'm a woman," Makenna replied. "But, as you can see by Mr. Hansen's letter, he has complete faith in me and in my ability to negotiate this arrangement."

"I don't know," Carr said, laying the letter down. He ran his hand under his sagging chins. "It's not that I personally have anything against doing business with a woman, you understand. But I've got my depositors to worry about."

"You would not be doing business with me," Makenna said with a sigh. "You would be doing business with Gabe Hansen. I am just his messenger."

"But you are a woman, Miss O'Shea."

"You keep telling me that," Makenna said. "Look," she added in a frustrated tone of voice, "have you ever made a loan on the strength of a telegram?"

"Well, yes, of course."

"Then you are doing business with whoever delivers that telegram to you," Makenna said. "And sometimes that's a mere youth. Am I right?"

"Yes."

"Then just regard me as the bearer of a telegram. But for certain reasons of confidentiality, Mr. Hansen didn't wish to use the telegraph system."

Carr picked up the letter and looked at it again, rubbing his chins once more. "Very well, Miss O'Shea, I'll have a bank draft made out to you for one hundred fifty thousand dollars."

"I would like it in cash, please," Makenna said.

"Cash? But, Miss O'Shea, that's a great deal of money for a woman...for anyone to be carrying."

"I realize that," Makenna said. "But I have the cloak of secrecy in my favor. And we must have cash as we are working against a deadline and would not have time to convert the draft into cash."

"Very well," Carr said. "How do you propose to carry that much money? It won't fit into your purse and I wouldn't recommend carrying it in one of our bags."

"I brought a portmanteau," Makenna said. "I shall carry the money in that." She pointed to the leather case which sat by the railing near the clerk's desk.

"It will take a few minutes," Carr said, excusing himself. "That's a lot of money to gather."

When Makenna left the bank one half hour later with the weight of the one hundred and fifty thousand dollars pulling at the suitcase, she had such a heady sense of accomplishment that she didn't even notice the closed coach across the street.

"There she is," Alexia said, pointing her out to the two men who sat with her. "I am certain that she has the money in that bag. You may keep whatever money there is. Just don't hurt her."

"You're a queer one, girl," one of the two men said. Both were Anglos and rather desperate-looking men, one with a large scar on his face and the other with a patch covering one eye. "If you don't want any of the money and you don't want her hurt, just what do you want?"

"I was told you'd do a job for me without question," Alexia said.

"She's right, Leo," the man with the scar said. "What the hell do we care why she's doin' this? If there's money in that bag, it'll be payment enough. And there sure as hell ought not to be any problem in takin' it away from 'er."

"Remember," Alexia warned again. "She is not to be harmed in any way."

"What if she puts up a fight?" Leo asked.

Alexia laughed. "Can't two strong men handle one woman who fights?"

"Not to worry, we'll take care of it all right. I was just wonderin', that's all. Come on, Waylon. We got work to do."

The coach tilted as the two men got out and one of them turned back to look through the window. "This here'll be the last time you'll ever see us, ma'am. I want ta tell you it's been a pleasure doin' business with ya."

"Good day to you, sir," Alexia said. She signaled for the coach driver to pull away and left the two men standing beside the street.

Alexia had been left to guard Makenna's purse one night on the train while the latter went to the ladies' lounge. She read the letter and realized that here might be a way to stop the hated railroad from cutting through the Tafoya land. Such an accomplishment would certainly make Bernardo take more notice of her, maybe even return the love she felt for him. There was needed only a way to take advantage of her knowledge and that way presented itself when, yesterday, she was taken on a tour of the waterfront.

"There are desperate men here who will do anything for money," her uncle told her as the carriage rolled past the waterfront saloons. "They are drifters, robbers, miners who have lost their claims, men with no hope nor ambition beyond the next day. It is not an area where one should long idle," he added. He spoke to the driver and the driver whipped the team into a trot.

This morning, saying that she was going to the Museum of Art, Alexia hailed a closed coach and returned to the waterfront. She found the desperate looking men lounging outside a saloon and offered her proposition. She would provide them with information that would allow them to acquire a great deal of money. All they had to do was take it. She wanted nothing other than the money to be taken.

As the coach rolled down the street, Alexia turned her head to keep Makenna from seeing her. For just a moment, she regretted the whole thing and almost yelled at the driver to stop and pick Makenna up before the robbers got to her. After all, she had gotten to know Makenna on the train and she liked her. But no, Makenna wouldn't be hurt and the money wouldn't be a personal loss. It would affect only Gabe Hansen and his railroad. And in that Alexia knew that she was doing a noble thing.

Makenna had chosen the St. Mark's Hotel because it was only two blocks from the Pacific Trust Bank. She increased her pace in order to cover the two blocks as quickly as possible. She was perfectly safe; it was broad daylight and no one knew what she had in the bag. But, nevertheless, she would feel much better once she reached the hotel.

As she approached the alleyway just before the hotel, a man lurched out of it. At first, he frightened her, not only by the suddenness of his movement, but also because he was a frightening apparition to behold. He was large, unkempt and unshaven, and wore an eyepatch over one eye. But the man was staggering about and he held an empty wine bottle to his mouth as if trying to milk one last drop. Obviously, the poor wretch was a wino, just coming awake from last night's intemperance.

"Hey, missy, would you buy a poor man a drink?" the man slurred, staggering toward her. He reached for her as if pleading and Makenna's attention was so focused on him that she didn't notice, until the last instant, the second man hiding in the shadows. He jumped out at her and pulled a canvas sack down over her head. She tried to scream but the scream was muffled by the bag. She felt a rope being wound around her tightly and then the case was wrenched from her grip. Next, there was a sharp pain as she was struck on the head and everything went black.

CHAPTER FIFTEEN

When Makenna regained consciousness, she found that she was tied and gagged and lying in a crude bed of some sort, the canvas sack gone from her head. The room seemed to be moving and she could hear creaks and groans as if from stretching rope and flexing boards. A dimly lit lantern cast flickering shadows across the room and, as she examined her situation, she saw, in addition to the bed where she lay, a table and chair, a chest, and a shelf with a handful of books. She was also cognizant of a very strong and most unusual odor. It had a bit of a fishy smell to it, though not so overpowering as to be unpleasant.

Makenna heard the rattle of chains. That sound she recognized immediately, having heard chains being used to secure cargo on trains.

"Cap'n, the anchor's aweigh," a voice called.

"Aye, we'll stand off Alcatraz Island for the night, Mr. Voyles."

A ship! She was on board a ship!

Makenna tried to cry out and strained against the bonds which held her, but she was unable to make more than a pitiful whining sound. She made no progress against the ropes whatever.

Makenna felt the throb of the ship's engines and realized they were moving, leaving for no telling where. My God, what would she do? What was going to happen to her? She thought of her father and felt heartsick.

The money!

Makenna tried again to call out but could manage nothing. She was suddenly aware of a painful bump on her head and realized that the money had been taken. What would Gabe do without the money to operate? And how did she get here and why was she here?

The door opened and a man entered. He was short but muscular and looked like a solid block of granite. He was bald but more than made up for it by the full set of chin whiskers. His mouth was clean shaven, however, with no mustache above and nothing below until far down on the chin. The light in the room was not bright enough to allow Makenna to determine the color of his eyes.

"Well, I see you are awake, Miss Burkhart," the man said.

Miss Burkhart? Who is Miss Burkhart? *Makenna thought.* That's it! There's been a case of mistaken identity. *She shook her head rapidly and the man removed the gag.*

"I guess we can take this off now," he said. "After all, we are in the middle of the bay. There is very little chance of anyone hearing you."

"Who is Miss Burkhart?" Makenna gasped as soon as she could speak.

"Oh, I see…you're going to plead mistaken identity, is that it?"

"I am not Miss Burkhart," Makenna said. "My name is Makenna O'Shea. And I can prove it."

"And precisely how do you intend to prove it?" the man

asked. "You have no identification on you. Do you have family in San Francisco?"

"No," Makenna said. "I'm from New Mexico."

The man laughed again. "New Mexico. That's as good a place as any, I suppose. Now, suppose we quit playing games, Miss Burkhart."

"Who is this Miss Burkhart you keep calling me?"

"All right, if you must hear it recited, Miss Burkhart, I shall accommodate you. Your name is Agnes Burkhart and you are from Boston, Massachusetts. You worked as a governess in a private girls' school and—must I go on? Do you realize by now that I know who you are?"

"But I'm not who you say I am," Makenna insisted.

"Look, Miss Burkhart," the man said gruffly. "You kidnapped four of those little girls, extorted money from their parents, and then killed them. There is no place in the civilized world where you can hide. Two Pinkerton men traced you to San Francisco and caught you yesterday. They put you on board my ship because it was the next one leaving for Boston."

"But that isn't true!" Makenna insisted. "My name is Makenna O'Shea. I came to San Francisco yesterday to borrow money for a railroad that is being built. I left the bank with the money and two men accosted me. They took the money and now I find myself here in this place. I don't know who you are or why you are so willing to believe that I am this Miss Burkhart you speak of but I am Makenna O'Shea."

"It is widely known that you are a persuasive woman," the man said. "But you'll find that I can turn a deaf ear to your lies."

"What is your name?" Makenna asked.

"I don't see why that should concern you."

"My God, sir, I am your prisoner! My life is completely in your hands! Am I not even to know the name of the man who may kill me at any moment?"

"You need have no fear on that," the man said. "You'll be taken back to Boston for a fair trial, that I promise you."

"Captain...I assume you are the captain of this ship."

"Aye, madam, that I am."

"Captain, if I am who you say I am, wouldn't it make more sense to send me back by train? After all, a train can travel from San Francisco to Boston in ten days. How long will it take you to reach Boston?"

"You've a point there and I raised the question myself to the Pinkerton agents," the captain answered. "But they explained that the trains'll not carry you without extradition papers and by the time those are signed you'll likely have made good your escape again."

"And you believed them?"

"I neglected to tell you, Miss Burkhart," the captain said coldly. "One of the little girls you killed was my own sister's daughter. I'll not be takin' a chance on your gettin' away again. That's for sure."

Makenna began crying quietly, big tears sliding down her face.

"The cryin'll do you no good," the captain said. "I'm immune to such pleadin'."

"Am I to be kept tied for the entire journey?"

"I'll untie you as soon as we are to sea," the captain said. "We'll spend the night anchored just off Alcatraz Island and get underway with the mornin' tide."

The despair of her situation nearly overcame her, and Makenna let out a pitiful cry and strained against the bindings once more, but to no effect.

"Captain," Makenna said quietly. "Describe these

so-called Pinkerton men to me."

"I don't wish to discuss it any further, madam," the captain said.

"Did one of them have an eye patch?"

"Yes."

Makenna sighed. "He was one of the two men who robbed me."

"This Miss Burkhart," Makenna went on, seeing the captain's shame and hoping to take advantage of it. "Do you have a picture of her?"

"No," the captain said. "But a very good description of her."

"Describe her, please."

"She's a beautiful young woman of nineteen or twenty, known to have very winning ways about her. She has brown eyes and red hair."

"Red hair? My hair is black," Makenna said.

"Madam, we are all aware of dyes which can change the color of a woman's hair," the captain said.

"The hair on one's head can be changed by dye. There is another place where the hair is the natural color."

"Madam, surely you don't intend for me to…"

"Captain, it's my only hope," Makenna said.

The captain took the lantern from the wall and moved it over the bed, causing the shadows in the small cabin to twist into grotesque shapes. He held the lantern over Makenna's stomach and looked at the junction of her legs. There was, glowing ebony in the lamplight, the small triangle of hair that proved Makenna's statement.

"Oh, my God," the captain gasped.

"Do you believe me now?" Makenna asked.

"Oh, my God." the captain said again. "What have I done?"

"You have made a mistake," Makenna said.

"Oh, what am I going to do?" the captain cried.

"Do? Why, you are going to let me go," Makenna said.

"No, I can't," the captain said. "Don't you see that?"

"What?" Makenna felt a new fear knotting at her stomach. "Why not?"

"Because now I'm guilty of abduction. If I let you go and you go to the authorities, I'll lose my license. I may even be put in jail."

"Captain, do you intend to add murder to your other crimes?" Makenna asked.

"Murder?" the captain asked. "No, who said anything about murder?"

"The only way you are going to keep me here is to kill me," Makenna said. "I've no intention of staying on board this ship."

"I've got to think." The captain walked across the room and put both hands on the desk and leaned against it for a moment. "I've got to think of something," he repeated.

"Put me ashore," Makenna suggested. "I don't know who you are. I don't know which ship this is. How can I hurt you?"

"I...I don't know," the captain said. Finally, he looked back at her. "I'm going to put you ashore on Alcatraz Island."

"Where is that?"

"It's right here in the bay," the captain replied. "You can catch a ferry in the morning. By then, I'll be gone."

"Thank you, captain," Makenna said quietly.

The captain quickly untied her and as her wrists were released, she began rubbing against the rope burns gingerly.

"I was given $250 for your passage to Boston," the captain said. He pulled an envelope from his pocket and handed it to her. "I'll give it to you."

Makenna was working on her dress but was unable to effect a modest enough repair to the damaged bodice.

"Have you something I can wear?" she asked.

"Yes," the captain said. "Forgive me, yes." He opened the chest, removed a bulky sweater and handed it to her. She slipped it on gratefully.

"Come," the captain said. "I'll put you ashore."

"Is there an inn or some lodging on the island?" Makenna asked.

"An inn? No, there is nothing," the captain answered.

"You mean I have to spend the night in the open?"

"I'm sorry," the captain said. "It's the only way."

On deck, Makenna saw the type of ship she was on. It had one mast forward and one aft and a huge smokestack right in the middle of the deck. A large paddle wheel protruded from each side of the ship. Under other circumstances, she might have found the vessel fascinating. Until now, she had seen only pictures or Currier and Ives prints of such ships.

"Mr. Voyles, lower a boat away," the captain ordered.

"Aye, aye, cap'n. Will you need a crew?"

"No. I'm going to put the lady ashore. The fewer of our men she sees, the better off we'll be."

"Cap'n, you mean you aim to let her get away?"

"We've made a mistake, Voyles," the captain said anxiously. "I no longer believe this woman to be Miss Burkhart."

"Then perhaps we should take her back to…"

"I'll make the decisions," the captain interrupted gruffly.

"Aye, aye, sir."

"And make ready to sail. We'll get underway as soon as I return."

"Cap'n, the tide is not yet in."

"We're not waiting for the tide," the captain said. "We're sailing immediately."

"Aye, aye, sir," Voyles said.

Makenna followed the exchange with disinterest. Her only thought now was to escape from this ship. If it meant that she would have to spend the night on some island that she had never heard of, then so be it. She intended to get away before the captain changed his mind.

The captain said nothing as they rowed from the ship to the dark island. There were only the sounds of the oars dipping water and rubbing against the oarlock. Finally, she felt the boat scrape against the bottom.

"Step out over the bow, madam, and you'll scarcely wet your feet," the captain said.

Makenna did as she was instructed without saying a word and no sooner was she out of the boat than the captain began pushing off for the return trip to the ship. He said nothing more to her, nor did she speak to him. She was thankful to be rid of him.

By the light of a full moon overhead, Makenna walked through cold water, which was only an inch or so deep and then reached the rocky but dry shore. She climbed up a small path until she reached a level place, then she turned to look back at the sea. The boat was nearly returned to the ship, and already smoke was coming from the ship's stack. It was a completely black silhouette and Makenna knew there would be no way she could ever identify it.

"Who is there?" a voice suddenly called.

Makenna felt a spasm of fear and turned toward the voice.

"Identify yourself, at once, or I will shoot," the voice said.

"No, don't shoot," Makenna said.

"Advance and be recognized."

Makenna moved hesitantly toward the voice.

"Halt," the voice said.

Makenna saw a man moving toward her carrying a rifle. As the man got closer, she noticed two things about him. He was quite young and he was a soldier.

"Good Lord, it's a girl," the soldier said. "Who are you? What are you doing here?"

"My name is Makenna O'Shea," Makenna said. "I was...abducted and put aboard that ship. But I managed to talk them into freeing me. I...what is this place? I was told it was uninhabited."

"It's a military prison, ma'am," the soldier said. "You just stand still, ma'am. I don't know what to do about this."

"What's going to happen to me?"

"I don't know, ma'am. I've got to report it," the soldier said. He turned his head to one side and cupped his hand to his mouth. "Corporal of the Guard, Post Number Five!" he shouted.

"Corporal of the Guard, Post Number Five," Makenna heard repeated in the distance and then even further away, so faint as to barely be heard, "Corporal of the Guard, Post Number Five."

"He'll be here in a minute, ma'am," the soldier said. "You just stay put."

"I'm not going anywhere, I promise you," Makenna said.

A moment later, Makenna heard someone approaching them.

"Halt," the soldier with her called. "Who goes there?"

"Corporal Robertson," a voice called.

"Advance, Corporal Robertson, and be recognized."

The approaching soldier advanced several steps.

"Halt," the soldier called again. Then: "I recognize you, Corporal Robertson."

"What is it, Tuttle. Why did you sound the alarm?"

"This here girl, Corporal," Tuttle said, pointing to Makenna as the man came closer.

"What? Who the hell are you?"

Makenna gave the corporal her name and explained how she came to the island.

"Well, ma'am, I don't reckon there's much we can do about that," Corporal Robertson said. "But if you'd like to come on back to the guardhouse, I suppose we could give you some coffee and a place to keep warm 'til morning."

"Will I be able to get back into the city tomorrow?"

"Sure," Corporal Robertson said. "I don't see any reason why not."

"Thank you," Makenna said. She turned to the private who had first challenged her. "And I thank you, too. You have been very nice."

"My pleasure, ma'am," the young soldier said, smiling broadly. "Most of the time out here on guard, there don't nothin' happen. This is somethin' I'll be able to talk about for a long time."

Makenna followed the corporal back along a moonlit path until they reached a small building that was made of rock. A welcome lamp glowed from within.

"What was it, Robertson?" a man asked as they stepped inside. "Was Tuttle wantin' his mama?" A second man laughed.

"No, sir, Lieutenant," Robertson replied. "Look what I got."

"Holy Jesus," the lieutenant said, seeing Makenna. Jumping to his feet, the lieutenant showed Makenna to a small, but private room where there was a bed and he offered it to her as a place to sleep. She accepted gratefully and slept soundly until the next morning. After a cup of coffee and breakfast served by the awed lieutenant, she was escorted to the ferry back to the city.

Once back in her hotel room, Makenna took a most welcome bath. The hot water helped to ease some of the physical abuse she had undergone but nothing could fill the ache in her heart over the loss of the money. She had not only let Gabe down but had added horrendously to his burden.

CHAPTER SIXTEEN

"Frankly, my dear, I'm afraid there is actually very little that I can do," the police captain said. He thumped his hand against the bowl of his pipe, dumping out the blackened tobacco, then began filling it anew. He was a big man with a red neck which seemed restricted by the blue tunic of his police uniform. He stuck a match to the bowl of his pipe and began drawing on it as he continued his conversation with Makenna.

"You see we are restricted in our jurisdiction to the actual city limits of San Francisco. Now if these two scoundrels have left town—and if they took as much money as you indicate, I'm certain they have left—then all we can do is get out a wanted poster on them."

"You mean you'll do nothing to get my money back?" Makenna asked in dismay.

"Oh, I didn't say that," the police officer replied. "We'll do all we can. I'm just being realistic when I tell you that what we can do, simply, won't be enough. I'm afraid you have lost your money."

"I see," Makenna said. She stood up and for a moment had to fight against an overpowering dizziness which threatened to make her faint.

"Are you all right?" the policeman asked anxiously.

"Yes, I'll be fine," Makenna said. "It's just that this has been quite a blow."

"I'm certain that it has," the police officer said. "Would you like one of my men to escort you back to the hotel?"

"No," she said. "I've nothing left to lose," she added, with a short, bitter laugh.

"I'm sorry, madam," the police officer said, rising. "I'm very sorry indeed."

Makenna left the police station and hailed a carriage to return her to the hotel. There was nothing she could do now except pack up and go home. She dreaded facing Gabe with this. He wouldn't blame her, of course, but his dream of building the railroad was over now. There was no hope left.

Makenna put her hand to her head, then leaned against the side of the carriage. She wanted to cry but there were no tears. She looked out at San Francisco. It was such a beautiful city and she had hoped to be able to enjoy it while she was here. The trip had started with such excitement, plans of building the railroad with Gabe, thoughts of seeing a glamorous city—and now it had all evaporated into a mockery.

As the carriage clattered along the street, Makenna suddenly noticed a large building with the sign: EMORY VAN ZANDT TRUST AND INVESTMENTS, INC.

"Stop—stop the carriage!" she shouted.

"Whoa," the driver called to the horses. "Yes, ma'am. Is something wrong?"

"No," Makenna said. "I've changed my mind. I want to get out here." She paid the driver, then left the carriage and started toward the Van Zandt Building. She had no idea what she was going to do but she knew she must try something.

Emory Van Zandt's appearance belied his fifty-nine years. He had a full head of silver hair, a face that was weathered but not haggard, sharp, piercing eyes, and a trim, youthful body. His healthy appearance was the result of a full and active life in his youth. He had been a merchant sailor when he heard of the gold strike in California and worked his passage to the gold fields.

He didn't make the big strike but he did manage to take over five thousand dollars in gold dust out of the mountain streams and he used that to start his fortune.

His first investment was in a ship, which was abandoned in the bay when the entire crew, including officers, went into the hills to make their fortune. The ship became a navigation hazard and the city of San Francisco confiscated it. Emory Van Zandt approached the city council and agreed to take the ship if the council would pay him $250 to get it out of the way. To his surprise, the council agreed and, three days later, offered him the same deal on another vessel. Emory outfitted both ships, found crews from disenchanted sailors-turned-miners, and went into the cargo business bringing goods into the rapidly growing area. Within one year, Van Zandt Shipping Lines had twenty ships.

When the railroad boom started, Emory Van Zandt had enough money to get in on the ground floor. He amassed control of the California Coastal Railroad through a very ingenious maneuver. By the law governing their charter, no one person could buy more than two hundred shares of stock. But that same charter required two million dollars of stock to be sold to the public before a government matching grant could be obtained.

A ten percent down payment was needed to buy a share of stock. Emory hit upon the idea of having his friends buy shares of stock, with him putting up the ten percent down payment. They immediately signed over the stock to him as security for the loan with the understanding that they would default on the loan, turning stock back to him. Within six months, he owned 750 shares, or seventy-five percent of all stock in the railroad, plus the two-million-dollar government grant to start building.

Emory did not get involved in the Credit Mobilier scandal. He was offered the opportunity but saw, immediately, that it was a sham and he wanted no part of it. It wasn't that he was so fiercely moral...it was just that he considered it poor business. It was his theory that good business practices were founded on solid foundations such as ships of the sea and actual railroad stock, not falsified equipment and phony construction gimmicks. His California Coastal Railroad was an immediate financial success and Emory Van Zandt had become one of the wealthiest men in the world.

"But what good does it do me?" he had often asked his friends. "I've got a rapscallion of a son who cares about nothing but gambling and a good time. I see no prospects of his ever getting married...he'll probably get himself shot by a cuckolded husband long before that...and I'll die without a grandchild to carry this on. It all seems such a waste..."

Emory sent Peter to New Mexico to participate in the building of a new railroad with Gabe Hansen. It had been his hope that Peter would learn something from Gabe Hansen, a man Emory admired and respected. He was exactly the way Emory had been in his youth and the old man had no doubt but that Gabe would be a success.

But it wasn't working the way he had hoped. He had it on good authority that Peter was spending most of his time in the whorehouses and gambling halls of Albuquerque and not only was he learning nothing from Gabe Hansen, he didn't even get along with him. Emory was about ready to abandon the entire project. Peter was returning to San Francisco tomorrow and Emory intended to tell him to stay home. He would grant Gabe Hansen an extension on the money he had already loaned him, so that he could find financing somewhere else and just pull out of all further business transactions with the railroad.

"Mr. Van Zandt, there is a young lady to see you, sir. A Miss Makenna O'Shea."

"Makenna O'Shea? I don't know a Makenna O'Shea. Who is she, some doxie trying to make a claim against my son? No doubt she is pregnant. Why do they think all they have to do is get pregnant, and they can come here and claim Peter did it to them, and I'll pay them off?"

"You have already paid off a substantial number of them, sir," his secretary, a small owlish-looking man, said.

"Yes, I know. All right, send this girl in."

"Very well, sir."

Emory leaned back in his chair and made a tent with his fingers as he waited for the girl to be shown into his office.

"Thank you for seeing me," Makenna said when she came in.

This girl was different, Emory noticed. She didn't have the look of dissipation about her that marked the other girls.

"What can I do for you?" Emory asked. He started to make a caustic comment about her relationship with Peter but checked it to see what she had to say.

"Mr. Van Zandt, my name is Makenna O'Shea," Makenna began, "and I am from Albuquerque." Makenna went on with the story, telling how Gabe had run into difficulty because of the trick Bernardo had played on him and how Peter had offered to advance the loan—but only after extracting a terrible price. She told about discovering a way to increase the government grant by serving the seven previously settled communities and how she had come to San Francisco to borrow money from the Pacific Trust against this new source of revenue. She concluded by telling how the money had been stolen from her the day before and though she avoided the incident of her abduction, she did explain that the police held out no hope for the return of the money.

"I see," Emory said after Makenna had concluded her story. "You've had a rough time of it. What do you want me to do?"

Makenna took a deep breath. "I want you to lend me the money," she said. "The new source of revenue we'll receive will be enough to cover our loss to Pacific Trust and repay you as well."

"Young lady, are you aware that under the terms of our agreement, I hold as security all funds due you by government grant?"

"You mean Gabe will have to pay you back all of the money he gets?"

"No. But he cannot use it as collateral for another loan. By the terms of our contract, I could foreclose on him right now, since he violated that agreement by securing a loan from Pacific Trust."

"No," Makenna said. "I didn't know that."

"Who discovered the way to increase the funds?" Emory asked.

"I did," Makenna said, adding quickly, "that wasn't Gabe's fault."

"I'd hardly call it a fault, young lady," Emory said. "I find much to admire in that. In fact, I find much to admire in you."

"Well, I...I thank you," Makenna said, smiling at the unexpected compliment.

"Miss O'Shea, you are a woman with a practical mind, I can see that. I have a business proposition for you. I have a way you can earn that one hundred fifty thousand dollars. It won't be a loan but an outright bonus."

"How?"

"By doing something for me."

"What is it? Yes, I'll do it," Makenna said.

"You haven't heard the proposition yet."

"What could it be? If you're willing to pay one hundred fifty thousand dollars for it, I'm willing to do it."

"I hope you are as enthusiastic about it after you hear the offer," Emory said. He leaned back in his chair and cleared his throat. "Miss O'Shea, I take it you know my son?"

"Yes."

"How do you get along with him?"

"I...we used to get along quite well. I must admit there's been a cooling between us of late."

"That's the way my son is," Emory said. "He has no substance, Miss O'Shea. He is all fluff. Oh, he's handsome and charming and makes a very good first impression on the ladies. You might even say he's a ladies' man of sorts. But he doesn't have the gumption for the long haul and it doesn't take women long to realize this."

"I'm sorry," Makenna said. "I didn't mean to offend you."

"Offend me?" Emory laughed. "My dear, I never find

honesty offensive." He stood up and walked over to a side cupboard and poured two glasses of sherry. He brought one to Makenna and handed it to her before he resumed his talk.

"Peter's mother died when Peter was quite young. I was living a pretty active life then and it was a bit too much for her. Peter has never known a good woman's love...nor, in fact, been subjected to a good woman's influence. I fear that has greatly deprived him of something important. And in so doing, it has deprived me of my own immortality."

"Your immortality?"

"Yes," Emory said. "My bloodline, Miss O'Shea. The blood that flows through me flowed through my father and his father and his father for countless generations. Is it to stop with Peter? It will if Peter has no children."

"What...what are you saying?"

"Quite simple, Miss O'Shea. Peter is coming to San Francisco tomorrow. I want you to marry him."

"You want me to what?" Makenna blurted, unable to believe what she was hearing.

"I want you to marry him," Emory said again. "If you do, I'll give you the money and you can give it or loan it to Gabe Hansen as you see fit. You will also marry into a rather substantial fortune. Enough to cause most women to jump at the chance, I imagine."

"Well, I am not most women," Makenna said angrily.

"Precisely my point," Emory said. "Believe me, I wouldn't make this offer to most women. But you have a rare quality about you that is immediately apparent to anyone with discernment. I feel you would be a very good influence on my son and, what's more important, an exceptional mother for my grandson. What do you say?"

"I say no," Makenna replied.

"I'm sorry to hear that," Emory replied. "I had gathered that you thought enough of Gabe to do this for him."

"I do," Makenna said. "That's why I'm refusing your offer."

"Look at it this way," Emory invited. "If you agree to marry Peter, Gabe will get the money and he will be able to complete his railroad. If you refuse to marry Peter, I'll foreclose immediately and he'll lose everything. I'll ruin him."

"You...you would do that?" Makenna asked in a small voice.

"Yes, my dear. I'm sorry if I have disillusioned you. But I am a businessman and I play by the rules. You can check on me if you wish. I've never cheated another man, but I do take every legal advantage, and I am a hard fighter."

"I see," Makenna said weakly.

"I want a grandson, Miss O'Shea," Emory said. "And I don't mean some bastard conceived by some doxie."

"I can't," Makenna said. "I can't do this."

"Look at it realistically. If you marry my son, Gabe Hansen will get his money and build his railroad. If you do not marry my son, Gabe Hansen will lose everything."

"You make it sound as if I have no choice," Makenna said.

"You don't have a choice," Emory said. "That is, if you care anything for Gabe Hansen and the people of Albuquerque."

"What about Peter?" Makenna asked.

"What about him?"

"Have you spoken to him about this? You know as well as I that Peter isn't the marrying kind. He may not go along with this."

"He will be here tomorrow," Emory said. "If he doesn't

go along with it, then you are free and clear. If you agree to my proposal, I'll give you the money anyway, whether he wants to get married or not. What do you say?"

"How soon can Gabe have the money?" Makenna asked.

"I'll wire my bank in Trinidad and have a courier deliver the cash to him tonight," Emory said.

"And if Peter declines tomorrow, Gabe keeps the money?" Makenna asked.

"With no strings attached," Emory promised.

Makenna let out a big sigh. "Very well, Mr. Van Zandt. You've got yourself a deal."

"I'll send you with my clerk to validate the transfer of funds," Emory said. "Peter arrives on the seven-o'clock train tomorrow morning. He should be here by eight."

"I'll be here when he arrives," Makenna said. Makenna left the office with a very thin, very fidgety clerk, and together they went to a telegraph station. The clerk handed the message to the telegrapher, "Will that be all?" he asked of Makenna.

"No," Makenna said. "I want to stand by the instrument as the message is being sent and wait on the confirmation."

"What good will that do you, miss?" the telegrapher asked. "It'll just be so many clicks to you."

"Nevertheless, I'll feel better if I do," Makenna replied, purposely not telling them that she knew the science.

Makenna listened as the message was sent. It was, as Emory Van Zandt promised, an order to transfer $150,000 by cash from the bank in Trinidad into Gabe Hansen's hands at End-of-Track. A few moments later, the reply came back confirming the order. The clerk wrote the message on a piece of paper and handed it to Makenna, though as she had read it as it was coming in, she already knew what it said.

"Thank you," she said, taking the message. She looked at the clerk. "That will be all now." Makenna spent the rest of the day in a daze. She wandered through the city looking at the sights without actually seeing them. She felt as if someone very close to her had just died but the shock was still too great for her to react to it. She went to an apothecary that evening and bought a sleeping draught to help her through the night.

Makenna was at the office of Emory Van Zandt by seven-thirty the next morning waiting to see Peter. Emory breakfasted daily in his office and he offered to share the rolls, eggs, and coffee with Makenna as she waited. She declined his offer for all but the coffee.

"Mr. Van Zandt, your son is here," his secretary said at eight o'clock.

"Ask him to come in, please," Emory said, wiping his mouth with a linen napkin.

"Hello, Dad; damn, it's good to get back to civilization for a while," Peter said, coming through the door. There he saw Makenna and stopped short. "Makenna! What are you doing here? I wondered where you went."

"I came to San Francisco on business," Makenna said.

"Yes? I'll bet it has something to do with the fact that Gabe Hansen needs money. He's changing his route, Dad, but I've got him right where I want him."

"And where is it that you want him?" Emory asked.

Peter laughed. "Begging for mercy," he said. "I'm going to take that railroad away from him."

"Why?" Makenna asked.

"Why?"

"That seems a fair question," Emory said.

"Because I don't like him," Peter said. "He's such a...a

builder, a dreamer. He makes me sick."

"Because he's all the things you aren't?" Emory asked.

"If you want to say that," Peter replied, "I won't try to deny it. I'm right about why she is here though, aren't I? She asked you for more money. Did you give it to her?"

"I did."

"It figures," Peter said. He laughed it off. "Ah, what the hell. I guess it doesn't make any difference."

"I made a deal with Miss O'Shea," Emory said.

"What kind of deal?"

"I gave her the money on the condition that she would marry you."

"That she would marry me?" Peter asked incredulously. He laughed and looked at her. "Dad, are you serious?"

Makenna felt her heart leap for joy. Peter was about to slough the whole idea off as preposterous.

"Yes," Emory said. "I'm quite serious."

"You want me to marry her?" Peter said. He put his hand on his chin and looked at her.

"Sure," he said finally. "Why not? That should get Gabe's attention."

CHAPTER SEVENTEEN

When the money was delivered to Gabe, he had just about reached the desperation stage. He owed so much for rails (the price had gone from $151 per ton to $163 per ton) that the supplier sent a personal courier with the last shipment to collect the amount due. He also had to order dynamite for blasting. Nitroglycerin was cheaper but it was also much more unstable. Dynamite was relatively new but, already, had proven to be the safest and most effective way for construction blasting. On top of that, he had a payroll to meet, so the $150,000 was put to immediate use.

"Why do you suppose Makenna sent the money on ahead?" Kellen asked.

"I think she knew how desperately it was needed," Gabe answered. "It is just like her to think of such a thing."

"'Tis going to be a happy day when I see my daughter married and I hope it will be to you, Gabe Hansen," Kellen said. "I intend to give her a weddin' the likes of which has never been seen in this part of the country. What do you think of that?"

"I'll leave that up to you and Makenna," Gabe laughed. "I would like to have her as my wife but don't you think she should have a say in who she marrys?"

"Of course, Laddie, but she'll be comin' 'round," Kellen said.

"Send word to me as soon as she returns," Gabe said. "I'm going to Pie Town to get started on the blasting. We should have rails laid to there within two days."

"Aye, lad, I'll deliver her right to you," Kellen promised.

Pie Town was a small settlement that had been founded when silver was discovered in the Mangas Mountains. At its peak, it was never larger than a thousand people and now that the silver had just about played out, it had decreased in size to fewer than one hundred residents. But it was a previously established settlement and, therefore, qualified under the Railroad Grants Act to increase the amount of funds due the railroad.

Pie Town was now enjoying a new boom as word had reached them that the railroad would be coming through. Some of the railroad camp followers, who had been constructing tent cities along the route, moved their operations into many of the abandoned buildings of Pie Town, and there was even talk of hiring a city marshal. As the track had not yet reached Pie Town and Gabe wished to be there for the blasting operation, he had to rent a room in the newly reopened hotel, renamed the Railroaders' Hotel.

"I located some dynamite which was left over from the silver mining," Bull told Gabe as they ate their supper in the hotel dining room that night, a supper consisting of beefsteak, eggs and coffee. The same menu applied to breakfast and lunch as well and, for a moment, Gabe envied the fifty or so Chinese who were on the blasting crew and who were right now camped just out of town eating their own cooking and enjoying its varied fare.

"Good," Gabe answered, shoving a fork of scrambled

eggs into his mouth. "I have ordered enough to move a mountain, so we shouldn't lack for it."

"Have you heard from Miss O'Shea?" Bull asked.

"Yes, as a matter of fact, I have. I got the money last night. All the bills are paid; we have money for the payroll and enough materials and equipment to get us underway again."

"That's good. You know I didn't want to say anything but I've had a bad feelin'," Bull said.

"About what?"

"Well, it's just that Peter left so soon after Miss O'Shea did," Bull said. "I don't know, it was as if he knew what she was going to try and do or somethin' and was bound to make trouble. I don't care an ounce for the son-of-a-bitch."

Gabe laughed. "I share your dislike for the man," he said. "But if he had it in his mind to queer the deal, he failed. He reckoned without Makenna's ability to get things done, I guess. I'm awfully anxious for her to return."

"You know what she's doin', don't you?" Bull said with a knowing grin.

"No, what?"

"Why, hell, boss, it's as plain as the nose on your face," Bull said. "She's buyin' dresses. And, I'll bet she's enjoyin' ever' minute of it."

Bull Blackwell was right about one thing. Makenna O'Shea was looking at dresses but he was wrong about the other. She wasn't enjoying every minute of it. In fact, she attended to every detail as if her heart would break and, during the fitting of a wedding gown, she had to dismiss the seamstress from her room because the entire affair weighed so heavily on her heart that she was moved to burst into tears.

"But Miss O'Shea, the wedding is tomorrow. If you are going to have a wedding gown, I'll have to complete the fitting now," the seamstress complained.

"I said leave," Makenna said again. "I have such a headache that I can't go on with this."

"Very well," the seamstress said in a huff. She gathered her pins and measuring tapes and withdrew from the room, muttering under her breath about the lack of consideration of some people. As she left, she nearly ran over Alexia Botin, who was at that moment preparing to knock on the door.

"Makenna, it is I, Alexia."

When Makenna saw Alexia, she could no longer contain her grief. Alexia was a friendly face to her, a face from the happy time on the train. She broke into tears and fell across her bed, wailing as if her heart were breaking, as indeed it was.

"Makenna, Makenna dear, what is it?" Alexia asked, her voice mirroring genuine concern.

"Alexia, oh, it's been awful," she said.

"What is it? What has happened?" Alexia asked. "You must tell me."

Makenna told her story, beginning with leaving the bank with the money, then being hit over the head and robbed, and then of her awful ordeal on board the ship.

"Oh, God in heaven, how you have suffered," Alexia cried. Her own heart was breaking, too, now, for she realized that she had been responsible for all this. Not intentionally, for she had specifically told the two thugs not to harm her. But she was responsible for it no less than if she had wielded the club and tied the bonds herself.

"But that isn't the worst of it," Makenna went on.

"But what more could there be?"

Makenna told of being forced into marriage with Peter Van Zandt in order to replace the money she had lost. "The money is there now," Makenna said. "And the railroad has gone on. But I am no longer free to marry whomever I want, for I must wed Peter tomorrow."

Alexia was heartsick. To think that she had caused this sweet girl all this pain and for nothing! For she had reckoned without Makenna's fierce determination and will. Alexia began crying.

"Oh, now," Makenna said, seeing the distress of her young friend. "Please, Alexia, don't cry. Oh, forgive me for burdening you with my troubles."

Makenna's genuine concern for Alexia's wellbeing made Alexia feel all the more guilty, and she was unable to stem the flow of tears for a long while. Finally, after crying into each other's arms like two schoolchildren, the women had spent themselves emotionally and were thus able to compose themselves once more.

"Alexia, will you be my maid of honor?" Makenna asked.

"Oh, but I can't," Alexia protested. "Wouldn't you prefer someone else? Someone you've known longer?"

Makenna laughed. "I know no one in San Francisco," she said.

"But I am Mexican," Alexia said. "To be your maid of honor, would not an Anglo be more appropriate?"

"You are my friend," Makenna said. "Nothing is more appropriate than that."

"I...yes, Makenna. I would be happy to accept."

"I apologize to you for asking you to do such a dishonorable thing as serve in a wedding where there is no love."

"There is no dishonor," Alexia said. "I am flattered that you ask me." Privately, she thought that there was indeed dishonor—but it was her dishonor to Makenna that troubled her.

"Will you be married in a church?" Alexia asked.

"No!" Makenna said resolutely. "As a child I had always thought I would have a church wedding. But for this charade, no. A justice of the peace will marry us in Mr. Van Zandt's office tomorrow morning at ten."

"Shall I meet you here?" Alexia asked.

"No," Makenna said. "Come to the office at ten. I will marry him and be done with it as quickly as I can."

"Oh, Makenna, how sorry I am that this awful thing has happened to you." Alexia put her arms around Makenna one more time.

"Thank you for your concern," Makenna. said. "And your friendship. It means much to me now."

Alexia left Makenna's hotel room with the guilt of her sin clutching at her heart like a vise. This was all her fault. She wished she could call back the past few days. God, if there were only some way to undo what she had done! Oh, if she could only see those two men again, she would... *wait a minute*, she thought. *An idea!* It won't undo what had been done but it would make her feel better.

Alexia went to the nearest Western Union office and sent a telegram to Bernardo. She begged him to come to San Francisco at once. It was, she said, a matter of importance, though it could not be discussed in a wire.

Emory Van Zandt represented wealth, so any occasion that affected him, regardless of the intent to keep it small, was of necessity a major social event. Thus it was that when news traveled through town that his son was to marry, hurriedly purchased wedding gifts began pouring in and the cream of San Francisco society made plans to attend the ceremony. Railroad barons, mining millionaires, shipping magnates, everyone within traveling distance were present in the Van Zandt Building the next morning. They began coming shortly after nine and, by ten o'clock, a sizeable portion of the wealth of the city was present.

Peter stood against the cupboard drinking quietly. He was on his third drink when his father came over to talk to him.

"Don't you feel it is much too early for that?" he asked.

Peter smiled laconically and held the glass aloft. A shaft of early morning sunshine passed through the glass, split into a spectrum burst of color, and projected a rainbow on the wall. "Early or late," he said, "it's all relative. Now on the one hand, you might say it is a bit early for drinking, while on the other, you might say it is a bit late for the charming bride. Assuming, of course, that she comes."

"You think she will not?" Emory asked.

"I don't know," Peter said. "It will be amusing to see whether she has merely taken your money, or if she intends to go through with her end of the bargain."

"Is that all this is to you?" Emory asked. "Amusement?"

"Yes, Father," Peter answered easily. "What is it to you?"

"It's hope, boy. Hope that some of her gumption will rub off on you."

One of the guests walked over to the two. He stuck his finger between the high-wing collar of his shirt and his neck and pulled it out as if to allow air to enter. He was a big man who looked out of place in his morning coat but the profits from his gold mine made him wealthy enough to belong with the crowd that had collected in the office.

"Say, Emory, what time is this shindig supposed to get started? I've got a shipment to look after."

"Ten o'clock," Emory replied.

The big man removed a watch and looked at it critically. "The way I make it, that's about two minutes from now. And I ain't seen no sign o' the girl yet."

"She'll be here," Emory said.

"I'll stick around a bit longer if you're sure o' that," the man said.

"Father has faith," Peter said. "If faith can move a mountain, surely it can move Makenna O'Shea."

Alexia stepped into the room then, and the conversation stilled. She was dressed in white and wore a mantilla. She was dazzlingly beautiful and most obviously Spanish.

"Yes, miss, what can I do for you?" Emory asked.

"Excuse me," Alexia said, speaking with a strong accent. "This is the office of Señor Van Zandt, is it not?"

"Yes, it is."

"I am here for the wedding," Alexia said. "I am the maid of honor."

There was an undercurrent of surprise, which moved through the guests. Peter laughed but Emory offered the girl a generous smile.

"Come in," he said. "Makenna isn't here yet."

"She is outside," Alexia said. "She will be here momentarily."

"Well, now," Emory said, looking back at Peter. "Are you still amused?"

"Quite," Peter replied.

Suddenly, there was a gasp. It came first from one of the women, then was picked up by others until it spread through all of them like a prairie fire before the wind.

"I'm not late, am I?" Makenna asked calmly.

Emory looked at her and, for a second, he was speechless. "Uh, no," he said. "You're right on time."

Peter began laughing and, though his laugh was genuine, it had a hollow ring in the room where so many others just stared in numb shock. Finally, Peter got his breath.

"Come right this way," he said. "I think red becomes you. And it makes a perfect bridal gown for this marriage made in hell."

CHAPTER EIGHTEEN

After the wedding, if indeed such a loveless ceremony could be called a wedding, the bride and groom and the guests adjourned to the decks of the Star of the West, the luxurious yacht of Jesse Phelps, a business associate and friend of Emory Van Zandt. Makenna would have as soon not gone, as she wished to give no personal seal of approval to what she had done, but she reasoned that the longer she was in a crowd, the longer she could delay the inevitable time alone with Peter Van Zandt.

The boat was luxurious beyond description. It had a polished teak deck, brass fittings, and a richly upholstered salon. Uniformed crewmen buzzed about serving drinks over ice, lighting men's cigars, and helping the ladies to negotiate the ladderways and bulkheads. A string quartet was set up to play lively but unobtrusive music for the background pleasure of the guests.

"Do you like all of this, my dear?" Emory asked Makenna.

"The boat is very beautiful," Makenna agreed.

"Would you like it as a wedding gift?"

"What?"

"I imagine Phelps has grown tired of it by now. He tires of his playthings rather quickly," Emory said. "At any rate, I am certain I could persuade him to part with it. I'll buy it for you and you could use it to take a long honeymoon trip to the Hawaiian Islands. How would that be?"

"No, thank you, Mr. Van Zandt," Makenna replied. "You have already given me my wedding present."

"You mean the hundred fifty thousand," Emory said.

"Exactly."

Emory Van Zandt laughed and put his arm around Makenna. "I knew you were the right girl the moment I laid eyes on you," he said.

Makenna had a strange reaction to the embrace of Emory. She felt in him a passion for life and a virile strength which were totally lacking in Peter. In fact, Emory reminded her much of Gabe Hansen.

The yacht took a grand tour around the bay and as they passed close to Alcatraz Island, Makenna thought about her terrifying experience offshore there just a few days ago. Was it just a few days ago? It seemed like ages. How different it was to see Alcatraz from the deck of a luxury yacht than it was to wade ashore from the longboat from the black ship.

It was late in the afternoon and the sun was slanting long low beams across the bay before Peter and Makenna were put ashore by the celebrants aboard the yacht. As the newly married couple left the deck of the yacht, they were showered with rice and toasted with champagne. Then, to Makenna's surprise, all the champagne glasses were smashed against the deck.

"What are they doing that for?" Makenna asked.

Peter laughed. "With very few exceptions, everyone you see on that deck is a nouveau riche. Their parents were all dirt farmers, store clerks, or laborers. Now that these people have money, they look for ways to display their wealth. Among the upper classes in England, glasses are broken after a toast, and they think that following suit gives them class. It is said that if one wants to find a party in San Francisco, go to the sound of crashing glass. To that I would add, do so and you will find a crashing bore."

"You don't like your father's friends very much, do you?" Makenna asked.

"I don't like my father very much," Peter said.

"Why not?"

Peter smiled the same slow smile that Makenna had come to regard as his trademark. "This way I am seldom disappointed," he said.

A phaeton with a liveried driver was waiting for them and it took them to the top of Nob Hill, passing one of the new cable cars that had already made San Francisco famous throughout the world. The carriage moved through a large wrought-iron gate, around a curving tree-lined and beautifully landscaped drive, to stop in front of the largest, most handsome house Makenna had ever seen. She looked at it in fascination, absolutely speechless.

"Be it ever so humble," Peter said sarcastically, taking in the house with a wave of the hand.

"Peter, you live here?" Makenna asked, numbed with awe despite herself.

"In a manner of speaking," Peter said. "This is my father's house. In my father's house are many mansions," he added. "For tonight, one of them may be yours."

They walked up the broad steps and through the double doors into the house. A huge foyer greeted them and a very wide stairway ascended to the second floor where a balcony overlooked the entryway. Makenna was cognizant of polished marble floors, mahogany banisters, rich wall hangings, and a great collection of statuary. Paintings hung on the wall climbing alongside the stairs. Servants seemed to materialize, then melt back into the house almost as if they were ghosts.

"There is an excellent view of the city from up here if you wish to see it," Peter invited.

"Yes," Makenna said. "Yes, I'd like to see it."

Peter led the way upstairs, then down a long hallway and out onto a huge balcony, which ran the full length of the back of the house. The back lawn was exquisitely landscaped with boxed hedges forming geometric patterns and statues and fountains surrounded by beautiful flowers of every hue. But the most breathtaking sight was of the city of San Francisco. She saw white houses clinging to green hills, and from this vantage point, she could see the sparkling blue water of the Golden Gate as well.

"Oh, Peter, it's beautiful," she said.

"I suppose so," Peter replied. "Come, I'll show you your room."

Makenna followed Peter back into the house and down the hallway, wide enough and long enough to have accommodated two of the railway cars where she and her father made their home. At last, he halted.

The carved double doors were shut and when Peter pushed them open to allow Makenna to step into the bedroom. She saw that it, like the rest of the house, was elegant beyond her wildest imagination. A large bay window bowed out, offering substantially the same view as was enjoyed from the balcony. The floor was covered in a very deep, very plush dark blue carpet. The walls were white, carved panels, trimmed in blue and gold. The ceiling was vaulted and decorated with paintings of cherubs, birds and flowers.

A large dresser with a huge mirror sat on one side of the room, flanked by other large pieces of bedroom furniture. There was a small dining area near the window, with a roomy closet-dressing room opposite. A canopied bed dominated the room and two servant girls stood nervously beside it.

"These girls will take care of anything you might need," Peter said. "I'm sorry, I'm not around enough to remember their names, but it really doesn't matter."

"Of course it matters," Makenna said, remembering the pains Gabe had taken to discover the names of the railroad workers. "What are your names?" she asked them.

"My name's Della, mum," one of the girls, a pretty young blonde, said.

"And I'm Madeline," the other supplied.

Both girls had English accents and Makenna commented on it.

"Yes, mum," Della said. "Mr. Van Zandt hired us from England. Paid our way over, too, he did."

"It was most generous of him, mum," the other added.

"My father is generous to a fault," Peter said sarcastically.

Makenna looked around the room again, then walked over to look behind a door. "What is this?" she asked.

"It's a bathroom, mum," Della said. "If you turn those knobs, the water runs right into the tub. There's no need to carry it in buckets."

"Oh, how marvelous," Makenna said, more impressed with that than anything else she had seen.

"Careful, Makenna," Peter warned with a laugh. "You'll get intoxicated by your new wealth and you'll forget all about anything or anyone in Albuquerque."

"I'll never forget my father or Gabe Hansen," Makenna said hotly.

"To be sure," Peter replied with an easy laugh. He walked over to a cabinet and opened the doors, revealing a large selection of liquor. He poured some whiskey into a glass, then looked back at Makenna. "Would you care for a wedding toast?"

"No," Makenna said. "I'm going to take a bath."

Peter laughed. "I rather thought you would," he said. He looked at the two servant girls. "If you would help Mrs. Van Zandt? I'll be back in a short while."

Peter left the room carrying the drink in his hand, still chuckling as if he alone was aware of some hilarious but very private joke.

"Mrs. Van Zandt," Della said. "Did you hear what he called you, mum? It must be a grand feelin', hearin' that for the first time."

No, Della, it wasn't a grand feeling. It is a feeling of bitter heartbreak, Makenna thought.

Later, after the bath and the toweling had left her body pink and clean, Makenna put on a yellow, silk sleeping gown.

"Oh, mum," Della breathed. "You are beautiful!"

"Thank you," Makenna said.

Makenna sat at the dresser mirror and brushed her hair with long luxurious strokes as she waited for Peter. Within a short time, the hair took on the sheen of burnished ebony and its jet blackness, her suntanned skin, and the pale yellow silk of the nightgown created a picture of loveliness.

The door opened and closed and Makenna saw Peter come into the room. He walked directly to the dresser and stood behind her, looking at her in the mirror. "You are a gorgeous creature," he said quietly. Then he turned walked away from her. The movement was so sudden that, for a second, Makenna didn't realize what was happening.

"Well, that's something he will never see," Peter said with a cold laugh.

"What? What are you talking about?"

Peter turned to look at Makenna. His face was twisted in hate. "He took my mother from me," Peter said. "He killed her when I was just a child."

"What do you mean he killed your mother? He told me she died."

"She did die," Peter said. "She died of overwork and exhaustion. My father was so busy making his fortune that he worked himself and everyone around him without letup. My mother was a delicate woman, not given to that type of life. He killed her as surely as if he had shot her. I was only eight years old at the time. From that day to this, I've hated him, and I've looked for some way to repay him." Peter laughed. "And now I've found the way. I'll deny him the one thing he wants more than anything else. You'll never bear his grandchild. Never. I'll give him all the bastard grandchildren he wants but no wife of mine will ever bear my child."

"How do you propose to prevent it?" Makenna asked.

"Simple, my dear," Peter said. "There are thousands of women who quite willingly warm my bed. I'll merely seek my sexual pleasures elsewhere, and leave you to stew in your own juices."

"Peter, my God, if you felt this way, why in heaven's name did you marry me?" Makenna asked. "If you had said no, your father wouldn't have insisted."

"And let everyone off the hook?" Peter asked. "No, my dear. I find this an exquisite form of torture both for my father and for Gabe Hansen."

"And for me," Makenna said.

"I'm sorry," Peter said. "I bear you no personal malice. It is unfortunate that you are caught in the middle. But look at it this way," he added, smiling brightly. "You are a wealthy woman now. I'll never deny you any extravagance, and I know my father won't. Enjoy life to the fullest, I certainly intend to. Take Hansen as your lover if you wish. It will be pleasure enough for me to deny him the right to marry you. There is only one thing I insist upon. Do not have a child. If you become pregnant, you must get rid of it."

Makenna sat numbed with shock over what she was hearing. She was unable to answer Peter, so stunned was she by his pronouncement. Peter turned back to her just before he left the room.

"Don't wait up for me, dear. This is my wedding night and something there is inside me," he mocked, placing both hands over his heart in the style of an overly dramatic matinee idol, "which cries for love. I'm going to find someone to share my bed on this, my wedding night. Good night."

Makenna sat in silence for several moments after Peter walked out of her bedroom. She stared numbly at the image in the mirror and then resumed brushing her hair.

She didn't cry. There were no tears left.

CHAPTER NINETEEN

"Fire in the hole!"

The warning drifted down from the rocky walls of the canyon and was picked up and repeated by someone closer. "Fire in the hole!"

The first two warnings were given by the Chinese workers who were placing the charges and a third warning was given by an American, just to make certain there was no mistake, that rang loud and true through the bright, New Mexico afternoon.

"Fire in the hole!"

There was an expectant intake of breath as everyone waited, for this was the warning that a dynamite charge had been placed and was about to be exploded.

The blast went off with stomach-shaking effectiveness and tons of rock crashed into the valley below, raising a tremendous cloud of dust.

"Look at that!" Bull enthused. "That blast was so clean you can just about go in and prepare your roadbed with a broom. I tell you, boss, them little Chinamen are somethin' to behold."

"They are doing an excellent job," Gabe agreed. "In

fact, it's beginning to look like we'll get to the territorial line as fast this way as we would have had we gone our original route."

"I'm glad Miss O'Shea come up with this idea," Bull said.

At the mention of Makenna's name, Gabe's eyes reflected a flicker of worry. Where was she? She had been gone for ten days now and, other than the receipt of the money, he had heard nothing from her. It was beginning to disturb him and he had even thought of taking off and going to San Francisco to get her. In fact, if he didn't hear anything within three more days, he might just do that. Three more days would punch them through the pass and the track laying could continue on schedule.

"You aren't gettin' a little worried about her, are you, boss?" Bull asked when he saw the reaction in Gabe's eyes.

"No," Gabe said. "I guess not. But I do wish she would come back. I would like her to be here when we cross the Arizona line. It'll be as much a victory for her as it is for us."

"Fire in the hole," they heard again.

"They got that laid in there fast," Gabe commented.

"I tell you, boss, those people could move that whole damn mountain if you wanted 'em to," Bull said gleefully.

A moment later, there was another explosion and more of the ledge that blocked construction of the railroad fell into the valley below.

The bartender picked up the two whiskey glasses and saw that there was nearly an inch of whiskey left in each of them. He shrugged his shoulders, then removed the cap from the whiskey bottle and poured the liquor back into its original container. The two men who had been drinking it wouldn't mind. They were upstairs right now with Tillie and Gracie. The bartender laughed. Tillie and Gracie knew their business all right. They had pegged the two galoots as having money from the moment they walked in and they moved to them like a bee to a flower. It was funny. They were a couple of the ugliest hombres he'd ever seen: one was missing an eye and the other had a terrible scar across his face. But they'd come into the Red Wood wearing new suits, the both of them, and spoutin' off about a diggin' they'd uncovered which made 'em their poke.

"Diggin's," the bartender snorted under his breath. "The only diggin' them fellas did was the diggin' it took to bury the hombre they took that money off of."

The bartender had no idea where the money came from, but he was ready to wager that it wasn't honestly obtained.

"*Señor*, a whiskey please," someone said.

The bartender looked toward the end of the bar and saw a handsome, well-dressed Mexican. He wore black, with silver and turquoise conchos, and a silver clutch at the neckerchief around his neck. His hatband was made of silver as well.

"We don't..." The bartender had started to say, "We don't serve Mexicans," but there was something in the demeanor of the man who spoke to him that caused him to stop in mid-statement. It could have been the man's eyes, cool and appraising, or his manner, confident and assured, or just the way he wore his gun. It was slung low and kicked out, the way a gun-fighter wore a gun.

"You were saying?" the Mexican asked.

The bartender cleared his throat. "We don't get many of your kind in here," he said lamely.

"You have no objections to my kind, do you, *Señor*?" the Mexican asked, smiling and holding a fire to the long thin cigar that protruded from his lips.

"No, no, of course not," the bartender said. He started to pour whiskey from the bottle he had just put the leftovers into.

"I prefer a new bottle, *Señor*," the Mexican said.

"Yes, yes, of course," the bartender replied nervously. Something about this man made him uneasy and as he started to pour, he saw that his hands were shaking badly.

"Allow me, *Señor*," the Mexican said, taking the bottle from him. The Mexican poured a glass and set the bottle back down. "My name is Bernardo Tafoya," he said. "I am seeking someone."

That's it! the bartender thought. That's what made him nervous about this man. He was a man hunter looking for someone. The bartender decided he would not like to be searched for by this man.

"What are you looking for?" the bartender asked.

"Not what, who. And there are two of them. I know only their first names. One is Leo and the other, Waylon," Bernardo said. He flicked ashes into a spittoon. "I know they come in here, *Señor*. I was told this by two people."

"Well, if you don't know any more than that, how can I help you?" the bartender stammered.

"One man has a patch over his eye. The other has a scar like so," Bernardo said, moving his finger along his face.

The bartender's eyes darted toward the head of the stairs at the room where the two men had gone with the women.

"I see," Bernardo said, smiling easily. "They are upstairs."

"I didn't say that," the bartender insisted.

"You didn't have to, *Señor*," Bernardo said.

"What do you want with them?"

"*Señor*, I believe you already know," Bernardo said. "I want to kill them."

Bernardo said the words quietly but, within seconds, it had spread all over the bar, and conversations, poker games, and just plain drinking stopped as the patrons all looked at the handsome Mexican.

"What did you say, mister?" someone asked.

Bernardo looked toward the speaker and saw that he was an older man wearing a badge.

"I see," Bernardo said. "You must be the sheriff."

"That I am. And I'll not allow any coldblooded killing in my town," the sheriff added—nervously because he didn't know how Bernardo was going to take it but resolutely because he felt it should be said.

"I appreciate that, Sheriff," Bernardo said. "I do not intend to make the kill in cold blood. I will first challenge them and give them an opportunity to give themselves up. But if they go for their guns, I'll have no choice but to defend myself."

"Fair enough," the sheriff said, clearing his throat. He looked around at the others in the barroom. "You heard the gent, fellas. He's promised me that it'll be a fair fight. I aim to let 'im brace the two men when he wants to and I'll make no move to the contrary unless in my opinion it ain't all on the up 'n up."

"That's the way it ought to be done, Sheriff," one of the others agreed.

Bernardo nodded and turned back to the bar.

The piano, which had been playing in the corner, and had stopped for the discourse, now began to play again. However, all eyes were on the top of the stairs and all conversation directed toward the upcoming gunfight. Within a moment, the piano stopped again, and everyone in the saloon waited.

The waiting grew more strained and the conversation soon petered out. Now there was absolute silence and when someone coughed nervously, everyone turned to look at him accusingly. The clock on the wall ticked loudly as the pendulum swung back and forth. Involuntarily, perhaps a dozen or so men looked at the clock as if it were very important to fix the time in their minds, the better for the telling of their stories later.

Whiskey glasses were refilled as quietly as everything else, the drinker merely walking over to the bar and holding his glass out silently.

More people drifted into the saloon, but they were met at the door, and a whispered exchange told them what was going on. Most who wandered in stayed, drawing on their beer or whiskey as silently as the others, and then waiting.

Waiting.

The tension grew almost unbearable. There wasn't a man in the saloon who didn't know what was going on upstairs and they waited the outcome of the drama in silence.

One of the men upstairs laughed loudly and another cursed. The women laughed and then there was the sound of footfalls as boots struck the floor. The door opened and the two men came out of the room, laughing and talking to each other. They had started down the stairs before they noticed the deathly silence and the eyes staring up at them.

"Leo, what the hell's goin' on?" one of them said.

"*Buenos dias, Señores*," Bernardo said pleasantly, stepping away from the bar and looking up toward the two men. "I believe one of you is named Leo and the other Waylon. Am I correct?"

"Who are you? What do you want?" Leo asked. He retreated two steps back up the stairs. Waylon, who was already at the top of the stairs, moved over behind the railing and stood looking down onto the saloon. The women, who had followed them out of the room, let out a gasp of fear and ran back into the rooms from which they had just come.

"My name is Bernardo Tafoya," Bernardo said. "Of course, that name means nothing to you now. But it is the name of the man who may have to kill you. You took one hundred and fifty thousand dollars which didn't belong to you and you beat a young woman, then turned her over to an evil ship captain."

"What's it to you, Mex?" Waylon challenged.

"Let us just say that I want to see justice done," Bernardo said. "Now, I want you both to throw down your guns and come to me with your hands in the air. I am taking you back to San Francisco where you are going to return the money and then give yourself up to the police."

"You talk like a crazy man," Leo said, laughing shortly.

"Leo, I don't like this," Waylon said. "I don't like this at all."

"Aw, don't worry about it none," Leo said, waving his hand toward Waylon. The two men stood rooted to their position for a moment longer. Everyone in the saloon continued to stare.

"Throw down your guns," Bernardo said again with quiet authority.

"We ain't gonna do it," Leo said.

Bernardo spread his legs slightly, then held his hand out, ready to draw. "Throw down your guns or use them," he said.

There was a silence the length of a heartbeat, then Leo yelled, "Get 'em, Waylon!"

At the same time Leo yelled, he started for his gun. But Bernardo's gun was out in a move so quick that it was later described as a blur. Bernardo's first shot sent Leo slamming back against the wall, then he tumbled forward and slid down the stairs head first, his gun rattling to the bottom of the stairs before him. Bernardo's second shot caught Waylon right between the eyes and his face grew blank in death just before he flipped over the banister and crashed back first through a poker table on the floor below. Neither Leo nor Waylon had managed a shot, though both guns had cleared their holsters.

"This here'n's deader'n a doornail," one of the men said, looking at Leo.

"Him, too," another said from near Waylon's body. He poked at him with the toe of his boot.

Bernardo holstered his pistol, then looked at the sheriff. "Sheriff, was it a fair fight?"

"Fair as fair can be, I'd say," one of the other men yelled. He was answered by a host of others and the sheriff nodded his head in agreement.

"Can I buy you a drink, Bernardo?" someone invited.

Bernardo looked back at them and smiled. "No, thank you. I have some hard riding to do."

"What about the money?" someone called. "Didn't you say them fellas stole a hundred fifty thousand? You'll be wantin' that back, I suppose?"

"I have it back," Bernardo said. "It was in their saddlebags."

"Did you hear that?" Bernardo heard someone ask as he left. "He had the money already but he braced them two anyway. That took guts, I'll tell you."

"Either that or he hated them two like sin," the sheriff answered.

They were both wrong, Bernardo thought as he forked his horse. It took neither bravery nor hate to do what he did. It took a sense of fair play. Bernardo was merely doing what Alexia had asked him to do, righting the wrong that she had done to Makenna.

CHAPTER TWENTY

Ten days after Miss Makenna O'Shea stepped onto the crowded, dusty coach at Albuquerque to begin her trip to San Francisco, she, as Mrs. Peter Van Zandt, stepped onto the private car that would take her back. The car was on a side track at the San Francisco railroad terminal and many of the same people who had come to the wedding were now here to see the newlyweds on their journey. They wandered in and out of the car for some two hours, bearing baskets of fruit and bottles of champagne. The whole thing took on the aura of a party and little groups would form, talk for a while, explode in a peal of laughter, then move through the car or along the station platform to form new groups, a few moments later to repeat the pattern.

Makenna was aware of the impromptu party going on in the lounge area of the car but she was in the bedroom with Della, folding and packing away her wardrobe. It was an entirely new wardrobe, paid for by Emory Van Zandt "as a wedding present," he said and picked out by Della and Madeline.

"Oh, mum, I do hope you like the lovely things Madeline and I picked out for you," Della said anxiously.

Makenna looked at the girl and smiled. Della, too, was a sort of wedding gift and she was returning to Albuquerque as Makenna's maid. "They are lovely, Della."

Della smiled in relief. "Thank you, mum," she said. "I told Mister Van Zandt that a fine lady such as yourself would want to select her own wardrobe but he insisted that Madeline and I do it for you."

"He knew that I wouldn't do it," Makenna said.

"Mum, you mean you'd turn down these fine clothes?" Della asked in surprise.

"That is exactly what I mean," Makenna said.

"Lord, mum, I've been in this country for two years and I've yet to understand you Americans."

Makenna smiled. "You mean we, don't you? You're an American now."

"Yes, mum," Della answered. "Tell me, mum. What's it like, this Alby...Alby..."

"Albuquerque?"

"Yes, mum. What's it like there?"

"Oh, I think it's beautiful," Makenna said. "Huge, red mountains with jagged canyons, magnificent sunsets, and the quiet, timeless desert."

"But the desert...isn't that just sand, mum?"

"Not at all," Makenna said. "There are cactus and desert flowers, which make it all so beautiful it's hard to describe."

"That's where Mr. Hansen is?" Della asked.

"How did you know about Mr. Hansen?"

"There's been talk," Della said. "Excuse me, mum, for tellin' you but I thought you might like to know."

"What kind of talk?"

Della cleared her throat. "It's been noticed that Mr. Peter spends his nights elsewhere. It did seem a bit odd but then someone explained that your marrying him in the first place was odd. The talk is that you wanted to marry someone else."

Makenna looked at the girl for several moments with a look of total resignation.

"Excuse me, mum," Della said in a frightened tone of voice. She was unable to interpret Makenna's expressions. "I had no right to speak."

Makenna smiled. "Don't worry, Della. I can't be angry with you for telling the truth. Yes, circumstances forced me to marry Peter Van Zandt. I'd rather not discuss them right now; anyway, I imagine, since you know everything else, you know the circumstances as well."

"Yes'm," Della said. She walked over to Makenna and put her hand on Makenna's shoulder. "Mum, the really terrible thing is, no one will know what an act of love your marriage to Mr. Van Zandt really was."

There was a bump as the private car was connected to the rest of the train. Makenna heard laughter and shouted good-byes and knew that the visitors had left the car and were standing on the platform waving good-bye.

"Here we go, mum," Della said excitedly.

The trip back was uneventful and Makenna passed the time by reading or chatting with Della. She had come to like the young woman and to admire her grit. Della's mother had died when Della was only sixteen years old. Her father was an alcoholic, though in Della's quaint words he was "a gentleman much in his cups," and he arranged for Della to take a position with a tavern keeper.

"But it wasn't a servin' girl he was wantin', mum," the girl explained. "It was a doxie, to keep his customers happy. So I ran away. Then I heard that there were jobs like this one in America, so I went to an agency and signed on. And here I am."

When they reached Albuquerque, the usual crowd was gathered at the depot to welcome the train. Makenna looked out at the crowd in a totally different respect now. No longer did it seem large; in fact, by comparison with San Francisco, it was pitifully small. Also, the sense of excitement, the promise of mystery was gone. Makenna had "seen the elephant" as her father would say. There was no mystery left to reveal to her and she had put away all her feelings forever by marrying Peter Van Zandt.

Makenna walked from the private car up through the coaches, so that when the train stopped, she would disembark with the coach passengers. No sooner had she set foot on the platform than she heard a whoop and her name shouted.

"Makenna, we're over here!" Gabe shouted.

Makenna saw Gabe and her father coming toward her. Before she could say anything, Gabe broke into a run and reached her in just a few strides. He grabbed her and kissed her and, despite the awful truth she was going to have to tell him or perhaps because of it, Makenna allowed herself the kiss, melting into his arms.

"Don't forget your papa," Kellen said, laughing behind Gabe's shoulder. "Save some of your affection for him."

"Oh, Papa," Makenna said. She was crying now and she went into his arms, holding him to her as tightly as she could. There was the old, comfortable and familiar smell of him that she had known since childhood: a combination of tobacco, Irish whiskey, train smoke, and just a hint of lye soap.

"There, there," Kellen said, holding his daughter and patting her affectionately on the back. "I never could understand what it was that made a woman weep so easily."

"Excuse me, mum, but Mr. Van Zandt is looking for you," Della said.

Kellen and Gabe looked at Della in surprise and then back at Makenna.

"This is Della," Makenna said. "She is my friend, and, uh, my maid."

"Your what?" Gabe asked with a little laugh.

"She is my wife's maid," Peter said, approaching them then. "Of course, Della prefers being called a friend but what that all boils down to is a maid. You know the old saying, a mule in horse harness is still a mule?"

"Your...your wife's maid?" Gabe asked, clearly puzzled by the conversation.

"Yes," Peter replied easily. He put his arm around Makenna. "Gentlemen, I'd like you to meet Mrs. Peter Van Zandt."

"Makenna, is this true?" Gabe asked in a choked voice.

Makenna hung her head without a word. Tears slid down her face.

A blood vessel began jumping in Gabe's temple and he stared at the two for a moment, then spun on his heel and walked away quickly, shoving the unfortunate people who happened to get in his way to one side.

"I must say, he wasn't a very good sport about it," Peter said with an easy laugh. "I don't believe he even offered his congratulations, did he?"

Makenna looked at her father. His face was flushed and his eyes flashed in anger. He began shaking and Makenna was frightened that he might have a seizure of some sort.

"Papa," she said, reaching for him.

"No," Kellen said, pushing her away from him. "I am not your papa. And you are no longer my daughter."

"Papa, please!" Makenna begged in one loud sob.

Kellen tried to jump back to avoid her and as he did so, he dropped one of his crutches. Makenna reached for it but Kellen grabbed it first, shoving her back angrily. "I don't need your help," he said icily.

"Oh, Papa, don't; don't do this," Makenna said.

Kellen settled his crutch, then turned and left, swinging along as quickly as he could manage on the crutches.

"My, they appear to be upset, don't they?" Peter asked, still laughing.

Della put her arms around Makenna, and Makenna, taking comfort where she could, cried onto Della's shoulder. "Come along, mum," the girl said. "Let's return to the car. I'll fix you a nice cup of tea."

"You do that," Peter suggested, showing no sympathy for Makenna's plight. "I'm going out to End-of-Track to see how the money is being spent. I'll probably get Rosie to put me up for the night," he added, "so you needn't wait up for me."

When Peter arrived at End-of-Track, he was amazed by the amount of progress that had been made since he left. The seemingly impossible mountain pass had already been negotiated and the track passed through Pie Town, Omega, Quemado, and was headed for Red Hill. They were, in fact, only twenty-five miles from the Arizona Territorial line and the men were laying track at a rate exceeding five miles per day. There seemed little that could stop them from crossing the line before the deadline, and once that line was crossed, the government grant would be paid and Gabe Hansen's railroad would be a reality.

Peter watched the work for a while. It seemed odd to him to realize that as long as he had been associated with Gabe Hansen's railroad, he had never before really watched the actual track laying operation. He had been so busy conducting his personal battle with Gabe that he hadn't allowed himself the luxury of watching. Now, however, that battle was over and Peter considered himself the clear-cut victor. Gabe Hansen was going to get his railroad built but Peter, by marrying Makenna, had certainly rendered it a hollow victory for Gabe.

"Get that cart up here!" one of the foremen called, and Peter looked back to see a horse-drawn cart being pulled along the section of track, which had been laid only moments earlier. The cart was loaded with sixteen rails, plus the exact number of spikes, bolts and rail couplings, called fishplates, that would be needed for laying the track. The cart was rolled out to the very end of the last pair of rails spiked down.

The bed of the cart was equipped with rollers, and the rails were pulled off easily and quickly, then dropped into place. A team of men walked between the rails using a notched wooden board to space the rails exactly four feet eight and one half inches apart and then the men with the hammers would drive the spikes home. No sooner was that rail laid than the cart moved out onto them and brought rails for the next section. After all sixteen rails were used, that cart was pushed off the track and a following cart came with sixteen more units.

Peter started back to his horse to return to the main camp when he saw the Chinese cook beginning to set up the kitchen for their evening meal. He had never before paid any attention to them, but today he saw one girl who made him stop and stare. She was very young, Peter would guess around fifteen or sixteen, and she was exquisitely beautiful. She had high cheekbones, not prominent but well-accented and, even at this distance, Peter could see that her eyes sparkled like set jewels, framed by eyelashes that were as beautiful as the most delicate lace. Her skin was smooth and golden and her movements were as graceful as a lily stirred by the breeze.

"You," Peter called, pointing toward the girl.

The girl looked up and smiled.

"Come here," Peter said.

The girl replied in Chinese and bowed low.

"What the hell, don't you even speak English?" Peter asked. He looked around and saw Long Li near one of the empty carts.

"Long Li," he called. "Come here."

Long Li hurried over. He bowed slightly.

"Ask that girl to come closer," Peter said, pointing at the beautiful Chinese girl.

"She is a cook," Long Li said.

"I know she is a cook. What the hell does that mean?"

"She is not an employee of the railroad," Long Li explained.

"No, but by damn you are," Peter said. "Now ask her over here."

Long Li shouted something in Chinese and the young girl came to them. She stopped about eight feet away and hung her head, though she looked at Peter through up cast eyes.

"Ask her to hold her head up so I can get a better look at her," Peter said. "She is a beautiful girl."

"Hold your head up, little one," Long Li said in Chinese.

"Does he like me?" the girl asked.

"Why should that matter to you?"

"I think he is very handsome. Should he ask to buy me as his wife, Leader, please say yes."

"What is she jabbering about?"

"She is afraid she will be punished for neglecting her

work," Long Li said.

Peter smiled at the girl. "You tell her I won't let anyone punish her."

"She is not your responsibility to punish or not, sir," Long Li said.

"By God, I can make her my responsibility," Peter said. "What is her name?"

"Orchid Blossom," Long Li said.

Peter looked at the girl a bit longer, then smiled at her again. He got up on his horse and touched the brim of his hat just before he rode away. "Good-bye, Orchid Blossom," he said. "I'll see you later."

"He does want to marry me," Orchid Blossom said excitedly. "Tell him yes, Leader. He is a very rich man, is he not?"

"He is also married," Long Li said.

"But he is rich enough to be able to afford two wives," Orchid Blossom insisted.

"That is not done in this country," Long Li explained. "Besides, you are a Chinese girl. Do you seriously expect someone like Peter Van Zandt would marry you? I do not say this to be cruel, little one, merely to instruct you in the facts of life."

"But he does like me, I know this."

"I do not deny that he likes you, little one. But what he has in his mind is quite different from what you have in your heart. You should avoid this one. Please, listen to me. I am much your elder and say these things for your own good."

"Very well, Leader," Orchid Blossom said with an edge of disappointment in her voice.

CHAPTER TWENTY-ONE

Peter didn't return that night. In fact, he had been gone for four nights when Makenna heard that the Arizona line would be crossed sometime during the next day, and she made up her mind that she wanted to go to End-of-Track.

"But, mum," Della protested.

"I told you to please call me Makenna."

Della smiled. "I know you did, mum...I mean Makenna. It just takes some getting used to, that's all. But what I was going to say, Makenna, is that you are just asking for more hurt, aren't you?"

"I don't care," Makenna said. "I've been a part of this operation all along and I'm going to see it through. Now you get the car ready to travel and I'll go get Dudley to pull us out there."

When Makenna first approached Dudley, he began to make excuses as to why he couldn't pull her car to End-of-Track.

"Dudley, you too?" Makenna asked. "Have you turned against me along with everyone else?"

Dudley cleared his throat and looked at the ground. "Makenna, girl, I reckon you got your own life to live, 'n it ain't really nobody else's business. It's just that no one can understand why you up and married that Van Zandt fella. Especially with him spendin' ever' night since you come back with Rosie or one of her girls."

"Regardless of my reasons, it's something done," Makenna said. "Now, Dudley, I'm asking you again, please pull my car out to End-of-Track."

Dudley sighed. "All right, Makenna. I'll do it. I don't know how Mr. Hansen's gonna take it. He might decide to fire me."

"He won't fire you," Makenna promised.

"We'll be leavin' in about an hour," Dudley said. "Be in your car."

"I will be and thanks, Dudley. I really appreciate this."

Makenna hurried back to the car where she found Della just finishing stowing the items that needed securing for travel. "Are we going to End-of-Track?" she asked.

"Yes," Makenna said, her eyes flashing in excitement over the prospect.

"Oh, that'll be wonderful," Della said. "I've never seen men building a railroad before. Are there many?"

"Hundreds," Makenna said.

Makenna was in better spirits as they journeyed to End-of-Track than she had been at any time since the fateful trip to San Francisco. Even if Gabe wouldn't speak to her, she would be seeing him realize his dream. She knew that she was responsible for his success and she would take a quiet pleasure in that.

Della and Makenna were chatting about the scenery through which the train was passing when the train came to a sudden halt. So violent was the stop that lamps and chairs tipped over and Makenna heard the crashing of dishes in the cupboard.

"Makenna, what is it?" Della cried.

"I don't know," Makenna said. "But hang on tight."

Both women were in seats that were secured to the floor, so they were spared the indignity and possible injury of being unceremoniously dumped over.

"I'm going to get out and see what's going on," Makenna said.

"Oh, please be careful," Della warned.

Once outside the train, Makenna saw a large bonfire on the track just in front of the engine. Dudley was out of the engine arguing with two men on horseback. Makenna hurried up to the front of the train.

"Dudley, what is it? Why is that fire on the track?"

"*Buenos dias, Señora!*" one of the horsemen said. Makenna recognized him as Santiago, Bernardo's friend.

"Santiago, what are you doing here?"

"I am most sorry for the fire, *Señora*," Santiago said. "But Bernardo insisted that we warn the train before anyone was hurt."

"Warn the train? Warn us about what?"

At that moment, there was a stomach-jarring explosion and Makenna and Dudley looked toward the pass to see a tremendous cloud of dust rising. Tons of rock and shale crashed down on the track, closing the pass.

"About that, *Señora*," Santiago said. "If the train had continued to go, you would have been hurt in the blast."

"Oh, no, you've cut the track!" Makenna said.

"*Sí*. Now the trains cannot run," Santiago said. "Engineer, you may drive the train back to Albuquerque. You will not be harmed."

Dudley sighed. "You'd better get back on board," he said to Makenna. "I'll take us back."

"No," Makenna said.

"What do you mean, no?" Santiago asked. "You have no choice, *Señora*. Your engineer cannot drive the train through the pass, she is blocked."

"I am going to see Bernardo," Makenna said.

"What?" Dudley asked, sputtering.

"Santiago, take me to see Bernardo, please."

"I don't know, *Señora*, he may not..."

Makenna suddenly noticed that Santiago was calling her *señora*, rather than *señorita*. "How did you know I was married?" she asked.

Santiago smiled. "We know," he answered, without elaborating.

"Well, no matter, I've been back long enough for the world to know," she said. "Santiago, please take me to see Bernardo. It's very important."

Santiago sighed and said something in Spanish. Finally, he patted his saddle. "Very well, *Señora*," he said. "But when Bernardo grows angry, you must convince him that I did not take you against your will."

"Makenna, girl, don't be crazy," Dudley warned. Makenna climbed onto the horse with Santiago and looked back at Dudley.

"Don't worry about me, Dudley, I'll be all right," Makenna said. "You go on back to Albuquerque. You can stop at Hickman and send a telegram to End-of-Track, telling them what has happened. That is if the wire is still up."

"But what are you going to do?"

"I'm going to talk to Bernardo Tafoya," Makenna said. Santiago and the rider with him slapped their legs against the flanks of their horses and the animals bolted forward. Makenna was sitting sidesaddle with her leg hooked across the pommel in front of Santiago, and it was an uncomfortable ride, but she made no complaint. After a couple of hours, they came to a small ranch, and Santiago borrowed an extra horse for Makenna. Thus the remaining journey was made much easier for her, though she was still close to physical exhaustion by the time they reached the Casa Grande, the Big House.

"Who is the extra rider?" Bernardo called from the porch. Then he recognized Makenna. "*Caramba*, why have you kidnapped her?"

"I asked to come, Bernardo," Makenna said. She swung down from the horse and then had to hang on to the saddle for a bit to keep from pitching over, she was so tired.

"You asked to come?" Bernardo said, coming to her assistance. "Why?"

"I want to talk," Makenna said.

Bernardo led Makenna into the big house and called for a glass of water for her. "Did you eat?" he asked Santiago.

"Some jerky," Santiago answered.

"Come, *Señora*, we are about to take our evening meal. You will join us. And you, Santiago."

"Thank you," Makenna said, following Bernardo gratefully into the dining room where the spicy aromas were already reminding her of how hungry she was.

"Hello, Makenna," Alexia said quietly. Sitting beside her at the table was Teresina.

"Alexia! What are you doing here?"

"Don Esteban is my uncle," Alexia said.

"Oh, what a wonderful surprise," Makenna exclaimed. "I never expected to see you again."

"*Señora*, you are not as surprised as we," Bernardo said. "Tell me, why did you come here?"

"Bernardo, please. Let her have her dinner before you badger her with questions," Alexia said.

"Yes, yes, of course," Bernardo agreed. "You must

forgive me, *Señora*. Please, eat and then we will find room for you. Tomorrow, when you have rested, we can talk."

"Thank you, Bernardo," Makenna said.

The meal was eaten in a very relaxed atmosphere with Bernardo and Santiago teasing not only each other but Alexia and Teresina as well. Even Makenna came in for some good-natured teasing as Santiago told of her storming off the train demanding to be taken to Bernardo.

"Ah, *caramba*," Santiago said. "Her eyes flashed such fire that I feared for my life if I refused."

After the meal, the diners adjourned to a large room that Makenna would have described as a parlor, though it was decidedly less formal. Although Makenna had been at the big house before, there were many things she did not remember or had not noticed the previous time. Indian rugs decorated the floor and hung from the walls. There was also a rack of rifles against one wall and the antlers of antelope and horns of buffalo were mounted on decorative plaques. Don Esteban, Bernardo's father, had not taken the evening meal with them but he joined them in the room. He was tall and ramrod straight, with silver hair and flashing eyes. It was easy to see where Bernardo and Teresina acquired their handsome looks.

Makenna was introduced to Don Esteban and he smiled and kissed her hand graciously.

"*Señora*," Don Esteban said. "We are about to listen to a guitar concert. Are you familiar with the guitar?"

"Yes," Makenna said, "of course. Someone was always playing one somewhere as I grew up. A railroad worker or a cowboy. And I heard the guitars the last time I was here," she added hesitantly.

"But they played only chords to help them sing, am I right?" Don Esteban asked.

"Well, yes. What else is a guitar for?"

Don Esteban and the others laughed.

"Did I say something funny?" Makenna asked, a bit piqued.

"Excuse us for laughing, Makenna," Bernardo said. Makenna noticed the familiarity of the first name but didn't comment. "But you see," Bernardo went on, "the Spanish invented the guitar. And we didn't invent it to sing songs to the cows as do the Anglos."

"It is a concert instrument when in the right hands," Don Esteban said. "Forgive us for being impolite but it pains us to see the guitar misused as an instrument."

"Well," Makenna said, now curious as to just what a guitar could do that she hadn't heard before. "I must say that I am looking forward to this."

"Good," Don Esteban said. "Manuel, you may begin."

Manuel, whom Makenna had seen earlier helping to serve the meal, now picked up a battered guitar case and opened it. The case may have been battered but the guitar inside was exquisitely beautiful. The box was cherry red, giving way to soft yellow. It showed tender care and the way Manuel handled it, gently and with respect, told the story of his love for the instrument. He strummed the strings lightly, moving through an intricate chord progression that rose from the sound box and wove a pattern of melody as delicate as a lace doily.

Makenna sat quietly, listening in delight. She was amazed that this sound was coming from a guitar. It was as if she were discovering something entirely new. She was long familiar with the guitar but had never really known it.

Manuel went through the chord progressions a few times and then stopped. He hung his head for a few seconds, then started to play. The music spilled out, a steady, never-wavering beat with two or three poignant minor chords at the ends of phrases, but with an overall, single string melody, weaving in and out of the chords like a thread of gold woven through the finest cloth.

The sound was agony and ecstasy, joy and sorrow, pain and pleasure. It moved into Makenna's soul and she found herself being carried along with the melody, now rising, now falling. Perhaps it was the moment, the quiet, the softly lit room, the weight of her personal sorrow, but Makenna had never been moved so deeply by music before. She sat spellbound for several seconds after the last exquisite chord faded away.

"Now, she understands," Don Esteban said quietly as he saw the expression on Makenna's face.

"I will show you to your room," Alexia invited. "You must be tired."

"Yes," Makenna said. "Thank you, I am."

Casa Grande was a two-story stucco house with red slate shingles on the roof. It was a sprawling house, shaped somewhat like the letter "U," though with the wings at more of an angle. Makenna's room was at the end of the east wing and she followed Alexia down the long hallway.

"I can't tell you how good it is to see you here," Makenna said.

"It was a pleasant surprise to see you, too," Alexia said.

"Tell me, Alexia, would it be possible to have a bath?" Makenna asked.

Alexia laughed. "I have already asked for a bath to be drawn for you. I remember you told me on the train of your penchant for bathing."

Alexia opened the door and motioned for Makenna to enter. The room was large and comfortable, with a huge double window looking out over the lawn. On one side of the room, near the wall, was a large tub. It wasn't the type with running water as she had enjoyed for the few brief days she had spent in the Van Zandt Mansion in San Francisco but the steam rising from the water attested to the fact that it was adequately hot and would be very relaxing.

"Thank you," Makenna said when she saw the tub. "Oh, that looks absolutely heavenly."

"Good night, Makenna. I'll see you in the morning," Alexia said. "Oh, just hang your clothes outside your door. I'll have them cleaned and returned by the time you wake up tomorrow." Alexia smiled and pulled the door shut.

Makenna walked over to the tub. She saw not only the water but the towels, soap, toilet water and oils she would use placed on a bench beside the tub. She removed her clothes, hung them outside the door, and slipped gratefully into the water.

After the bath, Makenna toweled herself dry, then walked over to the windows. She pushed them open and looked outside.

A cluster of trees waved gently in the night wind and the leaves of one of them caught a moonbeam and scattered a burst of silver through the darkness. The fragrant scent of carefully nurtured flowers floated in from a nearby garden.

CHAPTER TWENTY-TWO

"Good morning, *Señora*," a short, dumpy woman said. Makenna recognized the woman as one of the house servants she had seen the night before. The woman was holding Makenna's dress.

"It is all clean and pressed," the woman said, smiling broadly.

"Thank you," Makenna said.

The woman hung the clothes on a hook on the closet door and pointed to the dresser. "Here is a basin of hot water, soap and towels, *Señora*," she said. "Breakfast will be served in twenty minutes."

She heard a knock at the door and thinking it was the maid again, called out.

"Come in," she called.

Bernardo opened the door and stepped inside. "Good morning, Makenna," he said. "I've come to escort you to breakfast."

"Thank you," Makenna replied. "I'm ready."

Breakfast was the same casual affair as dinner had been the evening before. No one had faint appetites and even Makenna, who so often restricted her breakfast to a cup of coffee and a biscuit, ate heartily of the veritable banquet offered her.

"Where's Alexia?" Teresina asked.

"I saw her riding out this morning," Santiago said.

"Riding out? Riding where?" Bernardo asked. "She took some coffee from the kitchen early this morning, *Señor*," one of the servants said as she delivered more eggs. "She said she wanted to go for a ride."

"That's odd," Bernardo said.

"Perhaps not so odd," Teresina said, her eyes fixed on Makenna's face.

"I am not being critical, my brother," Teresina replied in English. "It is just that it is obvious to all that Alexia loves you."

"Alexia loves you?" Makenna asked. "But I thought she was your cousin."

"Her mother married my uncle," Bernardo said. "We are not blood cousins. Alexia is but a child. She only thinks she loves me."

"Ah, *Bernardo*, some child," Santiago said.

"I...uh, excuse me," Makenna murmured. She got up from the table and left quickly, burning with embarrassment and guilt.

Alexia was her friend. Did Alexia consider her coming here to be a challenge? Yes, that had to be it. Makenna asked to come here, what other reason would there be in Alexia's mind?

Makenna had no sooner reached her room than she heard an urgent knock on the door.

"Who is it?"

"Makenna, it is Bernardo. Please, let me in. I must talk to you."

"No," Makenna answered.

The door opened and Bernardo stepped inside. "Go away," Makenna said. "I don't want to talk to you." Makenna walked over to the bed and sat down.

"Please," Bernardo said. He sat beside her and put his hand on hers. "Perhaps you feel like talking about the reason you came to see me?"

Makenna sighed. "I wanted to ask you to let the railroad go through," she said. "But now, I am so confused I don't know what to do. Sometimes I think I should go back to San Francisco and make a life for myself there."

"I will let the railroad go through," Bernardo said quietly.

"Of course, I don't know what I expected by coming out here, I just..." Makenna paused in mid-sentence. "Did you say you would let the railroad go through?" she asked.

"*Sí,*" Bernardo said.

"But why? You've been fighting it so hard, surely you don't intend to change your mind just because I asked you?"

"Makenna, I realize now that the railroad is not going to go away or find another route. If not Gabe Hansen, then another will come, and then another and yet another. If we continue to fight the railroad, soon there will be a killing. Then perhaps more killings until there is a war. I do not mind killing a man who should be killed. But the men who work on the railroad are honest men with no evil in their hearts. My men are honest men who believe in what they are doing. To put honest men into a war against each other means that only honest men are killed. That would be a sin. I will make no more effort to stop the railroad."

"Oh, thank you, Bernardo," Makenna said as she squeezed his hand.

"But if I do this thing, I feel that the railroad should make…concessions," he said, looking for the right word.

"What sort of concessions?"

"The railroad has land grants that extend one mile to either side of the track," Bernardo said. "This hurts the people who own small ranches. Some will lose everything they have worked so hard for. Perhaps Señor Hansen will sell that land to me so that I can return it to the small ranchers," Bernardo offered. "It was land that originally belonged to my family and we gave it to these ranchers. I do not feel good about buying the land back to give it away a second time but if Señor Hansen will not charge too much, perhaps I can do this."

"I'll talk to him," Makenna said. "I'm sure he'll be willing to do as you ask."

"Will he listen to you?" Bernardo asked.

"Yes," Makenna said. "I'll make him listen."

"Good," Bernardo said, smiling broadly. "Then let us call off this fight."

CHAPTER TWENTY-THREE

Makenna felt so good over having worked out a deal with Bernardo that she nearly forgot the incident at the breakfast table and didn't think of it again until she saw Alexia returning from her ride just before noon. She wondered how best to treat the situation but Alexia took the problem out of her hands.

"Makenna," Alexia said. "I must talk to you." Makenna felt apprehensive. She didn't want to talk to Alexia because she was afraid that it would lead to angry words. And she didn't wish to get into an argument with the girl she considered her friend. But there was really no way to avoid the discussion, so she took a deep breath and agreed to go to Alexia's room to talk with her. She stood just inside the door as Alexia paced about nervously, obviously seeking a way to begin the conversation. Finally, Makenna decided to begin it for her.

"Alexia, it is not for the reason you think, that I came," she said. "I am truly sorry if you misunderstood. And I didn't know you were in love with Bernardo."

"But you know now?" Alexia asked, puzzled by Makenna's statement.

"Yes," Makenna said. "I was told this morning. I—I want to ask for your forgiveness."

"My forgiveness, Makenna? Forgiveness for what?"

"Because my coming here has hurt you."

Alexia said. "It is I who must ask for forgiveness."

"Forgiveness for what?"

"The two men who robbed you and gave you to the ship captain," Alexia said. "They are dead now. Bernardo faced them down and killed them both."

"But...but how did he know about it?"

"I told him," Alexia said. "I told him their names and gave him their description."

"But, Alexia, how did you know all that? I only saw one of them and I didn't know the name of either of them."

"Makenna, please, you must forgive me," Alexia said, suddenly realizing that she had said much more than she intended.

"Alexia, what is it? What is it that you aren't telling me?"

"I sent the men to rob you," Alexia said. "I told them not to hurt you. I only wanted them to take the money from you. I had no idea they would do what they did. That is why I asked Bernardo to avenge you."

"But...why?

"I knew that the money was for the railroad," Alexia explained. "I thought that if you didn't have the money, the railroad wouldn't be built. That would please Bernardo. But I didn't want to hurt you. I didn't know they would do what they did."

"Alexia, what they did was nothing," Makenna said. "If that were all that happened I would count myself lucky. It was what came afterward that has done me the greatest hurt. I was forced to marry Peter. And you did this to me. You!"

Makenna turned and ran from the room. She sped down the hallway and out the front door. Finally, when she reached a hitching rail in front of the house, she paused to grab her breath.

"What is it, Makenna?" Bernardo asked, following her out the door. "Why did you run out of the house like that?"

Makenna looked at Bernardo with her eyes flashing anger. "Tell me," she said. "Just how much were you willing to pay Gabe Hansen for the return of the land? One hundred and fifty thousand dollars, perhaps?"

"She told you," Bernardo said.

"Yes," Makenna replied, looking away. "How could she have done this? And you? You let it happen."

"No," Bernardo said. "I knew nothing about it until it had already happened. I have the money now. I was going to tell you about it."

"When?" Makenna asked. "After you used it to cheat Gabe out of his land?"

"*Señora,* let us not lose sight of who is cheating whom here!" Bernardo said angrily. "Do not forget, it was my land in the first place."

"I need a horse," Makenna said after a moment. "May I borrow one?"

"*Sí,* of course," Bernardo said. "I will ride back to town with you."

"No, that isn't necessary."

"It is a long way back. Much could happen to a woman riding alone."

"I don't care what happens to me anymore," Makenna said dejectedly.

CHAPTER TWENTY-FOUR

After he finished, the man got up and began getting dressed. The bright moon was shining on the girl who had not yet moved from where she lay beside the ravine.

"It was good," the man said easily. "But it's over now, so you'd better get dressed."

The girl smiled up at him.

"Here," the man said, picking up the girl's clothes and dropping them on her. "Get dressed now."

She continued to smile but made no move to comply with his request.

"Very well, have it your own way." He reached in his pocket and took out two coins. "Here," he said. "You earned this." He dropped the coins on the dirt beside her.

The girl's face registered surprise, then twisted into an expression of rage. She picked the money up and threw it at him, then stood up and leaped at him, screaming in anger. "I am not a Biao zi!" She yelled. "I am not a . . ." she struggled for the word in English.

"Hey, what the hell? Have you gone crazy?" the man asked, surprised by the girl's sudden move. He fended off her charge, then pushed her back. Thrown off balance, she let out a short scream and fell backwards into the ravine, which cut a deep scar into the desert floor beside where they had lain. Her scream faded as she slid downward. When she reached the bottom, she was perfectly still.

"Are you all right?" the man called out running to the edge of the ravine. "What did you do that for, you crazy..." He stopped in mid-sentence as he saw her. There was no need to go on. Even in the moonlight, he could tell that the girl was dead. Her head was grotesquely twisted and her eyes were open and unseeing. Her neck had been broken in the fall.

"What the hell did you do that for?"

He instinctively looked around to see if anyone saw or heard what happened and then realizing that nobody would be there in the dead of night, he walked quickly away.

The five-thirty call rousted the work crews out of bed, and by six o'clock work was underway. The steel had been ringing for nearly an hour when Peter stepped out of Rosie's car and saw Gabe and Bull standing together near the engineering car. He adjusted his hat and tugged at his cuff, then strolled over to join them.

"Well, how goes the mighty railroad builders today?" Peter asked.

"Good morning, Mr. Van Zandt," Bull said.

"Morning, Van Zandt," Gabe put in.

"Have you any estimate on when we'll have the pass open?" Peter asked.

"No," Gabe said. "Why, are you anxious to get back to Albuquerque?"

"No, no, my dear fellow. But I am anxious to bring my wife out to join me. You know my wife, the former Makenna O'Shea?"

"Why do you want her out here?" Gabe asked. "Aren't you afraid that will interfere with your visits to Rosie's girls?"

"No, not at all," Peter answered. "Makenna is very understanding about that sort of thing."

"I'll just bet," Gabe said.

"My—don't tell me you are worried about my wife's sensitive feelings being bruised? I should think that would be the last thing you'd worry about, Hansen."

"I've got some things to do," Gabe said, flushing angrily.

"To be sure," Peter said. "Nothing must stop the railroad."

Peter laughed as Gabe walked away.

"Mr. Van Zandt, you ought not to ride Mr. Hansen like that."

"How touching," Peter said.

"I thought I knew Makenna better'n that, too," Bull went on. "What I can't figure is why she done what she did. I think they's somethin' to this that none of the rest of us know yet."

"Oh, most astute of you," Peter said sarcastically.

"You know, Mr. Van Zandt, I don't always know what all them words you say mean," Bull said. "And I ain't none too sure that I like it. But Mr. Hansen said let you be, so that's what I aim to do for the time bein'."

The smile left Peter's face and an evil glint flashed in his eyes. He looked at Bull coldly. "Don't ever get the wrong idea, Blackwell," he warned. "I wouldn't even try to fight a giant like you. I'd shoot you at the first move."

"Yes, sir, I reckon you would," Bull said. "But I reckon two or three of them little bullets in that pop shooter you carry wouldn't stop me before I broke your neck."

"Shall we try it then, Mr. Blackwell?" Peter asked.

"Bull, Mr. Hansen wants to see you," one of the men called from the front of the train.

"I reckon not," Bull said easily. "At least not now."

Peter watched Bull walk quickly to the front of the train and he stuck his hand in his pocket to keep it from shaking. The truth was, Bull was probably right about not being stopped easily. Especially with the gun Peter carried, a short barrel .25 caliber special. It was potent enough to do the job and, in fact, had done so on more than one occasion. But the greatest advantage was in its size. That gave him the advantage of having a concealed weapon but he had to trade that advantage off in the amount of stopping power of the bullets. And, of course, with Bull Blackwell, even the advantage of a concealed weapon was negated since Bull, as well as everyone else on the railroad, knew that he carried one.

The shakes stopped but the nervous sweats did not and Peter reached for his handkerchief to mop his brow. It aggravated him that his handkerchief wasn't in his pocket. He didn't know if he forgot it this morning or if he dropped it somewhere.

Long Li watched the work of his crew with satisfaction. Two hundred bodies welded together to function with one mind. His mind, he thought with pride. The Chinese were looked down upon as if they were something less than human. They ran laundries, cafes, or worked as house servants, and that was the extent of their existence. Except for the railroad. They had been proving their worth on the railroads and, through the railroads, were leaving behind a monument to their race. And of that, Long Li was inordinately proud.

A small elderly Chinese man approached Long Li, stopped at a respectful distance and waited, as was dictated by the social order of his station, for Long Li to recognize him.

"Yes, Wei Shan, what is it?" Long Li asked. Wei Shan was one of the cooks on the Chinese kitchen staff.

"Leader, there is much sorrow in the kitchen," Wei Shan said.

"Sorrow? Why is there sorrow?"

"Come," Wei Shan said.

Long Li followed Wei Shan along the track and down the elevated roadbed into an area where a collection of crossed poles, suspended pots, fires and smells made up the Chinese kitchen. Wei Shan pointed to an old woman who was crying.

"Old woman, why do you weep so?" Long Li asked.

"I weep for my daughter," the old woman answered.

"You weep for Orchid Blossom? Why?"

"Because she is dead," Wei Shan said. "Come, I will show you."

Long Li followed Wei Shan from the camp and they walked approximately two hundred yards across the desert floor. Finally, they came to the edge of a ravine. Wei Shan stopped and pointed. "She is down there," he said.

There, in the bottom of the ravine, Long Li saw her. Orchid Blossom, who had been so beautiful in life, was grotesque in death. She was nude and already her young, hairless body was being discolored by the sun. The cuts on her body were puffed with dried blood and insects crawled around exploring the strange creature that now lay in their domain. Her eyes were open and bulging, shining with opaque blackness. Her head was twisted sharply to one side and a large, discolored knot showed where the neck had been broken.

Something flashed in the sun near Long Li's feet and he picked up two coins, examined them curiously, then dropped them in his pocket.

"When did you find her?" Long Li asked.

"A short time ago, Leader," Wei Shan said. "Her mother said nothing about the girl being gone for a while, thinking perhaps she was taking a walk as she sometimes did. But then she grew worried, so she came to see me. I searched and found her here."

"Wei Shan, have you noticed any of the Americans, the round eyes, talking to Orchid Blossom?"

"No, Leader. Do you think a round eye did this thing?"

Long Li stuck his hand in his pocket and felt the two coins. "Yes," he said.

"Will you tell the round-eye chief of this?"

"No," Long Li said. "If justice is to be done, we must see to it ourselves and in secret."

"But the round-eye chief is an honest man, is he not?"

"Yes, he is honest, as is my friend Bull Blackwell. I believe also the one who talks with wires is honest. But Orchid Blossom is our responsibility. Do you agree?"

"Yes, Leader."

"Tell the mother of Orchid Blossom to finish with her weeping and say nothing of this," Long Li ordered. "And get clothes for the girl's burial from her mother. I will get shovels and we will bury her here."

"Yes, Leader," Wei Shan said, starting back to the kitchen camp at a trot.

Long Li stood there for a moment longer, looking down at the body of the young girl. Orchid Blossom was such a beautiful girl and filled with such curiosity. He felt heart-sick over the tragedy.

Long Li turned to walk back for the shovels. Just as he started back, he saw something white lying in a bed of prickly pear cactus. He bent to pick it up and saw that it was a handkerchief. The handkerchief had, obviously, been left there by the guilty party.

Long Li examined the handkerchief closely and saw a laundry number. He smiled. "So, my friend," he said under his breath. "You have signed your work."

CHAPTER TWENTY-FIVE

The rockslide, which Bernardo had brought down into the pass, was causing Gabe immense difficulty. The terms of the railroad grant act specified that continuous track be laid for every mile claimed. So it would do little good to reach the Arizona town of Springerville by the deadline if the pass were still blocked.

"The only way you're going to get the rock out of here in time is blast it out," Bull insisted.

"There is no dynamite available," Gabe said.

"Buy some more."

"That's what I mean," Gabe said. "The dynamite plant in San Francisco is out of production because of a fire. All the existing stockpiles from Chicago to the west are gone."

"How about black powder?"

"Maybe," Gabe said. "But it requires eight times as much black powder to do the job. If we could get that much together, the time required to fuse it and set it is so slow, I don't know if it will do us any good."

"We've got to try," Bull said. "I don't see that we have much choice left, do you?"

Gabe sighed. "No, we have no choice left," he agreed.

He pinched the bridge of his nose and leaned back in his chair. "Bull, why don't you ask Long Li to come see me? His men are going to handle it, so we'll need his thinking on this."

"All right, boss," Bull said, unwinding his huge frame from the chair he had been sitting in. As he started out the door of the engineering car, he saw Long Li and Kellen approaching the car. "Well, how's that for service?" he asked. "Long Li is on his way in here right now."

"Good," Gabe said.

Long Li and Kellen came into the engineering car and exchanged greetings with the two men who were already there.

"Long Li, can your men move that rock with black powder?" Gabe asked.

"Can do," Long Li said. "But much work for black powder, maybe cannot do in time."

"The way I see it, we don't have much of an option," Gabe said. "There is no more dynamite available anywhere. We'll have to use black powder."

Long Li studied the pass for a long time. "Boss Hansen, can you get nitro?"

"Nitroglycerine?" Gabe asked. "Are you serious?"

"Nitro very strong stuff," Long Li said. "More strong than dynamite."

"And much more dangerous," Gabe said. "All you have to do to make nitro go off is sneeze."

"But nitro can do job," Long Li said. "Black powder, maybe cannot."

"God, I don't know, Long Li," Gabe said. "I want this railroad built but I don't want to build it over bodies of my men."

"Not to worry, Boss Hansen. Just Chinamen," Long Li

said, eyeing Gabe carefully.

"What the hell do you mean!" Gabe exploded. "Chinamen, Irishmen, German, they are all the same and I don't want any of them killed."

"There are those who do not feel that Chinamen are the same as other men," Long Li explained.

"You know damned well I'm not one of them," Gabe said.

"I'm sorry I tested you," Long Li apologized. "But not to worry about men. I will set the charges myself."

"Long Li, you sure you want to do this?" Bull asked.

"Yes," Long Li said.

"Bring this in and you've earned yourself double wages," Gabe promised.

"I wish now to ask a favor of you," Long Li said.

"You've got it," Gabe replied, not even inquiring what the favor was.

"Orchid Blossom has been murdered," Long Li said.

"What?" Gabe shouted in surprise. "The beautiful young girl who works in the kitchen? Who did it?"

"That I do not yet know," Long Li said. "But I believe I will soon be able to find the answer to this question. I want to send a telegram to San Francisco."

"Certainly, send as many as you want," Gabe replied. "Would you like me to start an inquiry?"

"No," Long Li said quickly. He smiled an apology for being so blunt. "Please do understand, I know you want to help but I think the fewer people who know this, the easier will be the task of discovering the murderer. I beg of you to say nothing. It should not go beyond the ears here."

"Very well, Long Li," Gabe said. "If you want it that way. We are pretty much our own law here, so I'll let you handle it however you wish."

"Thank you, Boss Hansen," Long Li said. He handed a piece of paper to Kellen. "If you please, Mr. O'Shea, send this message to Wah Ching in San Francisco."

"Wah Ching? Isn't he a Tong chief?" Bull asked. "Long Li, you aren't getting involved with Tongs?"

"Only to ask that he answer a question for me," Long Li explained. "I have done many favors for Wah Ching and feel that I can ask a favor of him."

"What's the message?" Kellen asked.

"I found a handkerchief near the girl's body," Long Li explained. "It has a laundry mark and that is good identification. Wah Ching can determine who the number belongs to."

"Is it a San Francisco number?" Gabe asked.

"Yes, it has the Chinese character for San Francisco," Long Li explained.

"That shouldn't be too hard," Kellen said. "How many of our people would likely have San Francisco laundry marks?"

"About three hundred," Gabe said. "I hired most of them from that area, remember?"

"Oh, yes," Kellen said. "I see what you mean. Very well, Long Li, I'll get this right off."

"No," Long Li said. "First, order the nitroglycerine, then send this message. I will examine the best places to use the nitro now. I thank you, gentlemen, for your help."

Bull and Gabe watched Long Li leave the car and climb the hill to examine the rubble, which covered the pass.

"He's a hell of a guy, you know that?" Bull said.

"Yes, he is," Gabe agreed. "Bull, you know most of these men. Who would do such a thing as murder that girl?"

"I don't know, boss," Bull answered glumly. "I thought I knew them all pretty well and, I swear, I can't think of a one who would do it. Of course, get a man liquored up enough and you never can tell what he might do. I'll tell you this, though, whoever the son-of-a-bitch is, I'd like to have his neck in my hands right now."

When Makenna returned to Albuquerque, she was bone weary from the long ride, and she went immediately to the car where she and Della were living, and straight to bed. Della was deliriously happy to see her not only because she was worried about Makenna but because she was beginning to worry about herself being ill-equipped to long survive the rigors of living in such an inhospitable country.

Makenna slept the rest of the day and the entire night away without awakening once. Only the aroma of breakfast lured her back to consciousness the next morning and when she sat up in bed, every bone in her body ached.

"How do you feel, mum...I mean, Makenna?" Della asked, bringing a hot cup of tea to Makenna while she was still abed.

"Oh," Makenna moaned. "I feel as if I have been run over by a locomotive."

"I am so glad you returned," Della said. "I've been frightfully lonely without you."

"Has Peter been in touch?" Makenna asked.

"No, mum. I've heard nothing from anyone. Dudley, the railroad engineer, brought the car back here and here I've sat. I've been frightfully worried for fear something had happened to you. Did you see the brigand?"

"The brigand?" Makenna repeated, rubbing the back of her neck.

"Yes, mum. You know, the Mexican fellow who was responsible for blowing up the pass?"

"You mean Bernardo?" Makenna asked, smiling at the English girl's description of him. Then when she recalled what she had discovered about Bernardo, her smile faded.

"Yes," she said. "I saw him."

"Oh, what is he like?" Della asked. "Is he dashing and romantic?"

"I suppose you could say that," Makenna answered. "Why would you ask such a thing?"

"Oh, I should like ever so much to meet someone like that," Della said. "He could place me on the back of his horse and we would ride off into the sunset."

"Della," Makenna said, laughing. "I didn't know you were given to such romantic fantasies."

"Oh, yes, mum; it's the only type entertainment a poor girl like myself has." She blushed slightly, realizing that she had divulged one of her fantasies. "Would you like breakfast now?"

"Have you eaten?"

"No, mum."

"Good, then you can eat with me," Makenna replied. "After breakfast, we'll go into town and I'll show you all the sights of Albuquerque."

"Oh, that will be delightful," Della said. "I do want to get out of this car. Not that it isn't ever so posh, you understand, and I deeply appreciate having such a nice place to live, but…"

"I understand," Makenna said. "You're getting what we call cabin fever. You need to get out."

"Yes, mum."

The two women spent the morning shopping, visiting the Emporium, the Ranchers' Mercantile (which had a sign advertising "Goods for all mankind"), and any other such shops as took their fancy. They ate lunch in the hotel dining room and were given a private booth in the corner. Thus it was that they were unobserved when a group of men came in for lunch and started a conversation that the two ladies could not help but overhear.

"He's ordered nitro," one of the men said. "Nitro? Why, he's gone plumb loco. Nobody works with nitro anymore. That stuff'll kill you quicker'n anythin' I can think of. Why'd he go and order nitro?"

"They say it's the only way he can clear the pass in time. There isn't any dynamite to be found, 'n' black powder'd be too slow."

"He got anybody kin handle it?"

"That Chinaman's gonna do it for 'em."

The other men laughed. "Hell, if that's all, it won't be no great loss if he does blow himself up. The world's got plenty o' them Chinamen."

"As long as they're blowin' people up, it's too bad they couldn't blow up that goddamn Peter Van Zandt 'n his new wife."

"What, you mean Makenna O'Shea?"

"Makenna Van Zandt now," the first man said derisively.

"Oh, Makenna," Della said quickly, putting her hand across the table on Makenna's hand.

"Shh," Makenna warned, placing her fingers across her lips.

"Listen, Makenna's all right. I remember when she and her papa worked here. She's got spunk."

"That ain't all she's got," another said, his voice obviously colored by lechery. "I remember when she used to go down to meet the midnight train."

"Yeah, well, she's like all the rest of them. She sold out to the highest bidder. She married that Van Zandt fella 'cause he's rich."

"I just can't believe that about Makenna. Hell, I've knowed her since she was a little girl and I tell you if she married Van Zandt, there was a reason behind it!" another said.

"How's Hansen takin' it?"

"I guess it's just eatin' away inside of 'em. They say if he was a worker before, why you should see him now. He's drivin' hisself near to death."

"You know what it is, don't you? It's her bein' here in that fancy private car that Van Zandt's got her set up in. It's knowin' that she's so close and yet so far, in a way of speakin'."

"If the girl had any concern for him at all, if there was ever any love between 'em, why she'd'a never left San Francisco."

The conversation of the men changed to other things then and Makenna felt relieved that she would not be subjected to any more of their painful talk.

"I've a mind to tell them a thing or two," Della whispered hotly.

"You'll do no such thing," Makenna said, putting her hand on Della to restrain her. "Please, just sit very quietly until they've had their lunch and left. I don't want them to know I'm even here."

"The very nerve of them," Della fumed. "If they only knew what you really did for Mr. Hansen, they would change their minds."

"Della, I'm no longer sure I did the right thing at all," Makenna said. "I fear I made a terrible mistake and perhaps I've compounded it by coming here. The men are right. We shouldn't have left San Francisco. We're going back tomorrow."

CHAPTER TWENTY-SIX

The nitro proved to be almost as difficult to come by as the dynamite. So volatile was the substance that an accidental explosion of the stuff once wiped out a city block in San Francisco, killing fourteen, and shattering windows throughout most of the city. Because of that, San Francisco now had a very strict ordinance prohibiting not only the manufacture but the very presence of the explosive within its city limits. Many other cities had followed suit and had it not been for the nearby Madden Mining Company, which had some on hand, Gabe might have had to resort to black powder after all.

Gabe bought all the nitro the Madden mines had on hand and Bull had a car built especially to transfer it. It was really a classic of ingenuity and Bull showed it off proudly.

A second deck was built on an ordinary flatcar. The second deck was mounted on leaf springs so that it would take up whatever shock the flatcar's normal suspension let by. Four poles were erected on the second deck, and an intricate basket of ropes was constructed between the poles. Nestled in the rope basket was a large box. The box was stuffed with cotton and the idea was to place the nitro container inside the cushion of cotton.

"Your own mother would be safe on this car," Bull boasted as he showed the car to Gabe.

"Well, you don't have to worry about my mother," Gabe replied. "Just you. You're the one that's going after the stuff."

"I thought you'd say that," Bull said, grinning through a grimace. "All right, boss, when do you want me to go after it?"

"Right now would be as good a time as any," Gabe suggested.

"Boss, someone's ridin' into camp carryin' a white flag," one of the workers shouted.

Gabe looked in the direction indicated and saw a coal-black horse approaching. The rider was sitting erect and proud and carrying a pole from which fluttered a white flag.

"Son-of-a-bitch, it's Tafoya!" Bull swore. "Who's got a rifle?"

"Wait a minute," Gabe said, putting a restraining hand on Bull's arm.

"Well, what the hell does he want?" Bull asked.

"Let's find out. Let him through, boys," Gabe called.

There was a mumble of protest and a few exclamations of curiosity as the horseman rode into the camp. He reined his prancing animal just short of Gabe.

"You are *Señor* Hansen," the rider said.

"Yes."

"I am Bernardo Tafoya," Bernardo said. He smiled broadly. "May I dismount?"

"I suppose so," Gabe replied. "But you aren't exactly a welcome sight around here, Tafoya. What do you want?"

"I want to go somewhere you and I can talk."

"It's a trick, boss," Bull said. "Don't listen to him."

Gabe looked at Bernardo and smiled. "Bull, he is here

in our camp surrounded by our men. What possible trick could he have up his sleeve?"

"I don't know," Bull said. "But I don't like it."

"I assure you, *Señor* Blackwell, I have no trick up my sleeve," Bernardo said easily. "I do have a proposition which I hope will interest Señor Hansen. It will bring us peace."

"I'll listen to your proposition," Gabe said. "In the meantime, Bull, you take the engine and go get the stuff."

"The stuff?" Bull asked.

"You know, your special car?"

"Oh, oh, yes," Bull replied. "I'll get right on that."

"Come into my caboose," Gabe invited. He led the way and Bernardo was right behind him, carrying a pouch of some sort. Once inside, Gabe offered Bernardo a chair. "What is your proposition?" he asked.

"As you know, I have expressed an opposition to your railroad," Bernardo started.

Gabe laughed and pointed toward the pile of rock and rubble that covered the rails running into the pass. "Is that what this was? An expression of your opposition?"

Bernardo returned Gabe's laughter. "You have a sense of humor," he said. "I like that in a man, whether he be a friend or an enemy."

"But you aren't here to listen to my jokes," Gabe said.

"No, *Señor*, I am not. I am here to strike a bargain with you. I want to buy back the land that your railroad has taken from the small ranchers."

"Buy back?" Gabe said.

"*Sí.* The government land grant gives you land for one mile on each side of the right-of-way. I know the government says it is their land to give. But before it was their land to give, it was in my family for over two hundred years. My family gave it to many other people to bring civilization to this country. Now, with the railroad, those people will have no homes."

"Bernardo, you may not realize that I have had to borrow heavily to build this railroad," Gabe explained. "The land grants along the right-of-way have been pledged as collateral. Legally, it is not my land to give to you. Or to sell either."

"But it will be your land when the railroad is completed and the debt repaid?" Bernardo asked.

"Yes," Gabe said. "Assuming that I complete the railroad within the prescribed deadline. As you know, I've had some difficulty in making that deadline."

Bernardo smiled. "We will offer you no more difficulty, *Señor.* When the railroad is completed, will you sell the land then?"

"No," Gabe replied.

"I see," Bernardo answered, his mouth a tight line.

"I'll give it to you," Gabe said.

Bernardo broke into a big smile. "You will give us this land, *Señor?*"

"Yes," Gabe said. "It is important to me now, only in that it helps to secure the loan for construction. Once the railroad is completed, I will have no further need of it. Giving it to your people may help this area to develop. That can only be good for the railroad."

Bernardo stood up and grabbed Gabe's hand. He began pumping it furiously. "Makenna is right. You are a fine man."

"Makenna?" Gabe asked, puzzled. "You've seen Makenna recently?"

"*Sí*," Bernardo answered. "Oh, and that reminds me, this is for you." Bernardo handed the pouch he had been carrying to Gabe.

"What is it?" Gabe asked.

"Open it, *Señor*."

Gabe opened the pouch and looked inside. It was filled with money.

"Look at this," he said. He dumped the money onto a table. "How much is here?"

"Very nearly one hundred and fifty thousand dollars," Bernardo said. "I think only about one hundred had been spent by the time I got it back."

"Got it back? What are you talking about?"

"*Señor*, this is the money Makenna borrowed from the Pacific Trust Bank," Bernardo explained.

"It can't be," Gabe said clearly puzzled by the turn of events. "I've already received that money. That's what we're working with right now."

"No, *Señor*," Bernardo explained. "The money you are working with now is the money Señor Emory Van Zandt paid Makenna to marry his son."

"What?"

"*Sí, Señor*," Bernardo said. "This money," he pointed to the money on the table, "was stolen from Makenna after she borrowed it. She went to see Emory Van Zandt to try and borrow more but he refused to loan her any. Then, when he discovered that you had borrowed from Pacific Trust, he threatened to close your railroad immediately. However, he gave Makenna a choice. She could marry Peter and he would not only call off the foreclosure but would give her the money you needed or she could refuse to marry Peter and you would be put out of business that very day."

"And so she—?" Gabe started but he was unable to finish his sentence, so struck was he with shame over the things, he had said and thought.

"*Sí Señor*. She married another to save you."

"My God," Gabe whispered. "How could I have been so blind?"

"Makenna loves you so much that she was willing to give you up for what she thought would be your happiness. *Señor*, I hope you will not make her sacrifice be in vain."

Gabe smiled broadly. "It won't be in vain," Gabe said. "I'm going to go after her."

"Good, *Señor*," Bernardo said. He stood up. "Now, I must deliver the good news to my friends, that the land will be returned to them when the railroad is completed."

"Oh," Gabe said. "Yes, that's right. Bernardo, I can't go after Makenna now. I must finish the railroad by the deadline or default and all the holdings, including the right-of-way land grants, will go to my backers. Please, you must do something for me."

"*Sí, Señor*. What is it?"

"Go see Makenna. Tell her of our conversation. Tell her that I'm coming for her when the railroad is finished."

"*Sí, Señor*, I will do this thing. *Adiós*."

Inside the engineering car, Peter Van Zandt stood at the window and peeked through the curtain as Bernardo rode away. There was only one other person in the car with Peter— Kellen O'Shea who was sitting near the telegraph instrument.

"I wonder what that Mexican wanted?" Peter asked.

"I suppose Gabe will tell us in good time," Kellen replied. "Maybe it's good news."

"Good news?"

"Maybe he's decided to quit fighting the railroad."

"Ha," Peter laughed. "I don't think that is likely to happen."

The telegraph began clacking and Kellen transcribed

the message. "Hey," he said. "This is a break. We're about to discover who killed Orchid Blossom."

"What? Who killed who? What are you talking about?" Peter asked.

Quickly, Kellen explained about the death of Orchid Blossom. He told how Long Li had found the handkerchief and wired to San Francisco for an identification check on the laundry number.

"It's about to come in now, as soon as the lines are cleared," Kellen said. "Whoever owned that handkerchief killed Orchid Blossom."

Peter remembered then that, earlier, he had missed his handkerchief. "That's silly," Peter said. "You mean to tell me that you think you can determine the killer just through a handkerchief?"

"It's obvious that whoever left that handkerchief out there killed her," Kellen said.

"But a bunch of numbers, what does that prove?"

"The Chinese are very thorough," Kellen said. "They've got a number for every customer they've ever had. It's simply a matter of looking it up."

"But that wouldn't be any good in a court of law, would it?"

"It'll be good enough in our court," Kellen replied. "We have our own law."

"I...Kellen, listen, there's something..."

"Shhh, it's coming in now," Kellen said.

Kellen hunched over the instrument, transcribing the dots and dashes. After a moment, he looked up at Peter with an expression of shock on his face. "It's you," he said quietly.

"It was an accident, Kellen," Peter said quickly. "I didn't mean to kill her. I don't know what got into the girl. I gave her some money and she went berserk. She attacked me for no good reason. I just tried to shove her away from me and she...she fell down that ravine. I swear to you it was an accident!"

"Then why didn't you say something when it happened?" Kellen asked.

"I was afraid no one would believe me," Peter said. "Anyway, what difference does it make?" he shrugged. "I mean she was Chinese; it's not like an American girl got killed or anything."

"She was a human being." Kellen said. "Same as us."

"Kellen, why don't you pretend you never received that wire?" Peter said. "I'd make it worth your while. How much money would you like? Ten thousand? Twenty thousand? After all, you're my father-in-law now, it would be keeping it in the family."

"What in the hell did my daughter ever see in you?" Kellen asked, his mouth twisted in a contemptuous snarl. He reached for his crutches. "I'll let Gabe decide."

As Kellen stood and turned his back to leave, Peter saw a ball peen hammer that had been left on Kellen's desk by one of the construction crew. Peter picked the hammer up, then coldly and calculatingly brought it smashing down on Kellen's head. He caught Kellen as he collapsed, then dragged him out onto the car platform. He looked around quickly and, upon seeing no one, flipped Kellen's body over the edge of the platform. Kellen's head struck the track and his crutches fell beside him. Peter smiled. It would look as if the old man had simply lost his balance and pitched off the platform onto the track.

Peter returned to the desk and tore the page off the message pad, slipped it into his pocket, then left the engineering car before anyone else saw him.

CHAPTER TWENTY-SEVEN

"I'm sorry, Mrs. Van Zandt," Wayne Gerhard said as he sorted bills of lading. "But it is against line regulations to attach any private car to a Western Pacific passenger train without specific authorization from our home office in Kansas City."

"Then get permission from the home office," Makenna said.

"I told you, I will send a letter."

"Can't you send a wire?"

"No," Gerhard said. "The regulations say that permission must be obtained in writing from the home office and authorized by the senior superintendent's signature. A wire is not the same thing."

"I want to leave here now," Makenna insisted

"I'm sorry. There's nothing I can do."

"Very well, I'll ship this car to San Francisco as freight. You can clear that here."

"You would have to be attached to a freight train," Gerhard said.

"I don't care," Makenna said. "Our car has everything that we will need. Besides, it will only be to Denver. Once we reach Denver, we'll change trains and, fortunately, lines as well."

Gerhard sighed and ran his hand over the top of his head. "Very well, Mrs. Van Zandt," he said. "I'll attach your car to the nine-forty-two freight. Please be ready."

"We will be ready," Makenna said. She returned to the car to tell Della the news and to help prepare the car for shipment.

They ate a light supper, then spent the evening talking until about nine-thirty, when Makenna heard the whistle of the approaching freight. "This is it," she told Della. "I'd better go see the trainmaster and make sure he notices that we are being shipped."

Makenna stood on the platform as the train approached. The arrival of a freight train didn't create nearly the excitement of a passenger train, so Makenna was practically alone as the giant 2-6-2 engine pounded by, throwing sparks and spraying steam. Car after car of the dark boxcars and flatcars slipped by until the train finally stopped. Makenna walked back to the only car showing light, the small caboose, and waited for the trainmaster to disembark.

"Well, hello, Makenna," Ross, the trainmaster said with a warm smile. "It's been a while since I saw you, lass. How is everything? How is your father?"

"Papa is just fine, Mr. Ross," Makenna said. She handed the trainmaster a shipping order.

"What's this? Don't tell me you're working for the WP again?"

"No," Makenna said. "This is a shipping order to attach my car to this train to pull it to Denver."

"Lass, you want to put a private car on a freight train?"

"Yes," Makenna said. "I've already paid the shipping

fee."

"But why, for Christ's sake? There are two more passenger trains leaving here today."

"Mr. Gerhard said that I can't attach to a passenger train without specific written approval from the home office."

"Hogwash," Ross said. "Station masters do it all up and down the line. The home office never says a thing about it. They welcome the revenue."

"Well, you know what a stickler Mr. Gerhard is for regulations," Makenna said.

"Come along, lass, we'll talk to him," Ross invited.

Gerhard was scribbling in a large ledger book when Makenna and Ross went into the depot.

"Gerhard, what is this business about attaching Makenna's private car to my train?" Ross asked.

"She paid the fare," Gerhard answered without looking up. "She's entitled to have her car moved."

"Yes, but by a freight? My God, man, there are two passenger trains leaving out of here tonight. Attach her car to one of them."

"That's against regulations," Gerhard insisted.

"To hell with that," Ross exploded. "That regulation is consistently disregarded by every station master on the line."

"Not by this station master," Gerhard insisted.

"I'm not sure but what that's been overridden by now anyway," Ross said.

"Until I get a regulation superseding it, I intend to follow it as it is written," Gerhard replied.

"Gerhard, do you know what we've got here?" Ross asked. "We've got a forty-car freight with no provisions to connect to a passenger car. The coupling isn't even designed for that. It would be dangerous to attach this girl's car to the end of that train."

"She doesn't have to go," Gerhard said.

"Makenna, I'd advise you to wait," Ross said.

"No," Makenna replied resolutely. "I intend to get out of here tonight. I don't care if you have to jerry-rig the coupling. I just want to leave. Please, hook up our car."

Ross sighed. "Very well, Makenna. I'll pick up your car."

"Thank you," Makenna replied.

***

"Here you are, boss," Bull shouted as the engine and special car pulled into camp. He hopped off the car and ran over to Gabe. "She rode as safe as a babe in its mother's arms. It's a good thing, too, not only for my sake, but because I'm told there's not another ounce of the stuff this side of Cincinnati."

"I'm glad you made it back all right," Gabe said quietly.

"Well, you don't look glad," Bull said. "What the hell's wrong?"

"In there," Gabe said, pointing to the private car which had been his but which he had given to Kellen to use. "Kellen's in there."

"In there? Why didn't he come out to meet me?"

"He's dead," Gabe said.

Bull's face registered his shock. "What happened? Did he get sick or what?"

"He fell off the back of the engineering car," Gabe said. "His head hit the track."

"Was he out on the platform when the car was being moved?" Bull asked.

"No, the car hasn't been moved. He just fell off."

"You mean to tell me he just walked out there and fell off?" Bull said. "I don't believe it. You know how well he handled himself."

"I know," Gabe agreed. "It does seem hard to believe. But the evidence speaks for itself."

"Well, I'll be damned," Bull said. "I really liked the guy. What about Makenna? Shouldn't she be told?"

"Yes," Gabe said. "Of course, Peter should tell her but I don't know where he is. I'll go in first thing in the morning to tell her. There's no sense in upsetting her tonight."

"You're probably right. You want me to go in with you in the mornin'?"

"No. You stay here and supervise the blasting," Gabe said.

"Speaking of blasting, where's Long Li? I thought sure he'd want to be here to see his new firecrackers."

Long Li was at that moment confronting Peter Van Zandt. He had told Peter that he had something of urgent importance to discuss with him and asked that Peter come to the tent the Chinese cooks used. They were alone in the tent and Long Li studied Peter's features for a long, silent while before he spoke.

"You killed Kellen O'Shea," Long Li finally said. It wasn't an accusation; it was a simple statement of fact.

"What? Don't be ridiculous," Peter sputtered. "Why would I kill him? He was my father-in-law."

"You killed him because he discovered that you murdered Orchid Blossom."

"Old man, you've gone crazy," Peter said.

Long Li put his hand in his pocket and withdrew two coins. He showed them to Peter. "I found this money by the girl's body," he said quietly. His words slid out smoothly as if lubricated by the finest oils. There was something strange about them and, for a moment, Peter was puzzled. Then he realized what it was. The man who normally spoke only in pidgin English was speaking as clearly as an Oxford scholar.

"You've lost your accent," Peter said.

"I want to be most certain that you understand my every word," Long Li said.

"All right, so you found that money by the girl's body. What does that mean?"

"I know the girl was attracted to you," Long Li said. "And you were quite obviously attracted to her. Her interest was emotional, yours was carnal. When you finished with her, you offered to pay her money. She was offended and attacked you, so you fought her off. In so doing, you broke her neck."

"I don't know what you are talking about," Peter said.

"This is all conjecture, to be sure," Long Li went on. "But I found a handkerchief at the scene with a laundry mark. I believe it was your laundry mark, Mr. Van Zandt. I believe Mr. O'Shea received verification of that from San Francisco and you, somehow, discovered it. So you killed him. But I still have the handkerchief, Mr. Van Zandt, and as soon as another telegrapher is available, I shall ask that the message be conveyed to me."

Peter's hand flashed to his shoulder holster but even as the gun was coming clear of leather, Long Li's hand was there. A very quick thrust of Long Li's hand sent Peter's pistol into the air. Long Li brought the back of his hand across Peter's face then, so fast as to be almost one blow, he slapped Peter's face with the palm of his hand.

"No!" Peter shouted, suddenly terrified by the strange behavior of a man he had so long regarded as practically subhuman.

"Do not worry, Mr. Van Zandt," Long Li said. "I do not intend to kill you. That would be too quick and too painless. I am going to watch you suffer the turning wheels of justice. Before, when there was only the Chinese girl involved, I could not be certain that justice would be done. Now, with the death of an Occidental, I think there is every possibility we will be privileged to watch you hang by the neck until you are dead."

Long Li opened the cylinder gate on Peter's pistol and ejected the shells. They fell to the ground, one at a time, until all six lay there.

"Good day, Mr. Van Zandt." Long Li returned the pistol to Peter, who slid it back into his holster. He turned and quickly left the tent.

"Ah, there you are, little buddy," Bull said, stepping into the tent a moment later.

"Bull, most gratified to see nitro not explode you," Long Li said. The words and rhythm of his speech pattern returned to the Long Li everyone knew.

"You ain't no more gratified than I am, little buddy. Anyhow, I got the stuff here, 'n it's ready for you as soon as you are."

"Now I am ready," Long Li said. "I have hole prepared for first charge. I will take the nitro I need into position."

"Don't waste any of this stuff, buddy," Bull said. "This is all there is."

"I should be able to do it in three explosions," Long Li said.

"Well, let's get on it," Bull said, leading Long Li to the nitro.

"It's getting a little late in the day," Gabe told Long Li, as Long Li climbed onto the car and looked at the vat of nitro. "Are you sure you don't want to wait until morning?"

"Time is running short, Boss Hansen," Long Li said.

"Maybe do one blast tonight and we catch up."

"All right, Long Li. Whatever you say," Gabe agreed.

Long Li took a detonating container from the package of containers that were designed for that purpose and prepared to transfer enough for the first charge. He ran a small blue flag up on a pole, then looked back at Gabe. "Boss Hansen, more better everyone get back from this car until I have nitro I need. When I have the nitro, I will take blue flag down."

"All right, you heard the man," Gabe said. "Everybody get back, all the way around the bend in the tracks!"

Everyone in the crew followed Gabe's instructions. The engine backed away along with the workers. Word was sent through the rubble-closed pass to the other side, to inform those who were still on the far side of the pass not to come around until they got further word. That included Rosie's girls.

"You ever handled nitro, boss?" Bull asked as he and Gabe watched from a rock ledge. They were so far away that Long Li was no more than a small figure in the distance.

"I've assisted," Gabe said. "How about you?"

"Are you kiddin'? Could you see me wrappin' these big mitts around a container of nitro? I'd set it off just by holdin' it."

"I've never seen anyone who could work with dynamite better than Long Li," Gabe said. "If he is that good with nitro, we'll have no worries."

"If he ain't that good, he'll have plenty of worries," Bull said.

"What's takin' him so long?" someone asked.

"You don't hurry that stuff up," Bull said.

"Hey, boss I nearly forgot. We left Kellen back there in

his car. But I guess it shouldn't matter to him.

"I don't know," Gabe said. "I'm going to hate having to tell Makenna about the accident, I know that."

"Hey, he's put the flag down," someone said. "Can we go back?"

"Let's go," Gabe said.

The crowd of workers moved slowly back down the track, but even before they reached the camp, Long Li was already out the other side, climbing up the mountainside to lay in the first charge.

Peter had climbed the mountain when everyone else left the camp. It was easy to slip away in all the confusion and, now, he was several hundred feet above the pass and above the point Long Li had marked for his first charge.

Nothing had worked out as it should for Peter. He had not wanted to be associated with this foolish railroad venture in the first place but he took it because, in so doing, it allowed him to put a great deal of distance between him and his father.

At the thought of his father, Peter's stomach reacted. He hated his father...oh, how he loathed him. He was always holding others up to Peter, extolling the virtues of hard work, honest enterprise, and ambition. Ambition and hard work had killed Peter's mother. Afterwards, there was only his father to goad and taunt, cajole, push and hound him, to mold him after his own image.

But Peter rebelled. He purposely stood for everything his father was against and hated everything his father stood for. It had been a victory of sorts to marry the girl his father had chosen for him and then sit back and deny his father the grandchild he so desperately wanted.

Then when things seemed to be going their best, a

simple little sexual act with a simple Chinese girl had backfired. It was baffling to Peter. How had it gotten this far? He had been sampling the favors of Chinese girls since the onset of puberty and it had all been made possible by a few coins. Why was this one different? Did Long Li mean to imply that this foolish little girl actually thought that he, Peter, could love her? Was the girl that stupid? If so, it was probably a very lucky break for him that the girl had been killed.

But it wasn't lucky that he was caught. He should have paid more attention to what he was doing. Dropping the handkerchief there had been a very careless blunder. But the blunder could be corrected. Kellen was dead and now only Long Li remained. And soon, he too would be dead.

Peter checked the boulder beside him and dug the crowbar in beneath it. He had taken the bar from the tool car, intending to use it as a weapon against the Chinaman. But then he got a better idea. If he could dislodge a few boulders and start them toward him, Long Li would be trapped. The boulders wouldn't even have to kill him, just make him move out of the way. As volatile as the nitro was, that would be enough. A rapid move would cause the nitro to detonate.

Peter raised up and saw Long Li approaching the blasting site. He waited one more minute until Long Li was in place, then moved around behind the rock. He began pushing on the bar, straining against it. Finally, it began to move, a little at a time and then all of it. With it went a couple dozen other rocks, not quite as large but big enough to start an impressive slide.

The slide was large enough to be noticed from ground level. Gabe saw it first.

"Oh my God, Bull, look!" Gabe said, pointing to the rocks, which cascaded toward Long Li.

"Long Li!" Bull yelled. "Look out!" There was just time for the echo of Bull's voice to return to them, haunting in its tone of horror, and then a stomach-jarring explosion erupted on the side of the mountain. Tons of rock and dirt slid down the mountainside and, when the smoke and dust cleared away, Long Li was no more.

CHAPTER TWENTY-EIGHT

For the first leg of the trip toward Denver, Ross rode in the private car with Makenna and Della. Ross was fifty-one years old and Makenna had known him since she was a very young girl. She knew him to be an honest and open man and she had always liked him. They talked about amusing incidents from the past but Makenna noticed that Ross managed to slip in the fact, more than once, that his wife had died. He said this, ostensibly, to Makenna but in such a way as to ensure that Della heard it as well because, despite the difference in their ages, it was obvious that Ross was quite taken with her.

"You must have an awfully responsible job, Mr. Ross," Della said. "Rather like being captain of a ship, I would imagine."

"Please, call me Caleb," Ross said. He beamed under the girl's interest and smiled as broadly as a schoolboy who had been noticed by the prettiest girl in class. "Yes, it is rather important—Emma, that's my late wife, Emma, she's dead now, you know...I'm a widower..."

Makenna hid a smile from the two of them. This was at least the fourth time he'd mentioned it.

"Emma used to say that having a job this responsible kept me young. And you know, I believe it does. It keeps you alert physically and mentally all the time."

The train slowed to a stop.

"Oh, dear, not again," Makenna said. "Why do you suppose we have stopped?"

Caleb Ross pulled his silver-cased Elgin Engineer's Special watch from his pocket and flipped it open. "We're waiting for the southbound Midnight Flyer," he said. "Passenger trains have the right-of-way on the line. We have to pull over for all of them."

"Well, then shall I serve some tea?" Della asked.

"That would be nice," Makenna agreed.

"Thank you, ma'am, I take that most kindly of you," Ross said.

They just had time to finish their tea before they heard the Midnight Flyer approaching on the adjacent track.

"Right on time," Ross said, looking again at his watch.

The engineer of the Midnight Flyer blew his whistle in greeting and the great train rushed by at fifty miles per hour, smoke and steam trailing back in long wisps, great driver wheels pounding at the rails, and sparks flying from the firebox. The blast of air and noise from its passing shook the car like a cork bobbing on water. The lighted windows of the cars streamed by so fast as to be almost one long blur of light. Within a moment, the last car flashed by, and Makenna saw the red and green lamps at the train's end, already receding in the distance.

"Oh, my, how magnificent!" Della said. "I do believe that was the most marvelous thing I have ever witnessed!"

"I'll go see the engineer and see if we can't speed up a bit ourselves," Ross said.

"You can't walk up to the engine," Della protested.

"Suppose he started up while you were still on the ground? You'd be left."

"Oh, I won't be goin' along the ground, ma'am," Ross said. "I'll be going topside." He pointed to the top of the car.

"Topside?"

"He's going to go along the tops of the cars," Makenna explained.

"Oh, my, isn't that a bit dangerous?"

"Certainly," Ross said. "For someone who doesn't know what he's doin'. But not to worry, miss, I been runnin' the cars since before you was born."

Ross stepped outside, and just as the train got underway again, he climbed to the top of the car and started forward.

"Isn't he a wonderful man?" Della asked.

"He's very nice," Makenna agreed. "Even if he is pretty old."

"I don't care how old he is," Della said. "In England, I saw many proper gentlemen married to ladies who weren't a third their age. It's different for women."

"Oh, I wasn't finding fault," Makenna said quickly. "Besides, it's obvious that he likes you."

"Oh, do you think he does?" Della asked. "Oh, Makenna, wouldn't that be just too wonderful?"

Ross reached the engine cab and dropped down to talk with the engineer. The fireman had just restoked the furnace and was looking at the steam pressure. They both turned around when Ross dropped in on them.

"Didn't think you'd come up to visit us with the pretty ladies back there," the engineer teased.

"I've got a job to do just like you," Ross said.

"Hey, what was that?" the fireman suddenly yelled. He pointed ahead of the onrushing engine, and they saw a few random rocks sliding down a rock wall and rolling across the tracks.

"Did they clear the tracks?" the engineer asked anxiously.

"Yeah, I think so."

The engine flashed by the spot where the rocks had fallen and the three men in the cab breathed more easily.

"Must have been a deer or something kicked a few rocks loose," Ross suggested.

"Yeah, it happens all the time," the engineer replied.

But it wasn't a deer. Two hundred feet above the narrow cut through which the tracks ran, a small normally dry creek bed was straining to hold a raging torrent of water, the result of extraordinarily strong mountain rains. The normally dry creek bed now held ten feet of swiftly moving water, and trees and other debris rushed pell-mell downstream.

The creek bed wasn't large enough to hold the torrent, so in accordance with the forces of nature, the water was enlarging the creek bed, cutting its own channel. Dirt and rock had to be removed to widen the channel and it was from this action that the few rocks had fallen across the track. In addition to those few rocks, however, a tremendous cut was being hydraulically excavated where the creek made a long sweeping bend. The bend was right above a gigantic overhang that guarded the entry of the tracks into a long tunnel, known as the Munson Tunnel after its builder. Already rocks were beginning to drop onto the track though, so far, the fall was inconsequential.

"I came up here to see if you could get any more out of this hog," Ross said, using the railroader's term for a locomotive.

"Hey, what do you think you're in, a high-liner? We ain't pullin' passengers, Ross, we're pullin' freight. We ain't nothin' but a rattler."

"Yeah, but we're ridin' the high iron," Ross said. "And the regs say that any train on the main line may make as much speed as is safe to maintain."

"We'll give 'er what we got, Ross," the engineer said. "You gonna boiler head?"

"No, I'm goin' back to the shack," he said.

"Shack, my ass. You ain't goin' to the caboose," the engineer teased. "You're goin' back to the drone cage where them pretty ladies are."

"I might look in on 'em," Ross admitted.

"Well, you'd better stay up here until we clear Munson Tunnel. Get caught on top of the cars while we're in there and you'll get swept off."

"Much further?"

"'Bout a quarter of a mile," the engineer said. "The light'll pick it up directly."

The train pounded on down the track, the poles lighting up, then whipping by. Finally, the dark maw of the tunnel loomed ahead of them. Ross happened to look up just as they went inside and saw something that made his blood run cold.

"My God!" he shouted. "There's a landslide. Half the damn mountain is coming down!"

The engineer reached for the brakes and the locomotive wheels locked in place. The walls of the tunnel were painted orange from the glow of sparks that flew from the sliding wheels.

"No, that's no good, you've got to get us out of here! Open her up full!" Ross yelled.

The engineer released the brakes and slammed the throttle to full open. As the train had still been sliding forward, the application of the throttle allowed it to regain its momentum easily, and it shot ahead again.

Forty cars back the drone cage, or private car, in which Makenna and Della were riding, was caught up first in the train's attempt to stop, and then in the continued motion to go forward. That had the effect of "popping the whip," and the car, which had a coupling system designed for passenger use and thus was jerry-rigged to the freight, separated from the rest of the train. It continued to roll forward on its own momentum and, for several seconds, there was no indication of what had happened. But then it became obvious as the car began to slow. Della was looking forward and she saw it first.

"Makenna, the train has broken away from us!" she shouted.

"What?" Makenna ran to the front of the car and saw the train pulling away. She also saw the black opening of the tunnel and knew that they would probably come to a stop somewhere inside. That could be extremely dangerous. If the engineer didn't realize he had lost the car and they were left sitting on the track in the tunnel, the next train through could crash into them.

Makenna was about to voice her fear when she noticed an even more immediate danger. For this, she didn't have time to shout a warning, just emit a scream. The rock slide hit at about the same time they entered the tunnel and the car came to a smashing halt.

The sound was unlike anything Makenna had ever heard in her life. It was a terrible, wrenching, smashing sound, which seemed to go on forever. The windows of the car were broken, the top came crashing down, and the furniture was smashed. She and Della were knocked to the floor by the shock of the blast, then another crash shook the car, and for Makenna, everything went black.

The rest of the train emerged from the other side and

Ross let out a whoop of relief. "We made it through! Come on, pour on the coal, we've got to get to the next stop so we can send a warning about the tunnel being closed. There won't be any more trains tonight, that's for sure."

"We'll be in Colby's Switch in fifteen minutes," the engineer said. "He has a telegraph there."

"I'd better go back and see if our two passengers are all right," Ross said.

Ross climbed to the top of the first car, then began running toward the rear of the train. It was dark, and the train was making maximum speed, but Ross was at home here as the ordinary person is strolling down the street. He was agile and sure-footed, and he jumped from car to car with ease, until he stood on the last car and gazed down with shock at the sight that greeted him.

Makenna's private car wasn't there!

Bernardo was in the Albuquerque station when word came in. The Munson Tunnel was closed by a landslide and Makenna Van Zandt's private car was trapped inside.

"Is she still alive?" Bernardo asked, when he heard the news.

"They don't know," Gerhard answered. "There are tons of rock covering them. If they are alive now, chances are they won't be long. They'll smother."

"You've got to send a message for me," Bernardo said.

"No private messages during a company emergency," Gerhard said.

"But it's to the girl's husband and father at End-of-Track," Bernardo said. "They must be notified of this!"

"I'm sorry," Gerhard said. He opened a book of regulations. "It clearly states here that during the time of a company emergency, the wires must be kept clear for emergency messages."

"Damnit, man, this is an emergency message!" Bernardo insisted.

"It is not a company message," Gerhard said.

Bernardo thought of pulling his pistol and using it to force the man to send a message but he realized that he couldn't read telegraphy and there would be no way to verify it. There was only one thing left and that was to ride out to the pass. Bernardo winced as he thought of it. That was over forty miles and the only way there was by horse since there were no engines available.

Bernardo sprang to the saddle and urged Diablo into a gallop. As he rode out of town, bent low over Diablo's neck and raising clouds of dust behind him, he formulated a plan. There were at least two ranches between Albuquerque and the pass where he knew he would be able to change mounts. If he rode Diablo and the other two horses at full speed, he could reach the camp in about two hours. That would put him there by three in the morning. That could present a problem if they had a nervous sentry posted.

Bernardo rode into the first ranch at a full gallop. He rode straight to the corral, yelling as he rode in. By the time he had the saddle off Diablo and had selected another mount, a lantern appeared in the window of the bunkhouse.

"Who is there?" someone shouted in Spanish.

"It is I, Bernardo Tafoya. I must cover a great distance quickly. I am leaving my horse here, I must borrow one of yours."

Bernardo had finished saddling the new mount by the time the explanation was completed and he swung onto the fresh horse. "*Adiós!*" he yelled as he galloped away.

"*Adiós*, Bernardo. Go with God!" came the return greeting.

The second transfer went just as smoothly and, almost before Bernardo realized it, he was approaching the camp. He began yelling, calling Gabe's name, so that the sentry would not be surprised and shoot out of fear.

"Gabe, Gabe!" he shouted as the horse pounded into the camp at a full gallop.

The gandy dancers, who were sleeping nearby and who were awakened by the shouts, yelled curses at the man who had disturbed their slumber. The Chinese were also awakened and Bernardo could hear their voices babbling in excitement and curiosity. Gabe appeared at the back door of his caboose.

"Bernardo, what is it?" Gabe asked.

Bernardo dismounted and walked over to the car. He was breathing heavily, and his mount was covered with the white foam of a hard sweat.

"Look at your animal!" Gabe said. "You must have ridden as if all the demons of hell were after you!"

"I have ridden from Albuquerque in two hours," Bernardo said.

"Two hours? That's impossible," someone said.

Bernardo held up his hand. "Please, I've no time to talk of this. I have come about Makenna."

"Makenna? What about her?" Gabe asked.

"There has been an accident. I did not get to see her to deliver the message you wanted because she had already left for San Francisco. But there was a wreck."

"A train wreck? My God, is she hurt? Where is she?"

"I don't know if she is hurt," Bernardo said. "She is trapped in a place called the Munson Tunnel. There was a rockslide. They say tons of rocks cover her car. If they don't get her out soon, she will suffocate."

"Boss, how they gonna move that rock?" Bull asked. He

had been awakened by the noise and joined them in time to hear Bernardo's message.

"They'll have to blast it out," Gabe said.

"That's just what I mean," Bull said. "There ain't nothin' left to blast with, remember? We got it all and we ain't got much of it left."

"He's right," Gabe said. "Bernardo, there isn't any dynamite available. We'll have to use our nitro."

"Boss, are you crazy? Who are you gonna get that will work with nitro? You saw what happened to Long Li last night. I don't believe I can get any of the Chinamen to work with it now and I know none of the Irishmen will."

"I'll do it," Gabe insisted.

"You've never done it before." Bull said.

"I've assisted," Gabe replied. "I know what to do."

"Even if you could do it, you've got to get the stuff there."

"Fire up the engine," Gabe ordered. "I'll pull that special car you designed."

"Boss, that car was good for bringing it out here, but I only had to bring it from the Madden mines. That's about twenty miles, and it took me two hours to get it here. You've got more'n one hundred and twenty miles to go. At ten miles an hour, it would be too late by the time you got there."

"I'll pull just the one car," Gabe said. "I'll run at full speed. I'll be there in less than two hours."

"You pull that stuff at full speed and you'll be dead in less than two hours," Bull said.

"I have no choice," Gabe said. "I don't expect anyone to go with me. I'll run the engine myself."

"You'll need someone to fire it," Bull said.

"I will fire it," Bernardo offered.

"No offense meant, mister," Bull said. "But to shovel coal for this kind of a run, it's going to take someone with more muscle than brain. That'll be me, I reckon."

"I am going with you, Señor," Bernardo said.

"There's no need for you to take that risk," Gabe said.

"I am going," Bernardo said again, more resolutely than before.

"Very well," Gabe said. "I'll be dressed in a moment."

"Perhaps I should tell her father," Bernardo suggested.

"He's dead," Gabe said. "I'll tell you about it on the trip."

"I can think of no one else who needs be told, can you, *Señor?*" Bernardo asked pointedly.

"No," Gabe said. "I can think of no one else."

CHAPTER TWENTY-NINE

When Makenna came to, she heard sobbing. "Della?"

"Makenna, oh, Makenna," Della said. "Thank God you aren't dead. When I couldn't get you to answer me, I thought you'd been killed."

It was so dark inside the twisted wreckage of the car that Makenna couldn't see her hand in front of her face. "Where are you?" Makenna asked.

"I'm over here, mum," Della answered. "Close to where the settee was, I believe."

"Are you all right?"

"I don't know," Della said. "There is something lying across my legs, and I can't move."

"I'll try and get to you," Makenna said. She began inching forward slowly, picking through the rubble and the wreckage, feeling her way with outstretched hands. "Keep talking so I can find you," she said.

"What'll I say?"

"Anything."

"My name is Della Holmes, and I was born in Tilbury on the Thames. I came to..."

"I'm here," Makenna said, reaching the girl at that

moment. She put her hand out and touched Della's face. Della grabbed her fingers and squeezed tightly.

"Are you in pain?"

"No, mum, not really," Della said. "The fact is, I can't feel anything in my legs."

"Well, hang on, Della. We'll get out of here."

"How, Makenna?" Della asked. Her voice cracked. "I wasn't knocked out the way you were. It sounded like the whole mountain fell in on us."

"Gabe will get us out," Makenna said.

"Gabe?"

"Yes," Makenna's voice was firm. "He'll come and he'll get us out of here."

"Oh, Lordy, mum, I wish I had something like that to cling to. But I fear we're going to die in this awful place."

"No," Makenna said calmly. "We won't."

Makenna couldn't explain the calmness she felt. She knew that the odds were very much against their escaping. But somehow, she felt they would. And, just as strongly, she felt that Gabe was going to play a part in it.

The throttle was wide open and the engine was speeding at more than seventy miles per hour.

"This is faster than I've ever been in my life!" Bernardo shouted.

"This is faster than ninety-nine percent of the human race has ever been," Gabe replied. "How does our load look? The box hasn't slipped in the ropes, has it?"

Bernardo hopped back to the tender, then climbed up onto the pile of coal so he could see the one trailing car. He returned to the engine and yelled at Gabe and Bull.

"It is still as it was."

"We're going to have to stop in Albuquerque to make

certain the tracks are cleared ahead," Bull said.

"You know Gerhard," Gabe replied. "That son-of-a-bitch probably wouldn't give us clearance anyway. Just go on through."

"But if there's someone ahead of us, we're dead ducks," Bull said. "And if it's a passenger train, there'll be a lot of innocent people go with us."

"Slow the train down when we reach Albuquerque," Bernardo said. "I will jump off and have a talk with Mr. Gerhard. He will clear the tracks ahead."

"You think you can talk him into it?" Bull asked.

Bernardo smiled and patted his pistol. "I think so," he replied.

The train began slowing gradually as they approached Albuquerque, in order to avoid the shock of stopping too quickly. Such a stop could set off the nitro and destroy not only the train but a goodly portion of Albuquerque as well. By the time they rolled into the yard, they were traveling no faster than a man could walk.

"Son-of-a-bitch," Bull swore. "The damned switch is closed!"

"I'll open it," Gabe said. He pulled the brake lever and the train stopped. Gabe jumped down and ran to the switch, only to find it locked. "Bernardo!" he called.

"Yes," Bernardo answered. He jumped down and ran to Gabe.

"Can you use that gun or is it for decoration?"

Bernardo saw the lock, and without a word pulled his pistol and fired a shot. The padlock flew apart, and Gabe opened the switch.

"Get that track open ahead," Gabe said, starting back toward the train.

Bull opened the throttle as soon as he saw Gabe returning to the engine, so Gabe caught it as it was already rolling.

"What is this? What's going on here?" Gerhard yelled, running out to the track.

"Good morning, *Señor*," Bernardo said. "Perhaps you would be so kind as to return to your telegraph instrument and signal for the track to be cleared between here and the tunnel?"

"I will do no such thing," Gerhard insisted. "That is an unauthorized locomotive!"

"It is also carrying a great deal of nitroglycerine," Bernardo said. "So I'd advise you to clear the tracks."

"I will not."

Bernardo pulled his pistol and shot the hat from Gerhard's head.

"All right," Gerhard shouted in panic. "I'll clear the track. But if any trouble comes down from the home office, I intend to let them know that I was forced into it."

"You do that, *Señor*," Bernardo said, smiling at him.

Gabe blew the whistle in a series of short blasts, denoting an emergency, and the abbreviated train was almost up to full speed again by the time it cleared the Albuquerque yard.

The sun was barely full disc up, a bright orange ball still touching the horizon and painting the mountains with various hues of red and gold as they approached the Munson Tunnel. Gabe slowed the train down as they came around the final bend.

Suddenly, there were three sharp explosions and a flash of light bathed the engine cab!

"What the—?" Bull yelled.

"We ran over their warning torpedoes," Gabe said. "It's

just a signal that the track is closed."

Bull let out an audible sigh and then smiled. "Boss, I swear I thought the angel Gabriel had come for me."

Gabe pulled the brake and the train came to a full stop about fifteen yards short of where the tunnel entrance used to be. There was nothing there now but a large pile of rubble. Several people, men and women, were crowded around the collapsed entrance and Gabe recognized Caleb Ross. He called to Ross as he hopped down from the engine.

"Mr. Hansen, I didn't expect to see you here," Ross said, coming over to him.

"What's the situation?" Gabe asked.

"It looks bad," Ross answered. "There are two women trapped inside."

"Just two? How did everyone get out?"

"There wasn't anyone else," Ross said. "Makenna O'Shea had a private car and it was connected to the end of a freight. Her car separated just before we entered the tunnel. It rolled in, then was hit by the landslide."

"Separated? You mean the engineer snapped it off, don't you?" Gabe asked angrily.

"It was an accident, Mr. Hansen," Ross said. "Believe me, the engineer feels as badly about it as you do."

"I doubt that," Gabe replied. He walked up to the entrance, then climbed a pile of rock and looked around. "It's closed solid here, how about the approach from the other end?"

"Completely collapsed," Ross replied. "We'll have to go in from this end."

"Have you heard anything from them? Any contact?"

"No."

"Have you tried?"

"Yes, we've tried."

"Them girls is dead if you want my opinion," a by-stander said.

"I don't want your damned opinion," Gabe said angrily. He looked at the man. "Are you associated with the railroad in any way?"

"No."

"Then get the hell out of my way," Gabe ordered. Gabe climbed back down the pile of rubble and looked at the morbid crowd. It surprised him to see so many this early in the morning.

The relief valve on the engine he had brought in popped open and a loud stream of steam shot out. Several of the people who had been standing close to the engine jumped back nervously.

"Are you goin' to try and get 'em outta there, mister?" one woman asked. Gabe looked at the woman who spoke. Of an indeterminate age, she could have been anywhere between twenty-five and fifty. She wore a gray dress that hung shapelessly from her thin frame. Her hair had the color and texture of sunburned grass. Her skin was weathered and wrinkled and she held a baby clutched against her flat bosom.

Gabe felt some of his anger slide away as he looked at the woman. She advertised the difficult life of the frontier by her very appearance. Naturally, she was drawn to the scene of the accident. Anything, even something as potentially gruesome as a railway accident, was a welcome respite from the tedious day-to-day struggle of just staying alive.

"Well, are you, mister?" the woman asked again. "Try 'n get 'em outta there, I mean."

"Yes, ma'am, I'm going to try damned hard," Gabe said. "Ross, who is in charge around here?"

"As far as I know, I am," Ross said. "None of the line supervisors have showed up yet."

"Then let's get to work," Gabe said.

"Mr. Hansen, we've already dug around there. There's nothing we can do until we get some dynamite in. We'll have to blast that stuff out of there."

"You won't find any dynamite this side of the Mississippi River," Gabe said. "We'll have to do it ourselves."

"With what?" Ross asked.

"Nitro."

"Where are you going to find nitro? And how would you get it put here in time?"

"I've already got it," Gabe said. He pointed to the flatcar behind the puffing engine. "There it is."

"Good Lord! You mean you were carrying nitro when you came roaring up here?"

"That's right," Gabe said. He rubbed his hands together. "I don't suppose you've ever worked with it before."

"Not me, no sir!" Ross said.

"All right, I'll do it," Gabe said. He waved back to the engine at Bull. "Bull, help me find the best place to set it."

"You sure you can do this?" Ross asked.

"The way I see it, we don't have much choice in the matter," Gabe replied.

"I don't know…what if something goes wrong?"

"Ross, damnit, if we don't do something, those women are going to die for lack of air."

"Yes, but we don't even know if they are still alive."

"If they are dead, then it won't make any difference if something goes wrong," Gabe said angrily. "Now are you going to help or not?"

"I'll help," Ross said. "What do you want me to do?"

"Keep everyone away from that car," he said. "And

when I start laying in the charge, get everyone back out of the way."

"Boss, I think we can move this stuff outta here," Bull said. He had been examining the rubble. "This ain't no different from what we do every day. Just a matter of movin' a little bit of dirt."

"Where do you think?" Gabe asked.

Bull pointed to two locations. "If we can touch 'em off here and here," he said, "it should pitch this whole damned pile right off and into the canyon below."

"All right, help me get the holes ready. I'll plant the stuff by myself."

"Let's get started," Bull said.

The two men worked quickly, digging the holes for the charges, placing them in such a way as to direct the force of the blast where it would do the most good. Finally, after nearly an hour's preparation, they were ready to place the charges.

"All right, Bull, here goes," Gabe said finally. "You back the engine up and keep everyone the hell out of here."

"I'll keep 'em back, don't worry."

Suddenly several dozen rocks came tumbling down from the mountain top above them. They were relatively small rocks, and they bounced harmlessly across the track and the canyon on the other side.

"What was that?" Gabe asked.

"That's what caused this collapse in the first place," Ross said. "The creeks are flooding and causing rock slides."

"Damn, that's all we need." The image of Long Li being caught in a rockslide as he placed a charge last night came into Gabe's mind.

"Maybe you ought to wait," Bull suggested tentatively.

"Wait for what?"

"Wait for some more of the railroad people to get here. Maybe one of them can handle nitro."

"I'll do it," Gabe said.

"Then at least wait and see if there is going to be another rockslide," Bull warned.

"I don't figure we have time to wait. I've got to get those charges planted now."

"All right, boss," Bull said, shrugging his shoulders. "It's your funeral."

"Couldn't you have chosen a better expression?" Gabe asked with a short, nervous laugh.

Bull and Ross moved the engine and the curious back down the track and Gabe loaded two detonating containers with the remainder of the nitro. Once they were both loaded, he started climbing back up the hill to place them in the holes he and Bull had prepared. The footing was difficult and, once, he slipped and fell to one knee. He was unable to break his fall with his hands because he was carrying a container of nitro in each hand. Therefore, his knee struck a rock sharply and he felt an excruciating pain shooting through him. When he stood up again, the knee was throbbing angrily and a quick heat began to build just below the kneecap. It was painful but he could tell from the movement of the cap that it wasn't broken.

Gabe finally got the first charge in place and the detonating fuse attached. He limped over to the second spot when he saw a train approaching. The train stopped just behind the engine Bull had backed out of the way and a couple of men hopped out and started running down the track toward Gabe.

"Get back!" Gabe shouted. "Get back, I'm working with nitro!"

"Hansen, get down from there," one of the men ordered.

"Who are you?" Gabe asked.

"I am Chief Railroad Detective Mason Emerson. You are not authorized here, and I am ordering you down right now."

"You go to hell," Gabe called back. "I'm going to blow this rockslide out of here. There are two women trapped inside or haven't you been told?"

"I know there are two women in there," Emerson said.

"I intend to get them out."

"We'll get them out."

"How, by digging with your hands?"

"We have two cars of men with us," Emerson answered. "We'll dig them out."

"You don't have time," Gabe said. "They may be dying in there. Now get back out of the way so I can plant this last charge."

Emerson pulled his pistol and pointed it up at Gabe. "Mr. Hansen, I am ordering you down from there at once."

Gabe drew his arm back as if to throw the nitro. He pointed at Emerson and the man who had come with him. "Lay your gun down on the track and get the hell out of here or I'll throw this at you right now." he said.

"What? Are you crazy?"

"Lay your gun down, Emerson," he said. "You, too," he pointed at the other man.

"I don't have a gun," the other man said.

"Well, you better find one quick, because unless I see one lying there beside his, I'm throwing this thing at you."

The other man reached behind his jacket and pulled out a pistol, then laid it on the ground beside Emerson's gun.

"I'm glad you remembered where you left it," Gabe said. "Now, get out of here, both of you." Both men turned and ran back down the track. Gabe waited a few moments longer, then planted the second charge and attached the fuse to it as well. He strung the fuse back along the tracks until he was well clear of the area and then he lit it.

"Lordy, Makenna, what was that?" Della asked as the explosion shook the very ground.

"They're here," Makenna said excitedly. "They're blasting for us. Della, I told you Gabe would come."

The rock started shifting and sliding and the two girls could hear the car being ripped open. Dirt and small rocks started streaming in through the rent in the roof of the car.

"That's making it worse!" Della cried. "Oh, we're going to be killed!"

The car began tipping and tearing and more and more dirt fell in. Della reached for Makenna and held her tightly. The car tipped completely over and the two girls went sliding to the opposite side. Whatever had trapped Della's legs had now released them.

"Oh, Makenna, my leg, my leg hurts so," Della cried suddenly. "I think it's broken. Makenna, we're going to die here." She began to weep as she clung to Makenna.

Finally, the sliding rock and dirt stopped.

"I think it's over," Makenna said, her eyes tightly shut. Della was crying softly.

Makenna opened her eyes and saw Della. She put her hand down to touch the girl's face. "You'll be all right," she said, rubbing Della's cheek gently. "You've got an awfully dirty face though."

"Who wouldn't have a dirty face?" Della answered through lessening sobs.

"Dirty face!" Makenna suddenly shouted. "Della, I can see you! There's light coming in!"

"What does that mean?"

"If there's light, that means they've blasted through! Della, we're saved!"

"Makenna!" Gabe's voice called. "Makenna, are you all right?"

"Gabe, we're all right, we're all right!" Makenna shouted back.

Makenna heard the sound of wood being pulled apart and, a moment later, she saw Gabe's face staring anxiously down at her. She looked up at him and though tears were streaming down her own grimy face, she was smiling broadly.

"Listen," Gabe said as calmly as if they were sitting on a sofa in her living room, "I just wanted to say that I love you and whether you are married or not, it makes no difference to me. We'll work something out."

CHAPTER THIRTY

"He is in here," Gabe said. "I've arranged for his funeral to be held as soon as you give the word."

Gabe watched Makenna walk into the bedroom and look down at the body of her father who lay on the bed. Gabe had hired an undertaker to prepare Kellen so that Makenna could view him without undue shock. He had told her of the accident during the ride back to Albuquerque and comforted her tears as best he could. When Gabe considered all that Makenna had been through and how well she had withstood it, his admiration of her equaled his love for her. Even watching her kiss Bernardo good-bye at the depot in Albuquerque had not upset him. In fact, it seemed right and proper for her to show affection for him.

As Makenna looked at the still form of her father, she began remembering things about him, little things that now tumbled hack into her mind as sharply as if they had just happened.

She could hear a conversation, which had taken place ten years earlier.

"Makenna, girl, we'll be goin' out West I'm thinkin'. There's nothin' left for us here now."

"But, Papa, Mama's grave is here. Are we going to leave her behind?"

"Child, your mama isn't in that grave. She's here in our hearts, and that's where she'll always be. Just like me, when I'm gone. I'll still be right there in your heart."

"Papa, I don't want you to ever die."

"Honey, we've all got to die. We can't go to heaven until we do."

"Where is Peter?" Makenna finally asked.

"I don't know," Gabe answered. "I haven't seen him around since last night. In fact, I didn't even bother to try to find him when I heard you were in trouble."

Makenna looked over at Gabe. "I'm glad," she said. "Don't you know it was you I wanted to see while I lay trapped in that car?"

Gabe put his arms around her. "I'm awfully sorry about your papa," he said.

"I'm sorry he didn't live long enough to see us together like this. I know he would have approved, no matter what."

"Well, have you decided what you are going to do?"

"I'm going to divorce Peter," Makenna said finally.

"What about your church?"

"My conscience is clear," Makenna said. "I was never married to Peter spiritually or physically, Gabe. We were never…man and wife together."

"Somehow, I can't see Peter being denied his marital rights," Gabe said.

"I didn't deny them," Makenna answered honestly. "He is the one who abandoned the bed. Not once, since we've been married, have we been together."

"Why not?"

"He is a very odd person," Makenna said. She told Gabe about Peter's hatred for his father and how he intended to show that hatred by refusing to provide his father with a grandchild.

"You call him odd? I think he's crazy. Makenna, you'd better let me be with you when you tell him you want the divorce. I'm afraid of what he might do otherwise."

There was a knock on the door then, and both turned to acknowledge it. Bull was standing just on the other side.

"Yes, Bull, what is it?" Gabe asked.

"Boss, that damn telegraph machine is just going crazy down there, 'n' we don't have anyone here who can answer it."

"Oh, yes, we do," Makenna said.

"Who?" Bull asked.

Gabe smiled. "You're looking at her," he said. "Come on, Makenna, I'll put you to work."

The three walked back to the engineering car, then stepped inside. The instrument was clacking as they reached it and Makenna sat down behind it.

"What are they saying?" Gabe asked.

"They are just trying to get an answer from us," Makenna said. She opened the key and began working the switch. "I'm telling them that our original telegrapher was killed in an accident and I am just signing on. I'm asking what messages they have," she said.

There was a rather lengthy exchange of messages, then Makenna tore the message off the pad and handed it to Gabe.

"It's Emory Van Zandt's bank," Gabe said glumly. "They need verification of our intent to satisfy the terms of the railroad grant by the deadline or a statement that such terms can't be met."

"I thought we had three more days, the bloodsuckers," Bull said.

"We do," Gabe said. "But they need to either prepare the transfer of funds, or make arrangements to foreclose."

"What are you going to do, Gabe?" Makenna asked.

Gabe handed the message back to Makenna and walked over to the door of the car. He looked out at his work camp and at the mountains and desert he had tried to conquer. He sighed. "I don't know yet."

"Can't you blast that rubble away from the pass?" Makenna asked.

"No, ma'am," Bull said. "We used the last of our nitro in rescuin' you, 'n there ain't no more anywhere."

"Gabe, you sacrificed your railroad for me?"

Gabe smiled and returned to Makenna. He put his arms around her. "Believe me, it was no sacrifice. Don't you realize that you are worth more to me than a dozen railroads?"

"Yes, I think I do, now," Makenna said. "I just wish I had realized it earlier and none of this would have happened."

"What are you gonna tell 'em, boss?" Bull asked.

"Makenna, tell them evaluation is still in progress. I'll have an answer for them by five o'clock this evening."

Makenna began flashing the message back and Bull and Gabe left the car to look around.

"Have you got any ideas, boss?" Bull asked.

"Maybe," Gabe said. "Didn't I see a couple of the engineers going in for some coffee a short time ago?"

"Yeah, they're in there."

"I need to talk with them," Gabe said.

The two engineers stood when Gabe entered the tent. One of the kitchen workers had seen Gabe and Bull approach and met them with a cup of coffee for each.

"How's the girl holdin' up?" one of the engineers asked.

"She's doing fine," Gabe said. "In fact, she's working

for us now. She took her father's place as a telegrapher."

"It can't be a job with much security," one of the engineers observed.

"All may not be lost," Gabe said. "Have the tracks reached Springerville?"

"Yes," one of the engineers replied. "But that does us no good as long as this pass remains closed."

"Then we are going to open this pass," Gabe suggested.

"Mr. Hansen, we don't have more than a couple hundred pounds of black powder, and that simply won't do the job."

"It won't remove the old rubble," Gabe said. "But it will do the job I'm going to ask of it."

"What do you mean?"

"The blast that Long Li set off, even though not yet placed, may have opened up another possible route for us. It won't be a very good route; the gradient may just about be at maximum, but we can lay track across it and complete the line."

"You mean as a temporary measure?" one of the engineers asked.

"Sure, why not?" Gabe replied. "Look, there is no requirement as to mean gradient ratio, only that a continuous and passable line be built. This section would allow the passage of a locomotive and tender and perhaps a few cars. Hardly enough to be classified as economical but it will fulfill the government requirements. Later, after the grant has been paid, we can return here and excavate the original track."

"That might work," one of the engineers said slowly.

"All I need is a track which will allow a locomotive and a few cars to pass. If we have to, we'll establish this as a precautionary area and reduce speed to five miles per hour. Can you do it?"

One of the engineers opened up his case and removed a tablet and some engineering instruments. He began drawing circles and triangles and filling the pad with figures. He and the other engineer talked in the strange language of gradients and radials, tepetate earth, abutments and foundations, and mathematical formulas. Finally, they looked up at Gabe and smiled.

"We can do it."

"You mean our railroad is going to be saved?" Bull said with a joyous shout.

"I think so," the engineer replied.

"Now the question is, can we do it in three days?" Gabe asked.

"That question I can answer," Bull said. "If these boys will give me the plans, I'll do it. We'll go on twenty-four-hour shifts."

The two engineers drained the last of their coffee and set their cups down. "We've got to walk our new cut," one of them said.

"I'll get the material and tools ready for construction," Bull put in. "What are you going to do, boss?"

"Find Peter Van Zandt," Gabe said. "We have some important business to discuss and I don't mean about the railroad."

Within moments after the meeting in the mess tent, word had spread throughout the camp that a way had been found to save the railroad. There was jubilation everywhere and the men prepared to return to work as soon as so ordered. Laughter and joking filled the air.

It was gratifying to Gabe to see that the almost oppressive layer of depression that had settled over the camp after the death of Kellen and Long Li, and the fear that the railroad might be finished, was now gone.

Gabe searched everywhere for Peter but was unable to find him. Finally, he returned to the engineering car to speak with Makenna. "You haven't seen Peter, have you?" he asked as he stepped inside.

"No," Makenna said. "Why, have you spoken to him?"

"That's just it. I can't find him anywhere."

"I imagine he'll turn up soon," Makenna said. She was busy cleaning the engineering car. "Honestly, I don't think any of you ever picked up a thing," she said. "It's too bad poor Della is laid up with a broken leg. I could use her help out here."

"I guess we just sort of let things get away from us," Gabe said.

"At least the messages were filed," Makenna said, tearing the message from the pad, which she had received only that morning. "Thank goodness Dad was always very particular with that. I think it was because he knew he was so sloppy with everything else that...wait a minute, this is odd."

"What?"

"Message number two four five is missing."

"Two four five?"

"Yes, see, every message is numbered in sequence and placed here on this spindle. The last message up here is two four and the one I took today is two four six. Where is two four five?"

"Maybe there was a numbering error."

"No, these pads are preprinted with the numbers," Makenna said. She began looking around on the desk and in the wastebasket. "Message two four five is gone."

"What is the last message received before this?"

Makenna took down message two four four. "It concerns a shipment of railroad ties," she said.

"Makenna, that's the last message we received, I swear it is. Your dad showed it to me not more than an hour or so before he was killed."

"Maybe he got another message and was bringing it to you when he...when he fell," she said, fighting hard not to reopen the hurt of her father's death.

"It wasn't on him," Gabe said.

Makenna looked at message 246 and then held it against the light, in such a way as to see indentations on the paper. She sat down at the desk and began running a pencil over the page lightly, covering the whole page in gray-black lead. Soon, white marks began to appear where the indentations were, then words and figures. They were able to read: 27520287 is laundry number belonging to... and then it stopped.

"That doesn't make sense," Makenna said.

"I'm afraid it does," Gabe said glumly.

"What?"

"It means your father was murdered."

"Murdered? Why? Who would want to...?"

"Whoever that laundry number belongs to," Gabe said. He explained about the murder of Orchid Blossom and the handkerchief that had been discovered near the scene bearing the laundry number.

"When that message came back, whoever it was discovered it and killed your father," Gabe said.

"But who could it be? Papa didn't write it down and no one would know unless they could read telegraphy."

"There are over four hundred men in this camp, Makenna," Gabe said. "There is every possibility that some of them can read telegraphy and we just don't know about it."

"I'm going to see if I can find out what name is missing," Makenna said.

"How?"

"By finding the telegrapher who originated the message. He'll have a copy."

There was an urgent knock on the door and Gabe looked around to see one of the engineers. "We've got a problem, Mr. Hansen."

"With laying the temporary track?"

"No, sir, nothing like that. It's something else."

"What?"

"I'd rather talk with you alone," the engineer said awkwardly.

"You go ahead," Makenna said grimly. "I'm going to try and get to the bottom of this mystery."

Gabe left the engineering car and walked a little way with the engineer. The man was silent for several moments.

"Well, what is it?" Gabe finally asked.

"We found Mr. Van Zandt."

"Good, where is he? I need to talk to him."

"There won't be any talkin', I'm afraid," the engineer said.

"Why? What do you mean?"

"We found him when we were walking the new route. He's dead."

"Dead? How? Where is he?"

"Come along, have a look for yourself," the engineer said.

Gabe followed the engineer up the side of the mountains, across the pile of rubble, until he saw a small cluster of people standing around looking down at something.

"It looks like he was killed in the explosion that killed Long Li," the other engineer who had waited by the body said. "He's been crushed by rocks."

Gabe sighed. "It looks like you're right," he said. "The

question is, what the hell was he doing up here?"

"I've got an answer to that, too," the engineer said.

Gabe turned to look at him. "What?"

The man led Gabe a few feet away from the body and pointed to a crowbar lying on the ground. "Look," he said. "Mr. Van Zandt used the crowbar to start a rockslide. Mr. Hansen, he caused the rockslide that set off Long Li's blast, then he got caught in it himself. He killed Long Li."

"I see," Gabe said quietly.

"But why?"

"Why? For the same reason he killed Kellen O'Shea," Gabe replied.

"Should we bury him?" someone asked.

"No," Gabe said. "Have one of the carpenters build a coffin for shipping. We'll send his body back to San Francisco. His father will want to bury him, I'm sure."

"If this son-of-a-bitch killed Kellen, he don't deserve no decent burial," someone said.

"Look, he's dead," Gabe said sharply. "It doesn't make any difference to him now what we do. But his father is still alive and his father is innocent. So we'll have some concern for him."

"Yeah, I guess you're right," the man said. "All right, we'll send the son-of-a-bitch back." Gabe climbed back down the mountain and went into the engineering car to tell Makenna about Peter. When he got there, he discovered her crying.

"Makenna, what is it?" he asked, slipping his arms around her.

"I've just discovered whose name is missing. Gabe, I know who murdered my father."

"It was Peter," Gabe said quietly.

"It was Peter," Makenna went on. "How could he do

such a...you knew?" she asked, suddenly realizing what he had said.

"I didn't know until a few minutes ago, when I discovered that he killed Long Li. I knew it had to be for the same reason."

"My God, you mean he killed that poor little Chinese girl, and my father, and Long Li? Gabe, what sort of monster is he?"

"He's a dead monster," Gabe said.

"What do you mean?"

Gabe sighed and held Makenna closer. "It's all over. We've just found Peter's body. He was killed in the explosion that he set off to kill Long Li."

"Oh, Gabe, I was such a fool," she whispered against his chest. "I not only messed up our lives but I got three innocent people killed, including my own father."

"You did no such thing," Gabe said firmly, "and I won't let you think like that. We have to take life as it comes and deal with it in the way we think best. We've both plodded through but the important thing is, we have arrived here at this point, at the same time. We are together now and that's all that counts, isn't it?"

"Yes, that's all that counts," Makenna agreed with a broad smile.

EPILOGUE

Eighteen months later:

After the Southern Continental Railroad reached San Diego, Gabe Hansen built a second line to connect it with San Francisco. Gabe established his headquarters there.

He had built a luxury home in the Knob Hill district of the city and, today, he and Makenna were celebrating their son, Kellen's, first birthday. They had invited several friends, including Bull Blackwell, who was now Chief Supervisor of the railroad, his wife, Della, and their eight-month-old daughter, Bess. Also present were Bernardo Tafoya and his wife Alexia, James Farley, United States Senator from California, Isaac Kalloch, the mayor of San Francisco, and Emory Van Zandt.

Van Zandt struck the glass with his spoon, the resulting ring getting the attention of all present.

"I have something I want to say. I know that Kellen isn't actually my grandson," Van Zandt said, "but he is closest I'll ever have to one so I'll be treating him as such. I've put him in my will as my principal heir."

The others applauded, then Gabe spoke up.

"Emory, there's no need for you to do that. The railroad wouldn't exist without your support."

"Son, the advantage of being old and rich is you can do pretty much what you want to do. And I want to make Kellen my heir."

"Boss, I remember when you were fighting him for money," Bull said. "So why are you turning it down now?"

The others laughed.

Gabe smiled. "Why indeed?" he asked. He lifted his wine glass. "To Emory Van Zandt, one of the giants of the state of California."

"Here, here," the others said as they drank the toast.

When Gabe sat back down, Makenna reached over to take his hand.

A LOOK AT: THE CROCKETTS': WESTERN SAGA ONE

During the Civil War, they sought justice outside of the law, paying back every Yankee raid with one of their own. No man could stop them… no woman could resist them… and no Yankee stood a chance when Will and Gid Crockett rode into town.

After their parents are murdered by a band of marauding Yankees, Will and Gid Crockett join William Quantrill and his gang of bloodthirsty raiders to seek revenge on the attackers.

Someone's about to mess with the Crocketts', and that means someone's about to be messed with back. Will and Gid don't like getting shot at, especially by varmints who don't have skill enough to kill them.

The Crocketts': Western Saga 1 includes: Trail of Vengeance, Slaughter in Texas, Law of the Rope and The Town That Wouldn't Die.

AVAILABLE NOW ON KINDLE

ABOUT THE AUTHOR

Robert Vaughan sold his first book when he was 19. That was 57 years and nearly 500 books ago. He wrote the novelization for the mini series Andersonville. Vaughan wrote, produced, and appeared in the History Channel documentary Vietnam Homecoming.

His books have hit the NYT bestseller list seven times. He has won the Spur Award, the PORGIE Award (Best Paperback Original), the Western Fictioneers Lifetime Achievement Award, received the Readwest President's Award for Excellence in Western Fiction, is a member of the American Writers Hall of Fame and is a Pulitzer Prize nominee.